They Left One Tree

Carl Armstrong

* * *

This is a work of fiction. Names, characters, places, and incidents are products of the author's imagination or are used fictitiously and are not to be construed as real. Any resemblance to actual events, locales, organizations, or persons, living or dead, is entirely coincidental.

Dalea Publishing

First paperback printing: January 2022

First hardcover printing: January 2022

ISBN: 979-8-9853468-1-7

For anyone who walks alone and wonders

1

Some protests are doomed to fail. Shay's Rebellion after the American Revolution. Pacifists shortly before World War One. Tiananmen Square. The Carbon Tax Riots. Merchants striking against the Great Ladder Monopoly. The last dirt farmers. And now, the protesters in front of Chicago's only forest.

The court denied the final appeal. Every protester abandoned their sign or banner when they heard the news, and headed home. The wind blew most of their garbage towards the forest and deposited it all just inside the tree line. None of the nearby residents bothered to clean it up. Instead, they opened their windows and let in the sounds of the woods one last time, just as they had for centuries.

Late into the night, after everything else went silent, a breeze carried through the forest's trees as they performed one final orchestral score. Heavy cottonwood leaves flapped against one another. Maples and elms shimmered, and a solitary oak rustled and creaked. Eventually, that too died down. Then, only the silent silhouettes stood amid the moonlight.

Night gave way, and a single robin tried to fill the morning air. Every resident's eyes were puffy, red, and spent.

Jack Beauregard Wilson, all of six years old, fell asleep the night before, not realizing how his small realm was about to change. His whole world was this forest, which ran right up to his back yard. He lived in these woods and explored them every day on the ancient dirt paths that crisscrossed the hundreds of acres.

Well, maybe he hadn't investigated them all by *himself* but, together with his parents, he had walked nearly all of them. Every night after dinner, Jack explored them again in his young mind's imagination. He would run through the forest and weave fantastic stories as the birds spoke to him. He'd close his eyes and pretend to climb the branches of the tallest trees to peer out over the expanse—something his parents would never allow when they all went out together.

Everywhere he went, he told people of his

adventures in the woods. People listened and nodded, and the older folks who looked like his great-grandparents would always smile in a sad, distant way that confused Jack. They had the far-away smile when he talked about the beehives, the brown leaves, and the caterpillars. Those he let crawl all over his skin, because they tickled and felt funny.

"You are a very lucky boy," the old woman at the vertical farm always said to him, at the end of the weekly retelling of his stories.

"Thank you," Jack said, unsure of why he was lucky, but wanting to be polite all the same. "Would you come and see my forest someday?"

"*Your* forest! Oh, my. Now I must come to see this forest that belongs to a boy. And what have you named your forest? What do you call it when you enter?"

And at this Jack was quiet, for he had no answer. Never before had he thought the forest needed a name. He reached for his father's hand and gave it a squeeze.

The ancient woman laughed again, deep crow's feet lining her eyes. She leaned down and met Jack with clasped hands. "Oh, I'm sorry dear. I didn't mean to put you on the spot. I just remember the forests having names long ago, when I was your age and there was more than just one left. I thought yours might have a name too. It's quite all right if it doesn't."

Jack's father finished paying for the day's groceries and gave his thanks as they left the vertical farm's lobby and headed home. All the way back, Jack thought of what he could name his forest.

That evening at dinner, his parents opened the windows and the family ate in peace, each alone with their thoughts as the sounds from behind the back yard found their way to the table.

Jack had a name for his forest. He decided he'd tell his parents in the morning.

As Jack's mom and dad put him to bed, he noticed each had tears drying down their cheeks, although they smiled and told him they loved him, as they did every night. Together, they held hands while they walked out of Jack's room. His window was left open.

By the time Jack stirred the next morning, the work was almost complete. He had slept clear through dawn. A loud crash woke him with a start, and he looked out his window to the noise that roused him.

He screamed.

His mother rushed in, heedlessly knocking stuffed animals out of her way. She held him as he continued to scream and flail as his world crashed outside his window, one tree at a time. The foresters cut through centuries of wood and generations of memories, felling in haphazard fashion the cottonwoods, the maples, the elms, and all the rest. At the end, only the solitary oak still stood, with a small blue and white birdhouse hung on a lower branch. Jack had built it for Mother's Day a month ago.

A lagging forester saw the birdhouse, unhooked it, and gently tossed it into Jack's back yard. Then he looked around. Seeing only the lone oak, he powered down his chainsaw and walked away. As he left, he stepped over all of Jack's laughter, memories, and joy.

Twenty-eight years later…

Jack found himself running through the forest again, as he had so often in the past. The evening air cooled his face and his bare feet, even as the ground radiated heat from the earlier sunlight.

They laughed as they ran, holding hands and letting the well-worn paths lead them where they may. No birds called out, no insects swarmed above, and there was no noise from beyond the forest's borders. Neither the dancing leaves nor the occasional stream uttered a sound. The soft footsteps of four feet and the light laughter of her voice were all that Jack heard. These woods were timeless. He still knew every path and every turn. The years changed nothing.

Aramae's hand fit inside Jack's only slightly, but both were lined with the beginnings of time. Every moment passed in an hour, every hour an age. Occasionally, they would stop and remark silently, words unneeded. Jack's mind moved to a standstill and all clouds cleared from his thoughts. As he looked up through the silent spinning leaves, he saw the deep reds, purples, and oranges of the setting sun.

The bright orb spoke to him.

"Jack…Jack…wake up. We overslept. We've got to go, or we'll never make the shuttle. C'mon, Jack."

And like that, the forest winked out. The light turned from deep red to the bright yellow of midmorning, and Jack's mind squealed back to reality.

"Oh, crap. Betty, what time is it?"

"Quarter after nine. Come on, we've got to get going. The shuttle. The trip. Now."

"Mmph. Five more minutes. I'll be ready, I promise. Happy anniversary."

He leaned over and gave her a peck as his mind began to register all of the things he had to do in the next forty-five minutes.

Jack's dream faded back into the ether of his mind with the unbidden promise of a sequel. That realization brought Jack out of his sleepy haze more than the hot shower he stepped into or the hotter coffee Betty set out for him as he walked, half-naked and dripping, across their condo's floor. Jack looked out the balcony window and surveyed the day.

"You know, when we have kids someday, you'll have to put on more than a towel when you leave the bathroom."

"What, can't I do whatever I want, whenever I

want?" A wry smile appeared in one corner of his mouth.

"No. You can't. For instance, did you know that no matter how long you stare at that huge lake, our shuttle is still arriving in thirty minutes, whether we're there for it or not?"

"I wish I could hear the lake and not just look at it. If I slid this door open, you know what we'd hear? Tires. Humming inducers. The dull buzz of fifty million shuttles charging. Half a million rooftop windmills drowning out any hope of hearing a single bird. Peace, quiet, and a gentle breeze. Why can't we have all three at once? Remind me why we live in Chicago," Jack said. He cracked the sliding door open a little and let the noise creep in.

"Because, Mr. Sunshine, this is where all the fun stuff happens. It's your *academia*, remember? Everything in North America revolves around this place. Three hundred million people live here. Where else *would* we live?"

Betty's clipped reply caught Jack off guard. He froze and stared past one edge of their balcony, not daring to turn his head. Orbital cars crawled up the city's star ladder in the distance, its tight black ribbon stretching endlessly upwards into space. The ancient city sprawled out before him as he sipped coffee. *How did I wind up here?*

"Helloooo, Jack. Hey, I'm over here!" Betty said. "Were you going to say anything at all?"

"I heard you," Jack replied. Still without a firm

answer in his mind, but not wanting to press his luck delaying a response any longer, he fired from the hip.

"We could always move west."

Her empty coffee mug hit the countertop with such force that Jack feared it would shatter, impede their departure, and inflame things even more. The stoneware miraculously held, although somewhere in Jack's mind he doubted it could take a second hit like that and survive.

"I am *not* moving west. Are you crazy? There's nothing but ruins out there! Science outposts, derelict towns, and who only knows what sorts of wastelands populate that expanse. What is wrong with you!? What would possess you to even consider something so stupid?"

Even after six years, I haven't learned to keep my mouth shut. Jack took, and held, a deep breath before Betty continued.

"Where would we live? What would *I* do? How could we even think about raising kids out there?" Betty was oblivious to the closed expression on her husband's face.

The dull background of city life that filtered in from the balcony became nothing against her voice, and Jack closed his eyes right after shutting the balcony door. He exhaled.

For half a moment, he heard wind, leaves, and rustling. Bare earth pushed against his toes. He pictured a smile. Then he opened his eyes.

"I'm sorry. I didn't mean to upset you. It was an idle thought, nothing more. But it's not all ruins and the apocalypse out there like you think it is. I went to school out there, don't forget."

"How could I *possibly* forget? Your entire study is draped with holography crap. I walk in there and it's like I've magically moved myself to the middle of nowhere."

"It's great, isn't it?" Jack replied, his voice low.

"It's…different. I'll grant you that. Just don't go and expect me to set foot out there. Ever."

"Shuttle arrives when? Ten?"

"Yes. And if we aren't there, it'll leave for someone else. How close are you to being ready? I'm so glad we packed last night, you're never ready for anything."

"Ten minutes. I'll be ready to walk out the door in ten minutes."

"Whatever."

True to form, Jack spent the time getting dried and dressed. He threw his toothbrush into his bag once he was all done, then stole into his study and grabbed a small grey cube, no bigger than the coffee mug he'd held earlier. He added it to his bag in one quick motion, then left his tidied retreat, refilled his coffee, and walked out with his wife. The shuttle arrived in ten minutes.

"You know we've got to take the express now, right?" Betty said as they hustled down the hallway.

"Oh, shit. I hate, hate, hate the express." He furrowed his brow and, for an instant, wondered what might happen if they missed the shuttle's call time.

Not wanting to experience a repeated verbal blast, he screwed himself up for the impending ordeal.

"It's fine, you big sissy. Honestly, I have never understood why you don't like the express."

"Just full of compliments today, aren't you?"

Betty shot him a glare as they rounded the corner and were confronted by two massive sets of doors. She waved her hand in front of the set to the right, motioning that they intended to go down.

Jack stood there beside his wife, palms sweaty, tapping a foot against the inside of his shoe with increasing speed. His tapping matched the vibrations emanating from the doors before them until, at last, the elevator car arrived. The doors parted.

The elevator car looked remarkably unchanged from elevator cars of past centuries, with a few differences. Old elevator cars would have been completely empty, but in this one sat two banks of seats against its far wall. Additionally, large white bins were bolted to the floor in three of the four corners. The car's walls all had pleasant digital projections of the surrounding city, giving the illusion that the walls were windows. Even the elevator doors maintained the illusion, with barely a seam visible from the inside.

Jack and Betty strapped their suitcases into the bins, closed and latched the bin covers, and made sure the lights on top glowed green, to show the luggage was secure.

The fourth corner of the car had no bin, but neither did it have the familiar rows of buttons on the wall that a traveler from centuries past might expect. Instead, there was a fourth white cube, smaller and shorter than the storage bins, with ten slots arranged in two rows of five, mimicking the seating arrangement for the ten black leather chairs against the back wall.

"You did remember your ID, right?" Betty asked.

"No, I figured I'd just hang on real tight," Jack said as he fished something out from his front pocket.

"Take a seat. I'll put them in."

She grabbed her husband's ID along with her own, then took the two gumstick-sized slivers of encoded metal and placed them into the two rightmost slots in the top row.

"I call window," Betty said. Armrests unfolded, and a lap bar rotated up from the floor for each of the two activated chairs.

"I'll have my eyes closed anyhow," Jack said. He sat and pulled the lap bar down over his waist until the cylinder's lit end changed from red to green. The armrests folded back down into position as Betty mirrored the procedure in the seat next to him.

Finally, everything and everyone was strapped in, and all indicator lights glowed green. They had six minutes until the shuttle arrived.

"I told you we'd have enough time. Nothing to it," Jack said as he turned to look at his wife. Her black shoulder-length hair obscured all of her face. Only the rounded end of a nose peeked through.

"The joys of being a Wilson, right? Five hundred stories up, a home most people would kill for, and a husband who would rather be on the ground, scratching through rocks and who knows what else."

"Let's just get to the shuttle. What's this car's name?"

Before Betty could answer, a firm British voice filled the space, replying everywhere and nowhere.

"My name is Alfred, sir."

Betty beat her husband to the reply. "Alfred, good morning. We need express to sublevel three, please."

"Of course, Doctor Wilson. Will anyone else be joining you today?"

"No, Alfred. Just the two of us."

"Thank you. Departure in ten seconds. I see everything is secured."

Betty turned and looked at her husband, who already had his eyes closed and was busy white-knuckling the ends of the armrests. Always the drama queen, she mused to herself. She looked back towards the city, admiring the enormity of the skyrise towers stretching to the horizon in three directions, while giant turbines spun over the surface of the great inland lake behind her. She tuned back to Alfred's voice as his countdown drew to a finish.

"Four. Three. Two. One. Release."

2

The movement of Earth's human population to cities began around the dawn of the twenty-first century, as rural communities across the globe drifted away from traditional agrarian roots. Drawn at first by the promise of a better and more modern life, the early migrators represented merely the beginnings of a trend line that, innocuously graphed, would belie the vast social upheavals underpinning its continuation, unimpeded for centuries.

By the time the migration ended, nearly every single person on Earth lived in one of the great star ladder metropolises near the stable places on the continents, sprawling to house tens of millions at their smallest, to hundreds of millions at their largest in Asia and North America. Of Earth's three billion humans, only a few hundred thousand or so remained out in the fringes, contributing to society through academia or the endless multi-generational work of caring for the shattered land in places so remote and inaccessible that modern AI couldn't penetrate it.

This massive demographic change fundamentally altered how cities structured themselves. Gone were the commutes, the ebb and flow of daily pulses of traffic, and the endless importing of goods and services to the faceless rows of superstructure skyrises. Production of everything needed for a city now happened *in* a city, with inter-regional trade narrowing to a commercial venture that speculated around luxury goods, much like during the spice trade or the age of the sail.

Ironically enough, it was sails once again that powered the massive freighters navigating the world's waterways, ghost ships remotely operated from far-flung port cities like Chicago or Memphis. Instead of harnessing the wind exclusively, the sails now also captured rays of sunlight to turn the propellers or charge the batteries, making the journey across an ocean cost nothing more than time.

The solar economy relied on this cheap, plentiful solar power, and more. It also needed massive, centralized population centers, and it needed star ladders to make the solar system accessible and economically feasible to the world's industrial, tourist, and scientific bases. Everyone wanted to get somewhere, but no one was willing to burn carbon to make it happen.

This meant vertical engineering reigned supreme. Hundreds of towering indoor farms dotted Chicago's skyline, providing local crops at a scale unimaginable in previous centuries. With concentrated populations, the infrastructure to disperse food and goods across entire continents evaporated, as did the need to farm tens of millions of acres of land. Even travel between cities was a short affair, slingshotting through low-Earth orbit from ladder to ladder. The average person spent their whole life inside the network of metropolises and never set foot beyond their borders, not even considering what existence looked like beyond the legions of towering constructs.

None of this history lesson really mattered at the moment to Jack. Like Betty, he heard Alfred's digital voice tick off the final seconds of the countdown. He also knew that in order to be on time for the shortly-arriving shuttle, they needed to get from the very top floor of their building to several levels below ground, a commute that might normally take fifteen minutes or more using a public elevator. Being over five thousand feet in the air meant waiting interminably long times for a car to arrive, and even longer for the multitude of stops it might make on its way down.

Fortunately, the top few dozen floors usually had a second option for the high-class, high-dwelling residents. Each floor had its own express car, designated exclusively for the floor's residents. These private cars were a step up from the public cars in comfort and amenities, certainly, and they also promised their users the swiftest possible trips. By forcing aside all other cars in the elevator shaft, like an emergency vehicle clearing a roadway, a private express car could monopolize a shaft for brief periods. As Alfred's voice ticked off those final seconds, the building's AI checked to make sure the shaft was clear to the bottom. Seeing and sensing no impediments, the AI released the braking clamps and cabling, sending Jack's heart into his throat and the express car into a controlled free-fall.

"Shiiiiiiiiiiit! I hate this!" Jack screamed as the elevator car plunged.

Betty laughed while the digital display of the elevator walls kept up with the plummeting joyride. After a little less than fifteen terrifying seconds, Jack felt the brakes begin to slow their descent to what he believed was a far more reasonable speed. The car entered the subterranean levels, and the lights and walls dimmed appropriately, fluxing to match the receiving floor. The car bumped to a stop and the trip ended, less than a minute after it began. They had traveled more than five hundred stories and nearly a mile of vertical space.

"Get me out of here," Jack said. The green lights

on their seats and bins changed to red, and the lap bars released, letting their occupants stand and unstrap their belongings.

"Oh, come on. That was fun!" Betty said. "It never gets old. Could you have imagined standing in a cramped elevator, forever, while we took the normal cars down? I'm so glad I married someone rich."

Betty went to her bin and unhooked the lid, her luggage unmoved.

"I wish I'd been quicker to get out of the condo," Jack replied as he pulled out his own bags. He wondered if he'd erred by bringing his cube with him. *Boy, I hope it survived the trip down.*

The doors slid open and they found themselves among several thousand other people, all lining various terminals.

"Time?" Jack asked. The two began making their way to the terminal with the giant "W" overhead.

"Nine fifty-eight. We're killing it today."

Betty's suitcases followed along behind her, rolling with the pair in quick succession through the "Z" and "Y" and "X".

"I bet you're happy you married a rich guy whose last name is at the end of the alphabet. If I were born as a MacPherson or a Lanii we'd never make it anywhere on time."

"If you'd been born as a Lanii, we'd get far fewer looks in restaurants, doctor's offices, and anywhere else your last name gets mentioned."

"You mean *our* last name."

"Right. You know what I mean. Sometimes I wish you'd change it."

"Wilsons did great things. If people have a problem with events from centuries past, that's on them."

Jack's quick defensiveness took Betty by surprise, as a few bystanders took notice of the name and began to look at the pair.

"Would you keep your voice down? You're attracting attention," Betty replied. "Where is the shuttle? It's nearly ten."

As if on cue, a slow shuttle approached their terminal, its aerodynamic chassis resting on top of four tires, looking ever so much like the personal cars of the ancient past. The shuttle's camera sensors scanned the faces of the crowd gathered near the "W" and stopped in front of Betty.

"Green, huh? I'd have pegged you for something more inconspicuous, like white," Jack remarked as their luggage loaded itself into the shuttle's storage. His bag decided to go in last, not wanting to get itself crushed by the collection of bricks Betty had apparently chosen to pack for the trip. As the trunk closed, nobody noticed the mild vibrations coming from his grey cube. Jack double-checked to make sure the trunk was closed all the way and then opened the passenger door for Betty. She hopped in and turned away from the stares of a half-dozen onlookers. Jack followed.

"When I selected green, dear, I thought you'd appreciate it. Something different, for once."

"Any upgrades? Maybe a hologram projector? We could spend the trip pretending to be anywhere we want."

"I honestly didn't look at any options when I booked the shuttle. I was on a break at the clinic and didn't want to spend it pouring over upgrades."

Jack closed the door behind him and, in doing so, cut off the prying eyes that now saw only reflections. He looked around the interior. The shuttle seemed as plain as could be, with the standard six white leather seats arranged in two facing rows, so that a party of six could converse with each other as if seated around a picnic table. Modern technology remained stubbornly unable to cure motion sickness, though, so the forward-facing seats at the rear tended to be the most utilized in all but the largest of parties. People preferred to squeeze four across the back row, rather than risk the unpleasant experience of a nauseated mess that everyone would get to share in for the remainder of a ride.

Jack and Betty occupied the back row. Each claimed their corner: Jack the right, Betty the left. As the shuttle got underway, they each reached towards the center seat's backing and unfolded a recessed armrest, giving them each their own personal space in which to stretch out.

"You know, I still don't know where we're going," Jack said at a near-whisper, as though the shuttle's soundproof interior somehow obligated library-level voices. "Are you going to tell me now that we're finally on the road?"

"Oh, I suppose. I'm surprised you haven't pestered me with questions about it for the last month. Every other year we've tried to guess each other's plans. I'm still winning. I think I'm up, what, three to one?"

Jack paused while counting back the years they'd been together: five years of dating, and now their sixth anniversary. Had it really been so long? A dozen years, give or take. They were both nearing thirty-five. Jack unconsciously rubbed a graying patch of the permanent two-day beard he kept.

"You're right. I suppose I've just been preoccupied with other things."

That was a lie. Jack had not looked forward to wherever they were off to. They had bickered more or less nonstop for months, and the idea of spending a week of vacation with his wife made his palms go all sweaty again. He knew deep down that he couldn't sustain this forever. Still, part of him hoped the trip could be a reset for them and offer a chance to get away from the routine of life in the continent's largest city.

"So should I guess, or are you going to tell me? Is it another cruise?" he asked.

Betty reflected on the trip from a few years back. "That was a fun one. You know, I'd never been to Memphis before that. I remember you woke me up in the middle of the night to show me the stars while we were on the road. That was a first for me."

"Yeah," Jack said. The memories flickered dimly in his mind. "You know, it'd been nearly a decade since I had seen the stars too. I used to look at them every single clear night in college out west. It was such a rare privilege to see them. I froze my butt off a lot back then."

"I remember you booked a shuttle with a moon roof for that Memphis trip and specifically left late in the day. I thought it was so odd, since you're usually such an early riser."

Jack grinned. "I seem to recall me making some lame excuse about why. You'd have never gone along with it, otherwise."

"You're probably right. I had never seen the sun set like that, either. It was the most peaceful shuttle trip I think I have ever been on. Waking up and looking through the open rooftop to see these...these little specks all over. This dim, constantly faint light piercing this totally black sky. I'd never seen anything like it."

"I remember that. The single moment of realization you had when you looked up. That was a great moment." *Too bad it didn't last.*

Silence filled the cabin. Jack felt his face fall, the grin from seconds ago now merely the remnant of an afterglow. He closed his eyes before it totally fled.

He found himself back in the woods in September, the trees making just a little more noise than usual as the leaves turned colors and began their slow drift to the forest floor. Gone was the summer's humidity, replaced by crisp breezes at midday, a sun that warmed but not quite enough to *be* warm, and the smell of early decay. He felt the corners of his mouth turn up just slightly. A slow exhale and he returned to the present, looking at Betty to see what she was going to say next.

Betty stared out her own window as the buildings passed by, their towering premises casting long shadows over the concrete canyons, the green shuttle, and the millions of others like it traveling in computer-controlled dull monotony. Every passenger knew their destination and arrival time down to the second, their shuttle trip filled with work or conversations, or for those on longer trips, the occasional nap while stretched out across the three-seat rows, taking advantage of the smooth ride and quiet cabin.

Jack turned from his wife to look out the opposite window and spotted one of Chicago's vertical farms as the shuttle drove north. It contrasted sharply with the rest of the skyline's boxy, geometric silhouettes. The enormous food farm began with a wide circular base and tapered as the stories rose, reaching its narrowest, smallest floor roughly four-fifths of the way up before widening again slightly at its peak. The entire building resembled a glass flower vase, and the green permeating through its windows from top to bottom only reinforced that. The rotating windmills on the rooftop could have been Lilliputian flowers to an imaginative child's eyes as they spun slowly, some thousands of feet above Jack and Betty's shuttle.

Jack visited a traditional farm once. At college, many years ago, before he settled on astrobiology as a major, Jack had considered terrestrial sciences. At one of his freshman seminar courses, the professor put out an opportunity, to anyone interested, to meet at the university's historical farm the next day. Almost nobody had ever seen food grown outdoors, under the sun, in fields of plowed earth. Aside from schools and research facilities, no opportunities to see such a thing even existed. Once they graduated, the chance would likely be gone forever. But most of the class's dozen or so members rolled their eyes at the thought of waking up early to walk across campus. Only a few, including Jack, were curious by nature. They quietly decided to head to the farm without informing each other. When Jack arrived at the far corner of the school, there were three others from class there, besides himself.

"So is Professor Amundsun coming out here, or is it just us?" one of the students asked. Jack hadn't come to know her well yet, in these first few weeks of the semester. She was quiet, observant, and had offered a couple of insightful comments the first week, but had otherwise been mostly mute, speaking little but seeming to take it all in.

"I didn't see him on the walk over here, and he said to be here at six-thirty, right?" Jack glanced at his watch and noticed he was on time, amazingly, given how unbelievably early it was. He glanced back to see the sun nearly peeking over the horizon.

"Have any of you ever been here before?" a third student, Farheed, asked as he sipped coffee from a bright blue steel mug.

"I haven't, although I knew it was here," the quiet girl answered. "I have a science course in that building over there, on the top floor, and there's quite a view. The professor is possibly the worst hologram presenter in the entire college. Anyways I'm terrified of falling asleep in front of all those people, so I get there early, grab a window seat, and spend the time looking outside. I tune into the lecture once in a while. I'm not missing anything. It's entry-level biogeology, and the hologram gets sent to me as soon as I enter the lecture hall. It's how he takes attendance. Archaic, really. There's nothing stopping me from bringing someone else's lenses with me or handing mine off to my roommate. We're in the same class."

"So why go at all?" Jack asked.

"I like the view," she quipped. "It's the only time I can get into the lecture hall, and there's nowhere else on campus that overlooks this whole historical sector. Plus, it's great for my imagination," she said, brushing back a few strands of long brown hair that had escaped her ponytail and were now blowing freely across her face in the breeze. She squinted as she looked at Jack, the sun beginning to rise behind him as morning pressed on. The squint forced up a pert freckled nose, and Jack was reminded of a mouse. A quiet, adorable, beautiful mouse.

"Maybe I could come some time."

More a statement than a question, it escaped Jack's mouth before he could fully form the implications of that thought, and he immediately felt his ears get very, very warm. He tried to recover. "I uh...um, I meant...oh man, my ears are burning," he said as he cracked a wide grin. He realized how he must look and laughed at himself.

"Are they? I can't tell with the sun right behind you," she said, covering well, not wanting to embarrass him into silence, and rather amused at how fast his ears had gone from summer tan to sunburn red. "As for someone coming with me...no one's ever asked before. You really want to sit through a biogeology class, just for the view?" She arched an eyebrow while continuing to squint, putting her arm out to better shield her face from the morning light.

"I think I'd enjoy it." Jack's mouth again moved faster than his mind, and the blush on his ears spread quickly to his cheeks. "Um. Oh geez. There I go again. By the way, I'm..."

"Jack. I know who you are. I pay attention, and anyways it's hard to forget the roll call, back on the first day. Your name perked up almost everyone at the end," she said, laughing as she spoke.

Jack cracked his signature smile a second time, the color leaving his cheeks a bit as his nervousness dissipated. "What's your name?"

"Aramae."

3

Some time had passed since the green shuttle brushed by the towering vertical farm. Neither Betty nor Jack had spoken, each alone with their thoughts in their separate corners. As the road slipped further north, they passed many more hundreds of skyrises, each one connected to others, with massive bridges weaving them together in a mosaic of urban fabric. Their shuttle passed the star ladder turnoff, and Jack began to wonder where they could possibly be going.

"Okay, I give up. We can't be going too far, because we just passed by the ladder exit. You hate sleeping in shuttles, so I know we'll be there by nightfall, and this one's not fit for that anyhow. What's the destination?"

Betty studied her husband for a moment before answering. "Oh, fine. Mackinac Island."

"How did you ever come up with that? I've never been there before. Have you?" Jack was only vaguely familiar with the resort and its throwback to a long ago era.

"I went once, when I was a kid. We spent a long weekend there. My parents insisted on shuttling over, and it was the longest ride I'd ever been on."

"But there's five of you, so...who rode backwards that whole time?"

"Not me! I absolutely refused to face rear. I remember sitting in the corner as the rest of them rotated through."

"So you chose the island because you went there as a kid?"

"I remember it was really different, just very calm and peaceful. Shuttles are still banned there. I thought you'd enjoy it."

"Thank you," Jack said. He reached over and held Betty's hand. "How long until we get there?"

"We've been going for what, an hour? I imagine three more to pass through the Wisconsinian Sink. And then maybe one more to the ferry?"

"What's a fair-ee?"

"We have to get on the island somehow. The shuttle drops us off and we take a boat across."

"The *water?*"

"Yeah, silly. You've been on a boat before."

"The thought terrifies me. I can't swim."

"You're kidding. All that you grew up with and your parents never taught you to swim? No pool? Nothing?"

"We did other stuff with our free time, my parents and me. You know that. Swimming just wasn't something we ever got around to."

"But we went on a cruise!? You never said anything!"

"That ship was huge. Nothing was ever going to happen. I never gave it a second thought. This little fair-ee sounds totally different."

Betty blinked a few times and looked at her husband, bewildered and unsure of what to say. "Well, it's a really *big* ferry," she stammered out.

Jack smiled. "I'll deal with it. You told me about it ahead of time. Now, at least, I can prepare. Just don't laugh when I stand right in the middle of the thing."

Betty blinked again. "Ooookay, Jack. Jack Beauregard Wilson, you are one strange man."

"I hate my middle name."

"I know," she said. *Never learned how to swim. Amazing. The man can talk about this world and every place else out among stars, but he can't tread water.*

She glanced at her husband and saw that he was gone, his gaze turned towards the window again as the buildings rolled by, looking at something far, far beyond her vision. *I wish you'd take me with you sometimes, Jack. Where do you go?*

Jack was indeed oblivious to his wife, just then. Not purposely, not with malice, but the thought of the ferry commanded his attention at the moment.

Although he hadn't said it, the truth was that on their cruise, he had been secretly anxious about being over open water and spent a good portion of the voyage perpetually buzzed off antihistamines. He never once looked out their cabin window or ventured onto their small personal balcony. Only his intense curiosity at traveling up the old eastern seaboard overrode his innate queasiness.

After departing from Memphis's massive trade port, their cruise ship had steamed through the Arkansas Shallows until it entered the Gulf of Mexico. Neither Jack nor Betty had ever seen the Gulf, and they were fortunate enough to see a whale pod on their second day of sailing east. The cruise ship hugged the coast and periodically stopped for SCUBA diving. The longest stop was a full day anchored over the ruins of Tallahassee, a popular spot for casual divers to survey the ancient city from above, peering down and marveling at the history right before their eyes. There were bigger ruins to visit, like Tampa or Miami, but they were further out to sea and harder to access, and anyways weren't along the cruise's route, which turned northward to stop at other drowned cities like Washington, New York, and Boston. At each turn, the divers would swim down and tour the crisscross of underwater city grids slowly succumbing to the ravages of saltwater and time.

While divers took some tourists below the surface, in either SCUBA gear or in one of a half-dozen small submersibles carried by the giant cruise ship, Jack stayed behind on deck. He wore a life jacket and spent his time timidly peering over the ship's edge to look down at the tops of the buildings, some of which were marked to avoid running over their spindly peaks. A cruise ship beached by one would be bad, but causing an ancient monolith to topple underwater was worse. Nobody wanted to imperil anything, from divers to sea life to research, or worst of all, future tourism revenue.

Jack spent many hours gazing at the underwater structures during the course of their cruise, and on these sojourns he brought out his drawing tools and paper. For all of the technological wonders that had advanced since these great cities stood in open air, drawing remained something done best by hand.

Using each coast on the distant horizon as a reference, Jack took advantage of his unique circumstance to draw the cities from a bird's eye view, except instead of sketching them in their presently murky states, his pencils pictured them as he imagined they once were, dry and full of life, testaments to an era long since passed.

Every major city the ship sailed over got a sketch: Tallahassee, then Charleston, Washington,

Philadelphia, New York, and finally Boston, on a trip that took a fortnight.

At each stop, Betty would join him and watch him draw for part of the time, interested to see him create something she herself could never envision. Each city took an afternoon and at their third stop, she came over to see his work.

"Can I take a look?" she asked. Jack sat facing the coast off the massive vessel's port side and looked down at his sketch pad. The wooden deck chair was alone, as though someone had purposely moved it away from all of the others.

"Hmm? Oh, hi," Jack said. He turned to see who the voice belonged to, as if anyone else he knew might somehow be on the same cruise. "I was just finishing this one up. What do you think?"

He shifted to one side of the chair and balanced the sketch on the wide armrest opposite his body, so Betty could take a look as she stood behind him.

"I think that's the best one you've done yet. Where are we?" She looked down and then up again towards the coast.

"We're sitting over Washington, D.C. at the moment. America's first capital. Actually, if my archaeology classes from long ago are correct, I think we're sitting right over the Washington Monument. Or at least, what's left of it," Jack said. He tapped a finger near the bottom of the sketch pad at a point he'd made, a single square with an "X" shaded into the middle of it.

"I don't understand. What're you pointing at?" Betty asked.

"This is the Washington Monument, and we're looking directly down on it from our bird's eye view. It was a giant, four-sided masonry column, one of the largest ever built, and it was a testament to the engineering of its time. I believe it's still standing down there now," Jack replied as he pictured it in his mind.

"And...okay, so I think I get it. That's the central point of the whole thing, it's what the bird is flying over in your drawing. And then everything else radiates out from it? What's that up there?" She pointed at a large, low, well-outlined building.

"That's the White House. That used to be the old President's residence."

"And that, with the round roof to the right?"

"The Capitol Building. Legislative branch seat."

"That's crazy. Weird. I mean, there's ten stories of water under us right now. Why didn't they just move the buildings to Chicago or one of the other old American capitals?"

"They never thought they'd need to. That's the simple answer."

Betty waited, knowing by now that Jack was likely just getting started.

He continued, "They believed they'd be able to engineer away the problem and hold back the sea. They did. For centuries, the Americans did everything they thought of, up and down both of the continent's coasts. Walls. Pumps. Raised roadways, raised buildings, relocated towns, massive dunes, synthetic reefs, genetically engineered mangroves, hundreds of miles of saltwater marsh. They did it all, and it worked. Around 2030, the ocean rise started affecting outlier towns and communities. Florida—those first places we stopped at used to be a state called Florida—saw the hardest and fastest changes. Florida was a lost cause, though. The entire place used to be a peninsula, and now it's ten thousand artificial reefs waiting for us to reintroduce coral. Have you seen a map of ancient America? It's amazing. It's like you're staring at another world. Almost none of it is recognizable on the coasts. Not like anywhere else in the world is either, really...but, but the east coast. Anyways. So they built but, one by one, every project failed. Not all at once. Not even all that close together in years, really. But inexorably, coastal cities emptied inland. Refugees from these cities migrated away for centuries. Can you imagine? A stream of people moving westward as a way of life. Everyone called it the Great Resettling. Everybody headed towards the center of the continent. That was before all of the carbon sinking began. So places like Cincinnati, Indianapolis, and Boulder—before the west dried up and emptied too—and Chicago. All of them swelled to accept migrants for *two hundred years*. There used to be states up and down this coast that are now remnants or memories, just lines on a history page. The Lost Thirteen. You remember that from school, right? Ironic, isn't it? Or sad, really. Like destroying a moon's or planet's earliest fossils. You can't get it back, ever. And we'll live our whole lives never seeing those cities dry out. A generation of fixers. And explorers. There's at least another century of restoring this, and the work is done by so few. The rest of us all fund it, sure, but meanwhile most of us live out our lives in fantastic, unbelievable cities that once were beyond imagining.

"There's these small, itty bitty populations of people repairing or sinking land, even fewer people steering asteroids back here for harvest because we can't mine Earth any more, and everyone else is oblivious to both, because the cities are so damn bright! Nobody can see beyond them. Where's this all left us? Not out in nature. We live in concrete and carbon fiber and condos. Not out in the stars—we can hardly see them, or even be bothered to look up and try.

"So we're left existing in this narrow slice of consciousness, with all these cities as the places people identify with. People forget why we all live here in the first place, and we forget what we're supposed to be doing, lost in this...day to day shuffle of people and materials..." Jack looked back from the coastline, stopping as his thoughts faltered and he came back to his present moment.

Betty looked on at her husband, who had just spoken for perhaps the longest continual streak she'd ever heard. "And if it wasn't for your family, nobody would be here to see any of this, Jack," she said.

Jack turned back to the coastline for what felt like an eternity. "The Wilson Legacy. What a joke. The only thing people remember about it is that we got blamed for killing half of humanity. Not that it saved the other half and opened up the solar system at the same time. No, sir. Everyone just remembers the bad."

"But you know the truth. Not everyone disdains the name, either. The academic world sees it for what it was. Overreach and greed by people who didn't understand what they were playing with."

"No, they certainly didn't understand. At least it's better now. Anyhow this isn't what you came over here for. Let's imagine what the rest of this city must have looked like," Jack said. He pointed to another part of his panorama. "So this was the Lincoln Memorial..."

And they spent the next hour before dinner exploring Jack's sketch, talking about the past, imagining the world as it looked long ago, and how it might look again.

By now the green shuttle had run quite far, leaving Chicago altogether after several hours of continuous driving, and had entered what was once vast farmland. Jack and Betty saw no crops, of course. No tractors and no barns, either. Only unending tracts of grasses and wildflowers, occasionally interspersed with groves of trees, greeted them along both sides of the road.

The Second Reconstruction stretched out before the couple. Begun well over a century ago, the greatest re-engineering in the continent's history sought to utterly reimagine and rebuild the land. Unlike the first Reconstruction, the second built no infrastructure and reversed no damage from warfare. Instead, as society migrated to a few cities, and populations dwindled everywhere else, people began the generational labor of rebuilding the continent's ravaged ecosystems. With an atmosphere that seemed stable after centuries of unintended manipulation, people finally took notice of the wreckage and the wasted land where crops no longer needed to grow. The Reconstruction movement was born. Taking a page from conservation groups long forgotten, the remaining governments seized nearly all property not in a population center and made plans to "improve" it, chiefly by valuing the ecosystems for the services they provided to the remaining cities.

The simultaneous and sudden rewilding of a continent even spurred a third Continental Congress, convening to map out a plan and the tasks each remaining government would undertake.

Staffed and attended by experts in science, policy, and development, the initial two-week meeting stretched into three months during the hottest summer to grip Chicago in decades, the summer of 2405.

The parallels to the previous Continental Congress were not lost among the attendees, who often smiled at history's six-century arc and the events that brought them all together. Jack's father himself attended, bringing his expertise in forests of the Midwest to the convention. Rather than the sidelong glances he got in most places when people learned of him, the delegates asked questions about his family, and his grandmother in particular, at nearly every turn.

At the end of three months' time, what emerged was nothing short of remarkable: A map of North America as big as a conference table, redrawn with no regard for politics, but instead outlined for broader goals. A forest here, a prairie there. Vast wetland tracts. Commitments to deploy armies of AI drones to do everything from removing millions of agricultural drainage tiles, to collecting and propagating seeds of thousands of plant species. Timelines to demolish nearly every single road, bridge, and rail line. A plan that closed the continent, outside of the major cities, to development.

The continent would, for the first time in a thousand millennia, be mostly free and wild. Devoid of even the original Americans, long since assimilated into civilization centuries ago, obliterating a once-fantastic mosaic of intimate knowledge, cultures, languages, and traditions.

Many attendees cried at the final adjournment,

realizing the work would take hundreds of years and many generations, and while they were all young enough to see some of the work bear fruit, none would see it end.

With most of the world's focus on the star ladders in the remaining cities, nobody paid any heed to the Second Reconstruction. As city-dwellers craned their necks skyward to the stars and the metal-rich asteroid fields, the work began largely unopposed. Barely anyone still lived in the countryside, and hardly any municipalities were left that needed lobbying.

Slowly, governments sold off vast tracts of their holdings to companies looking to cash in on the new carbon sinking economy. Eventually, only universities remained. They became outposts in the vast wilderness, examples of self-powering, self-regulating, and largely self-sustaining entities over the coming decades. Wind and solar, portable nuclear, small vertical farms, and some traditional land usage meant the universities of North America kept one foot in the modern age and one foot in the past.

Their remoteness let the universities tune out the din and churn of the megacities, their star ladders, and the exploitation of the solar system. The academics enshrined at these outposts could instead focus on teaching and shaping the minds of future scholars, thinkers, and scientists. They could examine their own planet, or the planets in their neighborhood, in quiet solitude.

Out in the rewilded places, these people once again found a consciousness that the cities had all but subjugated. A consciousness that, at this moment in the green shuttle, Jack desperately needed to get back to, although he did not recognize it.

"Hungry?" Betty asked. It was well past noon.

"Yeah, now that you mention it. What's on the menu?" He glanced at his wife for the first time in an hour. Their shuttle trip, powered from the road's induction system, would be fast and nonstop, like all shuttle trips.

"I figured we'd eat mid-afternoon, so I ordered something that would last a while."

Betty moved towards the center of the shuttle cabin, grasped a circular latch, and pulled straight up. A half-circle section of the cabin floor pivoted out and rotated around until Betty could raise it no further. Jack reached over and unfolded it, turning a half-circle into a full one and giving them a low table to eat at.

"Thank you," Betty said as she flipped down the middle of their shuttle's front seat and pulled out a small refrigerator. "It's Caesar salad, hard-boiled egg, and lemonade."

That wrested Jack fully from whatever latent thoughts he maintained about the grasses passing by his window.

"Amazing. That's like, the perfect meal for this trip." *Thank goodness she planned this and not me. We'd be eating the emergency rations under our seats.*

"A little intuition, a dash of guessing, and years of knowing you. Also, I didn't want to eat emergency rations again."

A snarky grin flashed across her face as they set up lunch on the circular table. Over the next hour, they managed to keep up a rolling conversation as they ate, Jack remarking at the apparent progress of the local rewilding while pointing things out to Betty. In turn, Betty talked about work at the clinic, retelling stories with a minute level of procedural detail that kept Jack doing more listening than talking for a good chunk of the meal.

"So what are we doing once we get to this island?" he finally asked during a brief pause, desperate to change the subject.

"Oh, well. There's all sorts of stuff to do. I figured we could check out the shops. They're all these really old, quaint stores that aren't like anything you'd see in the city. Check into the house we're staying at, stretch a bit. Maybe hop on a sailboat..." she trailed off as she remembered Jack's aversion to water.

"Um. Yeah, maybe something else after that too? Maybe there's a hiking trail somewhere?"

"You and your hiking trails. Every time we go somewhere, you've got to find out if there's a trail in the woods. How many times have there even been *trees* on our trips? Twice?"

"So what I heard you say is, that's a maybe to

hiking?"

"Sure."

"How much longer?"

Without waiting for Betty, the shuttle's AI intoned, "Destination in forty-five minutes."

"I always forget that thing's listening in," Jack muttered. "Thank you, green shuttle." He looked around the cabin, half expecting a face to materialize out of the floor.

"That's perfect; I'm going to nap. Can you clean up, please?" Betty reached under her seat for a blanket and pillow, and moved across the cabin to the rear-facing seats. She folded up the armrests and tossed the pillow against a corner.

"Thanks for lunch," Jack said. He stacked the empty containers and set them on Betty's now-empty seat before folding the table and rotating it home underneath the cabin's floor.

"You're welcome. See you when we get there," Betty said. She closed her eyes as the shuttle's AI polarized the windows, turning the cabin dusky. She was asleep in thirty seconds, a combination of the meal, the afternoon, and the shuttle's gentle rocking rhythm.

Jack looked on with a hint of jealousy, but only for a moment until his gaze turned back to the outside. The world beyond the cities was so vast and strange, and his curious mind continually imagined the landscape as it might have looked in the past: when horizons of rural farmland were all that was visible, or when the landscape looked much as it did now, only more primeval and less deliberate. *Richer. It was so much richer.* Bison herds, elk, bears, wolves, all roaming in numbers that Jack reckoned wouldn't happen for at least another century. He pictured a landscape with no roads and looked back towards Chicago to see a thin black line extend straight up to the sky, visible for hundreds of miles.

Star ladders had solved a tremendous slate of problems a century before. Permanently changing skylines around the globe, they became eternal monuments to ingenuity, engineering, and intellect. Ascending into the solar system became as routine and awe-inspiring as catching a train in generations past, when the continent first opened up to European settlers.

No longer limited to rockets and no longer burdened with a planet catapulting out of climatological control, humans collectively looked at the stars for the first time in almost half a millennium. Their itch needed a scratch. The unimaginable raw resources of the asteroid belt could substitute for terrestrial mining and halt the scarring of Earth's landscape.

A hundred years after the last terrestrial mine closed, the rewilders still quibbled with how to handle those scars. How do you repair an open pit mine a thousand feet deep? Or reforest a mountaintop cut flat? What does a place with no ancient analogue become?

The green shuttle rolled along for the remainder of its trip until it reached its destination. As the shuttle pulled up to a curb in another huge parking depot, Jack leaned across to his wife and gently jostled her shoulder to raise her from a deep slumber.

"Hey, we're nearly there. Wake up, sleepyhead," Jack said.

The shuttle slowed to a stop and the AI loudly announced "destination reached" to the cabin interior.

Betty looked around. "That was quick," she mumbled. The pair disembarked and waited while their luggage got itself out. Jack checked to make sure nothing got left behind.

"Did you clean out lunch?" Betty asked.

"Oh, thanks. Give me a second." Jack went back to the cabin and grabbed the containers. "Okay, shuttle. All belongings clear."

With that, they stepped away and the shuttle doors closed. The shuttle stayed there, vacant, waiting for it to be summoned elsewhere or commanded to a storage dock. Perhaps it would drive back to Chicago empty, or end up heading to another eastern city. Only the algorithms knew.

After freshening up, Jack and Betty sat on a bench in the cavernous great hall for a moment as Betty slipped on her lenses. People milled past, heading to and from their own shuttle rides.

"Any important messages?" Jack asked.

"Haven't gotten that far. Give me a minute." Betty's eyes moved about in an absent fashion as she flitted from place to place behind the eyepieces.

"Ever thought about switching to contacts?"

"Yes, actually. I have given it…quite a lot of thought," Betty said. "And the decision is still a no. I like…the ease of disconnecting with these. I don't care what the young…sters are doing. I also don't want things shoved in my eyes. Have you thought of joining the rest of society, or are you going to keep using that ancient cube for everything?" Betty fired back her reply even though she already knew the answer, having asked it dozens of times before.

"You're hilarious. And you know the answer to your question just as I knew the answer to mine. The cube works, and it's easy to fix or upgrade or replace parts, unlike your lenses."

Betty glanced at Jack with none of the distraction from moments ago. "Well, good for you. Anyways I've got no messages. When's the last time you bothered to check, yourself?"

Let's see…not this morning, I was running behind. There was that one yesterday from Harold, but whatever. Probably just something about next semester. Maybe I'll get to teach that exopaleoecology elective finally. Registration for next term is in what, six weeks? I'd have to polish up the syllabus.

Betty leaned over. "Hello, Jack. Earth to Jack."

Jack blinked. "Sorry. Messages, right. It's been a while. You're right, I should check."

He unzipped his bag and fished out the same grey cube he'd taken from his home's study much earlier. At a distance, it was just an ordinary grey cube, as unremarkable as an ancient Rubik's cube. Up close, though, numerous fine lines and sections of wear were visible. Small coverings slid out or off, and switches, toggles, or discreet sensor pads revealed themselves underneath. With everything buttoned up, even the most sensitive fingers would have trouble discerning the seams of the gunmetal surface. Minute pieces of debris lodged themselves in these spaces. Dust, skin cells, food, pollen: life's detritus. Every year, Jack would spend a few hours or so cleaning his cube, so the oddity remained remarkably well-maintained, considering the use it saw in his everyday life.

Opening a metal flap marked "thumb," Jack grasped the cube with his left hand. His thumb pressed against the revealed sensor pad, and his fingers squeezed with practiced ease. Equal pressure from five points around the cube triggered the boot-up sequence. Within seconds, Jack's ID was authenticated and he went to work checking his messages.

Another side of the cube turned on, and four small points projected a holographic interface out towards Jack. Tinged blue, the hologram let Jack interact with it however he saw fit. Unlike Betty's ocular lenses, Jack chose to manipulate the system with his hands. He made the display show a floating keyboard.

He put the cube between his legs on the bench and reached out a hand to grab the ethereal keyboard and accompanying screen, moving them around in the space until he was happy with their placement.

"Good lord, you know how to turn heads, don't you?" Betty's cheeks flushed as people slowed down to stare at Jack and his cube. "I have never seen anyone else continue on as you do. Everyone else checks things discreetly. Nobody uses these things anymore. And the typing! The next thing I know, you'll pull out an ink pen from your bag and start scrawling your reply. I'll never understand why you use something so...ancient."

Jack turned away from the blue-tinted holograms near his chest and looked towards his wife, pausing for a moment while considering his words.

"Be grateful there's no way to integrate a real keyboard into my setup, because if I could, I would. I didn't realize this caused you so much pain."

"No, but the looks we get. Every time you pull that thing out, it's like I'm on display."

"There's plenty of benches over there." Jack motioned across the way to where other people sat, expressions blank.

"That's just like you. Completely ignore what I'm saying, ignore how I feel, don't offer any solutions. Just fire back some useless reply. You know what? I think I will."

Betty stood, motioned for her luggage to follow her, and walked off.

First she asks if I've checked my messages and then she berates me for checking them. Feels like we're right on schedule. "It's not like I'm ditching my cube," he muttered.

Pushing all of that aside, Jack began combing through various accounts, letters, and messages. He remembered his friend, Dr. Harold Predmoor, and pulled up a vid. He muted it and toggled the captioning. Turning on an earpiece was too much hassle.

"Hi, Jack. Sorry to interrupt you like this, but I had a message from Boulder a few hours ago. One of the mining companies sent back a sample for someone to take a look at. Boulder sent me some scorch scans that were...well, pretty unbelievable. Give me a vid back when you can. Later."

The projection blanked and displayed the university's watermark. Jack quietly thanked his former self for upgrading the four projectors. Everything he'd just watched was totally private and free from prying eyes.

As the projection switched back to his university inbox, the message was nowhere to be seen.

That's odd. Did it have an auto-burn set?

Just as Jack speculated why Harold would bother with an auto-burn on a pretty routine correspondence, a new message popped into the interface, unbidden.

No sender, no subject, and it showed being sent only moments ago, while he watched Dr. Predmoor's message.

"What on Earth?"

He hesitated as he moved his hands over the phantom keyboard and pulled back several times while he pondered how the message before him was even possible. Every message should have a sender. Nearly discarding it several times without opening it, Jack couldn't get the idea out of his head that someone was waiting for him to read Harold's message and wanted to be sure to catch Jack's attention. Somehow, it felt safe.

He held his breath and exhaled. In the next moment, he opened it. The message was all text and only three lines long:

A find like this
Can't be verified.
Must come.

Jack read, and kept re-reading, the cryptic nine-word stanza, trying to puzzle it out. That it was related to Dr. Predmoor's first message seemed undeniable. But why the secrecy? Was this one from him too? Or was there someone else watching over his shoulder, trying to quietly catch his attention?

And why phrase it like this? It's very odd.

Something felt familiar, although he couldn't

place it at all. He let the back of his mind work on the idea as he zoned back in to the present.

Where was Betty?

Jack stood and looked around the terminal. Seeing the big overhead "W" nearby, he scanned around, first to the letters close to him, and then further afield. Q, P, N. No Betty. *Maybe she wandered off to go to the bathroom.* As his eyes dropped over the big letter "M," an idea crystallized and forced itself to the surface.

A, C, and M. Jack sat again and began to stare just as blankly as everyone around him, processing what his subconscious mind quickly figured out. Years had passed since he'd seen those initials, and as he struggled to accept that he knew the sender's identity, a flood of new questions crashed through his mind. Overriding all the others was a simple query: *why now?*

"I need to get to Boulder," Jack said as he powered down his cube and returned it to his bag.

"You're going *where?*"

A loud, shrill voice from behind froze him in his seat, and for a moment he closed his eyes. *Shit. Here we go.*

"Harold sent a message asking me to go out there," he said, conflating the two messages into one semi-truthful statement. *Well, it might be true.* "It sounded really urgent." The equivocation bought him some time to think as he waited for Betty to react.

"You're unbelievable. Absolutely unbelievable. Are you serious?" Several nearby people shifted. Jack wished they hadn't.

"Serious about what? Harold sent the vid. He says one of the mining companies sent down something to take a look at. You know how they are."

Again, Jack spoke in quiet half-measures, wanting to avoid the prying ears and de-escalate yet another argument with his wife.

"I don't care *what* they sent down. You're not going to Boulder."

Betty's voice now attracted everyone in earshot as the buzz of other conversations diminished.

"Is that so?" Jack replied.

"Yeah. You aren't going."

"Did you think I was talking about going right this instant?"

"Right now, later, whenever. It doesn't matter. You aren't going."

Betty stared straight at him.

Jack paused to consider his next move. He hadn't been thinking of leaving right then and there, but hearing Betty issue orders made him again reconsider spending a week of vacation with her. He certainly wasn't getting on any ferry with this hanging over his head.

"Hello! I'm talking to you!"

"No, you aren't. You're yelling orders at me. In public." Jack quietly looked up at his wife. He felt his ears burn.

"Oh, whatever. Get over it. Look, get up. We're going to miss the ferry otherwise. And don't sit there and complain about hating being on boats either, or whatever it is you're so scared of. I swear, you Wilsons might be loaded, but you're a pain in the ass in so many other ways."

People stopped in their tracks and began to crowd as Betty raged on, oblivious to her own spectacle. At the mention of their last name, all eyes turned to Jack.

If there were ever a time when Jack wished humans had learned to teleport items larger than quantum bits, this was it. There wasn't a bench big enough to crawl under or a throng of people large enough to jump into at that moment. The entire terminal halted and peeked over each other's shoulders to watch a woman scream at her husband in an incoherent rage. Having their last name broadcast for everyone to hear only magnified the scene, until Jack could no longer stand it.

He grabbed his belongings and began walking back towards the "W" as an unstated thought guided him. He shouldered past the dozens of people standing in his way. Some of them stared at him, while others turned their attention back towards Betty.

She continued to scream somewhere behind him, her voice somehow getting louder as he put more people between them. He scanned the fleet of shuttles for something just below his plane of thought. Finally, as the distance between Betty and him became too great for her voice to continue piercing, his eyes found their target: a green shuttle, right where it had been before. Jack walked to its side, opened the door, threw in his luggage, and dove in after, closing the door behind him. The luggage burst open on impact, but he didn't care. He exhaled, realizing he hadn't taken a breath in... thirty seconds? A minute?

What the hell are you doing, Jack?

I'm getting out of here. Right now, came an unbidden reply. *I can't believe I'm about to do this. I swore I'd never, ever use this.* "Wilson override privilege. Destination: University of Chicago. Wilson Science Center. Embark."

Looks like saving the world finally paid off for one of us. The shuttle started rolling. It slipped quickly away from the curb and got to speed, leaving behind a sea of staring faces. One woman, still screaming at her husband, took no notice.

4

The green shuttle went faster and faster, clearing the dropoff area and racing back south. Jack, finally alone, lost his composure and screamed. Not a scream at anyone, but a scream that led quickly to tears. As he curled onto his side, somewhere in the back of his mind a tiny rational thought peeped through, nearly drowned out by the bottled emotions now echoing through the small shuttle cabin. Emotions heard by no one and nothing, aside from the shuttle AI, which paid him no heed.

The cube, Jack. It's on.

He felt for his old grey cube through bloomed and blurried eyes, amidst the belongings scattered around the cabin. Finally, his fingers ran across it. Working fast, he pulled back the little thumb flap and pressed his finger against the tiny scanner, keeping the rest of his hand clenched in a thumbless fist. Three red lights lit up around the cube and Jack dropped it back to the shuttle floor. He was truly alone and, shortly thereafter, asleep.

A soft, golden light filtered through falling leaves as Jack became aware of his surroundings. Majestic trees displayed themselves in all their splendor, showcasing an array of color rivaled only by high prairie. Sunbeams shimmered through the pallet. Leaves twirled and spun as a master marionette pulled one billion tiny strings.

Jack strained to see past the trees and into the void beyond. Thick fog threw itself at every opening he thought he saw. One by one, the leaves stopped moving, and the rays retreated behind the canopy. The forest grew as a painted landscape: calm and motionless.

Overcome by his surroundings, Jack began to inhabit what his eyes and body sensed. He realized his feet no longer moved. Then, his arms. A heavy blanket crept over him.

He looked down at the blanket but saw no quilt. Red, orange, and yellow leaves instead covered him from neck to toe. He watched as the trees shed their leaves individually and all at once. Every leaf's path through the air concluded nearby.

Renewal and decay mixed in Jack's nose as he drifted off. In the moment before the leaves winked out of existence, a voice whispered, "Hold my hand."

Jack reached out, guided by an unconscious future, and found the warm, dry hand, ever so slightly smaller than his own. He held it as the forest closed with darkness.

Pink sky greeted Jack. He woke up disoriented and on his back, staring at the shuttle's roof. As he began to remember where he was, he looked down, half-expecting to see a pile of leaves at his feet, but found only his socks instead. Although he couldn't quite recall the voice that had whispered to him, his right hand felt warm while the rest of him stayed quite cool.

Time passed, the trance waned, and he sat up to look out the window. The sun hugged the horizon and the pinks of earlier morphed into deep reds and purples as it sank. Jack stared at it through the protection of the window's polarized glass, contemplated the slowness of it all, and wondered when he'd last seen a sunset. He thought back to college out west.

"Yeah, that had to be it," Jack said out loud. His voice pierced what had become a nearly silent background, the only other sound being the occasional vibration as the shuttle rolled over a rough patch of road.

"You should watch this one, Jack. There's nothing to interrupt," he said to himself. "Shuttle, pull off at the next available point."

What have you gotten yourself into, just leaving like that?

His mind wandered and he began to think about what he was going to do once the shuttle got back to Chicago. He could already see the city on the horizon, the slender star ladder soaring high, along with faint silhouettes of some of the other buildings. *I wonder if anyone's tried reaching me.*

Jack searched around the shuttle floor for his cube, still powered down, while he waited for the shuttle to come to a pull-off section. He found it as the shuttled slowed. His thumb smashed against the scanner again and he squeezed. The little cube popped to life alongside his anxiety, and Jack braced for a deluge of missed messages and notifications.

The shuttle jerked slightly and pulled onto the side strip of permeable concrete.

The cube remained silent.

The brakes finished and everything came to a halt. Still nothing. No vids, nothing missed. Nobody had contacted him. Jack exhaled. Several deep breaths later, he opened the door and made his way towards the horizon, away from the shuttle and off the road entirely. An enormous rock sat amidst a small strip of shorter grass twenty yards away, half again as tall as Jack and jutting straight into the air. As he headed towards it, he looked back and saw nothing and no one on the road.

I wonder how close the nearest person is. Five miles? Ten? The idea unsettled him for a moment as he pushed close to the boulder. The sun was nearly beneath the horizon and, if he didn't hurry, he'd lose the light.

He waded through knee-high grass. *Wow, look at those.* Hundreds of thin parallel lines etched themselves across the rock's flat surface, their white striations contrasting with the pink and black speckles beneath. He ran his fingers across them, tracing in his mind's eye the event that created them thousands of years ago.

The glacial megalith originated far to the north, much farther than he'd traveled today. At some point, one of the great ice sheets of Earth's past had dragged it along its underbelly for many hundreds of miles, scratching and scraping under thousands of feet of ice, until it eventually deposited the ragged rock in its present location.

Jack considered what the world looked like then, those prehistoric glaciers pushing down sea levels during their lives as much as the deaths of their more modern cousins had raised them.

His gaze returned to the setting sun. He scrambled up the rough, broken edges of the massive granite stone to a relatively flat section at the top and set his cube up to grab holograms. A few switches flipped, a few covers opened, and blue lights dimly blinked around the sides of the cube. He backed away and let the grey workhorse take in its own version of reality, capturing not just the setting sun but also the waving grasses, the swaying flowers, and the quiet breeze. The light held for a full twenty minutes while he sat beneath the cube, in a crevasse out of view of the cameras. As the sun sank beneath the horizon, Jack reached out to stop the capture. Twenty minutes of time and space retreated into the cube and copied itself into his files immediately, letting him relive the experience whenever he wanted. The big holo-centers would be ideal for these sorts of recreations but, in a pinch, his home's study would suffice. He could even show his students the facsimile, explaining the promise of better days for future generations. Or use it to simulate a field experience.

"Jesus, Jack. Your office. Get home."

Jack stood and stretched, and noted the thousands of fireflies bobbing just above the sea of grass. Like a cresting wave, they undulated with the breeze and flickered in and out of sight. Jack realized he hadn't seen something like this in years and took another quiet moment for himself. Then he grabbed the cube, offered the stone monolith one final brush of his hand, and walked to the shuttle. The door opened automatically with his approach. He got in. Through the opposite window, he finally saw another shuttle whiz by. With no sunlight and a new moon, he'd nearly missed it.

Several hours later, the shuttle deposited him in front of the university's science building. He shouldered a backpack. The suitcase he'd packed that morning extricated itself and followed close behind.

He hopped out to a noisy city, lit up like cities had been for centuries, with dots of light streaming out of windows, doors, streetlights, and gadgets. Unlike cities of old, however, Chicago had no need to worry about its energy supply. Long ago, renewable capacity outstripped even the most gluttonous human demands, as technologies like solar paint and no-loss batteries proliferated. Power outages were a thing of the past, much like lamp oil and wooden wheels. And while there was still light pollution, there were also quiet, dark places in every home, even in a city of three hundred million people.

The Wilson Science Center towered over him and everything else towered over it. Familiar streetlights shone down on the sidewalk as he approached the center's revolving doors. Trees grew over the lights to shield any stray beams. From a distance, the entrance glowed dimly, like a pixie in a forest deep at night.

This forest was, of course, dwarfed by the buildings around it, the trees engineered to grow in an artificial urban understory. Jack's brief walk along the sheltered path brought a few moments of peace. The busy city felt invisible under the canopy. If he stopped to look around, he could do so in solitude, much as he'd done along the highway. Even in a city with buildings a mile high, urban planners had purposely included green spaces.

They'd packed trees and pockets of smaller plants into every conceivable spot, in the ground and high in the air. By doing so, they'd brought nature into humanity, however artificial and managed it might be. The thick summer foliage muted incoming city noise as Jack walked. He heard sparrows flit from nearby branches and briefly saw a pair of yellow eyes peer out at him, no doubt a curious raccoon watching the path late at night.

"I wonder if Harold is even still here," Jack said to himself. "Why am *I* here? I could just go to bed and come back tomorrow morning."

Jack puffed his cheeks and slowly blew out the air. *Maybe I'll get lucky and she won't be there. Then I could get a quiet night's sleep.*

The churning in Jack's stomach made him pause at the foot of the steps. He sat down before heading inside, collecting himself and his thoughts. He faced the tree-lined path in the fuzzy dimness and looked at the sky, hoping to spot constellations.

This is such a joke. I see maybe thirty stars up there. "What am I doing?" *Today started out so well...or had it?* Jack closed his eyes. It was so hard to remember. The arguing felt like the arguments from yesterday and the day before that. What had started it all? It was so difficult to focus on the events. They just ran together in a tumbled, jumbled mess, leaving him anxious and wondering what would happen the next time he spoke to his wife. He couldn't keep this up every day, waiting for the next thing to go wrong, the next explosion, the next hour-long tirade about whatever he'd screwed up.

I can't keep hiding at work all the time, either. But if I bring any of this up, I'll just get told I'm being too sensitive, and I should just be more of a man about it, whatever that's supposed to mean. When's being married supposed to be fun?

"Jack? That you?"

A deep voice behind him startled Jack out of his thoughts. The roiling in his stomach momentarily coursed throughout his body as a wave of adrenaline passed. Jack stumbled badly as he spun around, nearly smashing his face into the pavement. He looked up and saw a friendly smile greet him as he recovered.

Dr. Harold Predmoor's curly white hair and dark skin made a negative of sorts to Jack's complexion. The man's antique metal glasses, round and curved with a thin gold frame, were something out of a history book. No far-off absent-minded look ever fell over Harold's eyes. The professor preferred his tech separate and apart from himself, much like Jack and his well-worn cube.

"Crap! Yes. Hi. You really startled me. How are you?" Jack looked around wide-eyed, glancing into the dark spots nearby.

"I'm fine, but you look like shit, Jack. What are you doing here? I thought you're supposed to be out of the city."

"So did I." Jack felt his ears warm and they were no doubt turning red. Jack wondered if his friend would be able to notice in the dim light. He looked down at the steps.

Harold regarded Jack for a moment. He'd seen Jack startle like that before, and he knew what it meant. *Poor guy. I don't think that man has been happy in…since college. Maybe by the end of tonight he'll be distracted enough to settle down and forget about her for a while.* "Do you want to talk about it?" *There's no way he wants to talk about whatever it is this time, but I have to try.*

Jack gazed up, wondering if he should drop such a weight on someone else. "No, not right now. Maybe later, though. Thanks for asking. Your message said something about a find?"

Analyzing asteroid returns was something Betty had never shown interest in, ever, even though it was a significant portion of what Jack did.

Harold smiled. *That was a not so subtle hint, wasn't it.* "You have no idea. Come on in, let's talk. Oh, and keep your shoes on."

Jack froze for a split second at Harold's last remark. He'd heard that same line once before, many years ago during their university days. Looking one final time at the sky, he began walking up the steps towards the revolving doors and remembered the time Harold had saved both their lives.

5

The transition of Jack's academic focus away from terrestrial science and agriculture, to astrobiology and exopaleoecology, happened as he neared the end of freshman year at college. Night upon endless night in Boulder, far away from any ladder city's evening glow, opened Jack to the circling stars overhead.

At first, the whole group of students from Dr. Amundsun's seminar class took to the evenings outside, when it was warm. The late sun meant the group could stay out for hours without regretting it too much the following morning. Fall semesters of freshmen years are often like that.

Each week the sun stuck around less. A minute here and a minute there. Or a few missed days added up, and the group shrank as some members found the night air a little less inviting. The long sleeves and jackets came out first, and then hats and gloves. The more clothes needed, the fewer people decided the experience was worth it, and folks found one excuse or another to find somewhere else to be.

Slowly but surely, the original group thinned, going from twenty to fifteen, and then to twelve. For a while that dozen held out, but after the first frost in November the dozen shrank to nine, and then eight, and then six. Jack was one who stuck it out, his childhood memories of exploring with his parents urging him to stay.

Of the remaining six, four were from the original group that had shown up to the farm one morning several months ago, when Dr. Amundsun stood them all up. There was Farheed, still with his blue steel mug, plus Jack, Harold, and Aramae. Ember and Hannah, two other girls who tended to talk whenever a silent moment happened in seminar, also remained. Their voices were always appreciated, even if Jack sometimes wished they'd use them just a little less.

These six remained constantly awed by the vastness of space and the sheer beauty of the stars and the Milky Way overhead. Even more mind-boggling to them were the planets orbiting so many of those faint dots of light, unnoticed and unseen, enjoyed in their obscurity.

"What do you suppose the Proxima Centauri colony sees every night when they look up?" Hannah asked as Thanksgiving approached. The group looked at her, their minds all imagining an alien sky around an impossibly distant planet, orbiting a faint speck of light above their heads.

Farheed sipped his tea, his breath barely visible against the galactic center behind him. "I imagine... that they look up every night. They look up at their stars and create new constellations for themselves. Some of them must tell stories to their children about the shapes in the sky and where Sol is. And so they're slowly weaving together a new tapestry of mythos on their world. And it's one where we are as much of a speck in the sky to them as they are now to us. But I bet they have an amazing, primeval view of their sky. There's not much there yet to drown it out. It's pristine."

"And incredibly far away. None of us here will ever see it with our own eyes," Ember chimed in with her thoughts, and the conversation steered in a new direction for a bit before silence filled the cold.

A fourth voice spoke, "That's okay with me. Just knowing that they're out there, that it's out there, is enough for me. Even if I know I'll never see it, it's comforting. It's comforting to know that there's over a thousand humans forever beyond the reach of any of us. Nothing we do will affect their world. That, that is calm."

The group all turned to Aramae, who rarely

chose to speak, even though the six of them had now been together for three months.

Jack picked up her gauntlet.

"I get the calm. I do. At the same time, it's incredibly bleak, don't you think? Look at all of these stars overhead. And that's only a fraction of them! And we've been looking at them and listening in every direction, in every conceivable way, for hundreds of years. Centuries. Two different *millennia*. Ancient-history lengths of time. And there's only one single star in this entire sky that we've ever, ever heard anything from. One. And it's only because *we* went there. Ourselves. All of these other stars, all of them, all these other planets orbiting out there. Millions of them that we've found, and the only thing we hear is our own human echo, whispering faintly. *Are we it?*"

Aramae stared back at Jack, the pair easily the quietest among the group, even when the group had numbered twenty. And here they were, revealing parts of themselves to the other. They regarded each other in the starlight for several minutes as the other four continued the conversation on their own. Neither broke their gaze as they searched in the dimness for any hint of what the other was thinking. A crinkled upturn in one corner of Jack's mouth and an almost imperceptible turning aside of Aramae's head passed unnoticed to everyone else, but each gesture reached their intended audience. Before they could get any farther, Harold spoke and pulled Jack back into the group.

"Hey Jack, have you ever gone to a Listener's meeting? There's a group out here that meets every so often. Think any of you would be interested?"

"I thought those were just a myth?" Hannah asked. Everyone else stopped talking. "Like, no one's been listening for a century, my parents always told me. I'd just read about them in books. Who listens?"

"No one," Farheed answered, "Harold's just pulling our leg, that's all. It was dangerous then, and it's even more dangerous today. It's a dead art." He held up his thermos. "Come, my tea is gone and it's past one. Let's head in. I've got an exobiology speech tomorrow and if I'm half-sunk, Doctor Tischler will finish the job and bury me." Farheed stood, capped his mug, and began walking back toward the dorms. Ember and Hannah followed close. Jack and Aramae meandered along, letting some distance grow between them and the rest, when Harold tugged at Jack's sleeve out of nowhere. Jack turned.

"I wasn't kidding," Harold said quietly, the rim of his glasses glinting in the faintest way. "When I started this year, I found out about the Listener group. It's real. Do you want to come? I've been going for the last couple of months and I think you'd be interested."

Jack's desire to catch up to Aramae dimmed slightly but still glowed. He stood frozen while he considered Harold's words.

"Yes. Find me in the morning," he stammered out. Turning back to Aramae, he saw she had caught up to the other two girls and was idly chatting with them.

Damn.

Jack found himself in the cafeteria's short line the next morning and grabbed his standard coffee and croissant.

Although the university enrolled only a few thousand students, owing largely to its uncommon science specialization, it boasted some of the best food at any North American school and had for generations. Nobody could quite put a finger on why. Maybe it was the elevation, high in the mountain air, some theorized. Perhaps the on-campus farm, growing food outdoors in dirt, gave the local harvests something extra, a certain *je ne sais quoi,* an essence not found in the more traditional vertical farms central to food production in every star ladder city around the world. Or perhaps it was something else entirely, an ethereal unknown that couldn't be touched or transported or tamed. Something embedded in the centuries of history of the school itself and the generations of students that passed through its halls.

Regardless, the coffee was good. Same with the croissants, and the eggs, and the soy bacon, the oatmeal, and anything else Jack could have wanted that morning. Simple fare always suited him best, though. Probably, he once thought, because it let him get outside and move around his forest as a little kid. It's hard to hike holding a bowl.

Memories of his childhood forest floated by as he absentmindedly sipped black coffee. He looked out the dining hall's panoramic windows and took in an ancient coniferous forest. Just like his memories, the morning scene was a little shrouded, the dining hall mostly quiet. The stillness of the open room, filled with tables and chairs, mirrored what Jack saw outside. The first snowfall of the year had arrived a few weeks later than normal. In the slowly brightening grey light, the sun gave the sky a very pale glow, illuminating huge snowflakes. These fell straight down, landing on trees and the forest floor below.

Without wind, the scene was serene, silent, still. Perfect for enjoying breakfast alone at a small table, joined only by an old wooden chair, layered with at least a dozen coats of varnish to smooth out a century's worth of early-morning routines.

Jack's spot in the dining hall that morning not only allowed the unobstructed view, but also provided no other seats near him. The table held a theoretical space for one more, but there were no chairs anywhere close by. Anyone who wanted to join him for a chat would have to work at it, meaning he'd likely screen out any idle, pointless conversations. Only someone who really wanted to talk would bother him. He smiled at the accumulating snow.

Metal screamed on concrete and sent a shiver through Jack like no blizzard could. The other scattered diners all jerked their heads towards the intrusion into their morning.

Ancient glasses and curly white hair, combined with a wide shit-eating grin, greeted Jack as he looked to see Harold purposely dragging a chair towards him with one arm. After a full minute, the screeching finally ended and Harold sat down across the small table. He pressed his shoulder against the panoramic window as though it were a wall.

"You're such a shit, you know that?" Jack said, smiling.

"What? I needed a chair. You oh-so-cleverly moved all of the ones near you away, so I grabbed one." Harold's impossibly wide grin persisted.

"You grabbed literally the farthest chair from me, you goof. And then you dragged it like a parent dragging a petulant toddler. And you made nearly as much noise." Jack ripped a piece of croissant and popped it in his mouth, rolling it around.

"I like to make an entrance. What can I say? By the way, I'm sorry about last night. I did the math as I got back to my room."

"That's okay. It'll work out."

Harold eyed his friend. "You really like her, don't you? She's cute..."

Jack felt his ears warm precipitously. "She's unique. And yeah, smartass, she's cute. It's just... hard to catch a moment with her, you know? We're both so closed off. I think. Either that or she's just closed off around me. I can never tell."

"It'll happen, Jack. Eventually. And anyways I didn't come down here so early to bust your balls about her. I figured it'd be quiet enough that I could tell you about the Listener meetings, and you had already left your dorm."

"Yeah. I'm interested. I definitely want to know more." A million and one questions raced through Jack all at once, but none of them formed enough to be spoken. He hoped Harold could just read his mind.

"Okay. Let's go with…what do you already know? About Listeners and everything. That'd be a good place to start. What have you heard?"

"I've heard only static," Jack said, "and seen nothing but noise."

Jack noticed Harold's eyes go wide as he recited the couplet known only to fellow Listeners.

"Are you crazy, uttering that in the dining hall? What if someone overhears? It's dangerous enough listening to the stars without *advertising it in public.*" Harold glanced around and kept his body calm, but his typically bellowing voice dropped and was barely audible. His dark skin looked suddenly paler in the light of the still-grey morning.

"One advantage to sitting alone. Unless there's someone literally in earshot, nobody can hear what we're saying. My cube's always set to counterjam. It's even making this window vibrate. Just one of those Wilson things."

Harold looked dumbfounded. "You mean that

beat-up thing I've seen you carry around? I thought that was just your interface."

"Oh, it is. It does a lot of other stuff besides get my messages and place vidcalls, though. It's rather exceptional, actually. I've had it for...oh, about as long as I've been listening. So since I was eight."

Harold sat back and scrutinized his friend's body language for a long minute. After unclenching his jaw for a third time, Harold arrived at a decision. "Grab that croissant, and one for the road. We're going for a walk. Get me one too, while you're at it. Should be easy enough to walk and carry one of those with me."

Jack chuckled softly and grabbed his coat, keeping the cube in his pocket untouched and running. He pocketed not two, but four croissants and topped off his coffee thermos. *You never know.* He hurried after Harold, who was already outside the cafeteria and heading down three flights of stairs to the hall's back door.

The exit led straight out into the boreal wilderness he had viewed from the window only minutes before. The door saw little use and attracted even less attention. No walkway or dirt path greeted them, just frozen ground and a quarter inch of the fluffy white stuff that swirled in the air, riding invisible waves. Harold had moved quickly and was out of sight by the time Jack exited. He followed the lone footprints into the pine trees.

Another piece of croissant vanished into his mouth as he entered the forest's edge and stopped to observe the silence. Snow from overhead slowly filled the canopy. It stuck to the branches and needles and pine cones here or there, in small amounts, but mostly made its way to the forest floor. The crystalline flakes reflected weak sunlight from every angle, filling the space with light and leaving nothing in the shadows.

Jack assumed his friend had his own reasons for getting out of the dining hall in a hurry and, absent any other tracks, was confident he would run into Harold, and only Harold, soon.

Sure enough, two minutes into the ponderosa pines and Douglas firs, he saw a small opening ahead where his friend stood. Jack paused, looked around, and felt nothing amiss. Harold's calm body language told Jack that there was nothing to fear. *Maybe the Listener meetings out here are remote enough to not attract attention.*

Harold, in fact, was looking at the sky: hat off, eyes closed, letting snowflakes fall on his face. His curly white hair took on a fuller appearance in the light.

I wonder how close I can get until he hears me. Hmm. I haven't played this game with anyone since I was a kid. And my parents knew I was playing. This could get interesting.

Glancing at the ground, Jack stepped out of the line of footprints and into fresh powder. His footsteps crept along, muffled by the snow. For a moment, he wondered if he'd regret wearing shoes instead of boots on their outing, especially if the snow kept up. Mindful of his joints, he tried to sense any potential cracking or popping that might give him away, but everything felt good. Harold hadn't budged.

Jack knelt and grabbed a line of the snow with a gloved hand, fashioned a rough sphere, and then made a second one as well. *I'm so glad I at least wore gloves.* He took aim and threw.

Half a second passed as Jack watched the snowball find its mark, hitting the end of a dead branch on a pine tree on the opposite side of the opening. Jack's aim was rewarded with a loud crack as the snowball shot the branch in two.

Harold's head snapped around in the direction of the noise, his eyes searching for Jack, momentarily confused and trying to make sense of the shapes under the canopy, looking for the human form.

Jack's fleeting window opened just long enough. He scooped up the second snowball and fired a rocket straight at Harold's broad back. The powder exploded into a thousand glittering shards and Jack got to watch as Harold spun around, jumped with a start, and nearly spilled over from fright.

"Jack! What!? How did you get over…oh, you jerk. I suppose that's payback for my stunt in the cafeteria?" Funny disbelief washed over Harold. "How long were you standing there? I never even heard you approach. I didn't hear you in the woods at all. How did you do that?"

"Many, many years of practice, starting when I

was very young. Until I was six, there was a forest in my back yard, and my parents and I spent a lot of time there."

The two were moving again, on some route that Harold apparently knew. Jack was content to follow and see where they would eventually end up.

"Your parents had a yard?" Harold finally asked. "Nobody has a yard, let alone a forest behind it. Where did you grow up?"

"The extreme western edge of Chicago, where the city never developed much or grew tall like the rest of it. We're talking a hundred miles from the lake."

Nearly everyone knew the basic layout and location of the city, much like centuries before, when nearly everyone knew places like New York City or Washington, D.C.

"And they owned a home and a yard? And a forest? Like something out of ancient urban history class? What do your parents do?"

"Well. The first part of that, that far west it's almost entirely carbon sink. All of it. Our house was one of just a few out that way. You don't travel very far east from there before getting back to the skyrises. Maybe a handful of miles, and in between is all tallgrass sink. So we were sort of our own little island, and stayed that way because some of the residents hold a lot of political sway. Otherwise, I'm sure someone would have taken over the place decades ago. Anyways the forest. Like I said, it got cut down when I was six. I didn't know it at the time, but someone, somewhere had unearthed some truly ancient land surveys. Like, seven hundred years old or something ridiculous like that. It showed the forest was originally prairie. And what with the push for accuracy from the Reconstructionists, it...well, my parents and everyone else fought the rulings for a couple of years, but eventually it had to come down for something more 'efficient and permanent.' I think they compromised by leaving the oaks and promising to reconstruct it as oak savanna, just to shut everyone up and leave a few of the big old trees. I remember they left exactly one. One tree. They cut the rest of the forest down and began reverting it. From what I think I heard, they even had some latent seeds germinate a few years after. Totally blew everyone's mind that they were still viable. Something like six centuries since its original state—never was tilled for dirt farming—but the trees were allowed to grow and it sort of got lost in time. It was an amazing forest to explore. I guess I never had anything to compare it to, really, until I got out here. It was all I knew. Which was still more than everyone else had easy access to. Anyhow I'm rambling here," Jack truncated himself, hoping the conversation would change topics.

"That's all great, but it still doesn't answer how you could afford that. The top floor of a skyrise doesn't cost what actual *land* costs to own. How high up the ladder are you?" Harold stopped and gazed at his friend, out alone, the two of them in the woods as the flurries began to fall just a little faster.

Jack shrank to the size of one of those snowflakes and the trees grew twice as tall. *Here we go. I hope I can find my way back to school.* "Um. Well, it's old money. My parents were teachers. My dad's side of the family is…"

"Loaded. Right. I get that. But how? Usually the rich flaunt it around and talk all about it. You definitely are uncomfortable," Harold paused. "You know what? I don't need to know. I can respect that." Harold began to walk again, towards the destination only he knew. The snow continued to increase and the wind started to bite.

Jack stood still. "I'm Rebecca Wilson's great-grandson. That's how we live in that house."

Harold stopped walking and stood, his back facing Jack, hands in his pockets. "And you think I'm going to hold that against you? Tell me, Jack. Did you personally kill three billion people?"

Jack looked down, focusing on the snowflakes. Working on his answer. "No. And neither did she."

"And if it weren't for her work, her discovery, it would be raining right now. And we'd both be soaking wet."

"That's tough to say, I suppose. But sure. It'd probably be raining. What difference does that make?"

"It means that those three billion people that froze or starved would have baked instead, or starved still, along with a lot of others, if not for your great-great-grandmother."

"Great-grandmother."

"Sure, okay. Whatever. So she goes and discovers how to turn carbon dioxide into oxygen and diamond."

"Graphite. Well, a certain type of graphite and a bunch of derivatives, but yeah."

Harold shrugged. "I never could keep it straight. So she discovers how to do...that. Really this incredible thing, right? I mean, that was the late twenty-second century. Greenhouse gas levels were way too high, and everything was going to shit really quick. People were terrified."

"Something like that," Jack said. He looked at his shoes, which were slowly disappearing as snow stuck to itself.

"Way crazy high," Harold continued. "That's about when the last glaciers went."

"Great-grandma Becky would tell me that they broke up when she was a kid. So I think they were long gone when she did her work and made her discovery. She always had loads of stories about the old coastal cities. Places like New York, Orlando. She actually visited them when she was a child. Like, the actual city, not the water-logged ruins. Anyways the last of the ice went when she was young."

Harold took several steps back towards Jack, his boots leaving heavy footprints in the snow behind him.

"Rebecca Wilson saved civilization, Jack. She got rich selling her discovery, and some people were very bothered by that, but it was hers to sell. I don't blame her. She took advantage of the situation and set your family up for basically *forever*. Didn't she also secure some special privileges from the government at the time?"

"Just some simple override commands. Nothing major. Stuff like near-AIs. I've never used it, and I don't think my parents have, either."

"Really? I'd use something like that constantly. Sounds awesome."

Jack shrugged, looked up at Harold, and back again at the snow. "Most everyone changed their names and swore off their heritage after the Great Drop. The whole world blamed her. Nobody wanted to be a Wilson."

"It was so long ago, Jack. The big air mining groups all scapegoated her. Anyone who studies history knows that now. It was a total hatchet job. Everyone got too greedy. Dreams of pulling money out of thin air, literally. Plus, they all wanted to be the first to get a ladder up, even ones that barely qualified."

"Yeah, well, you're forgetting. She owned stock in one of those groups and held considerable sway. She helped push them all to over-extract. By the time they hit one-eighty, it was too late. Everyone thought the northern tundra would release more latent methane for a while, but it never happened. Mammoths, man. Mammoths ruined it all. Nobody actually thought they'd have a huge impact."

Harold glared at Jack, letting the pun go unanswered. Good thing they knew how to get levels up again, huh? And here we are today. Thanks for telling me. I must have been daydreaming when the professor called roll on the first day."

The two set off again through the pines, Jack a step behind his friend as the flakes fell steadily enough to limit their visibility to perhaps a few hundred feet. Beyond that, the forest became impenetrably dim and grey, hidden behind an ever-changing patchwork of falling snow.

After another twenty minutes of hiking through the giant conifers, Jack stepped onto something hard, smooth, and flat. By now the snow was several inches deep, leaving the ground a uniform white. Several more steps felt the same. As he peered around at the frozen blanket, he understood.

"A road?"

"It used to be. Who knows how long ago."

Behind winter's veil were shapes familiar to Jack, squares and triangles and rectangles arranged in recognizable patterns, the silhouettes of homes barely visible from the roadway as Harold took the two of them straight up the middle of the street. On either side, they could make out the structures, now run-down and derelict. In most cases their decrepit frames, no longer plumb, leaned at just the odd enough angle to elicit an uncomfortable feeling in the stomach, as though the neglect and abandonment could somehow reach out and touch the two of them. Jack quickened his steps, the cadence of mutely crunching snow beneath his boots increasing as the pair moved further down the road. After several more minutes, Jack recognized enough bits and pieces to put together what he was walking through. *The odd flatness in front of each foundation, a rare post by the road, the relative monotony of the layout. This was a neighborhood.*

"People lived here," Jack whispered.

"Some still do."

Jack pondered this as they continued. Looking back once or twice, he could see his furthest footsteps fade to ripples across an otherwise unbroken expanse of white and grey. The old neighborhood, slowly disappearing into the forest, seemed content to let the pair pass through unhindered.

The road wound along the rolling terrain as it passed by collapsed or leaning houses. The snow continued, and after a while the old structures resembled white heaps more than anything else. In winter, it seemed, the forest had ways of covering up the past.

Harold's pace slowed and he began looking from side to side.

"Lost?" Jack asked. He ripped a layer off another

of his provisioned croissants.

"Not exactly. The snow is making it hard to reference things. We're close, don't worry."

"Close to what? There's nothing out here."

"Just wait."

"Croissant?" Jack offered one of the uneaten pastries.

"Sure, why not. Thanks."

The two of them stood in the middle of the long-abandoned road as the snow continued.

Jack watched his friend try to recognize the place, which became more difficult with each new moment. He wondered how they'd trek back to school with their footprints obscured. More time went by, more croissants vanished, and Harold wandered in the snow.

"Can you call it up on an overhead map, whatever it is you're looking for?" Jack asked.

"I could, but I'm not sure that'd help. I've never needed to look at one before. More importantly, the place is laid out specifically to look innocuous from orbit. It'd blend right in. We'd never see it."

Jack paused, "What if we could remove the snow?"

"Like, by hand?"

"Yeah. Start digging." Jack shook his head and smiled, and took from his jacket the small cube Harold had seen earlier that morning in the cafeteria. He flipped a few toggles and switches, opened a few covers, and up sprang his interface.

Shortly after, maps of where they were appeared in front of him. His cube's algorithms dug through satellite passes, ancient USGS surveys, old urban plans, and anything else it could find, compiling as much information as possible into a rendering program somewhere inside the cube's six square panels. No more than a minute later, the little holoprojector lights flickered to life, generating a world of blue lines which spread out several feet around and between them in all directions. Contour lines hugged small versions of the road, the trees, foundations of decrepit houses, and more, all there before them in three miniaturized dimensions. A faint red dot signified their location, and the four cardinal directions were marked in green all around the little world.

"That's quite the nifty toy you've got there. What else can that thing do?" Harold asked as he tried to find his bearings anew.

"Oh, it's got its uses. Never needed it for a hunt, though. I'm glad I brought it with us."

"I think I've got it. Can you zoom it in? Over here?" Harold asked. He pointed to a spot in space with his finger, breaking several of the blue contour lines with his motion. At that, the map zoomed in on the spot he'd pointed to, and the blue lines redrew themselves to show more detail.

"There it is," Harold said to himself, focusing on some point in space. "And based on where we're at...we go this way." Harold motioned with his head. "Thank you. I'd have never found the marker stones without this."

They trudged off towards what looked like an open patch of land, no doubt once a driveway from an era nearly beyond remembering. Jack felt the ground beneath his feet change as they left the road. He glanced at his cube, still lit up and throwing out thin blue lines into the snowy sky. Harold stumbled over something buried under the snowfall.

"Found it," he said, brushing away some of the snow with his foot. He cleared the rock's perimeter and stood back, examining its shape. He knelt, and with his gloved hand cleared away the top of the rock as well. Granitic pinks, blacks, and greys mottled and marred the white landscape.

"Did I see you fill that thermos with coffee? Right before we left?" Harold asked, without looking away from the stone.

Jack offered the thermos. "Yep. Want some?"

Harold took it and continued to brush the granite with his glove, cleaning out snow from the cracks and crevices endemic to the worn surface.

He unscrewed the cap, turned it upside down, and filled it with coffee. Slowly, he poured it over the granite and let the heat melt the snow in the cracks he couldn't reach with his fingers. With the last of the coffee, Jack could finally see what Harold had been searching for.

A faint irregular line etched its way across the granite edifice, twisting and turning between mineral crystals. It reminded Jack of erosion patterns from geology class. The etching wound down around one face of the rock and back up again, completing a circuitous path back to its origin and looking ever so much like a section weathered by repeated frosting, ready to heave and slough off after a few more years.

Harold took off a glove. He used his bare hand to rip the section of granite clean away with one smooth, practiced motion.

Jack stared at his friend, bewildered.

Harold laughed and tossed the rock section to Jack. "See? It's magnetic. Forms a perfect seal."

The hunk weighed far less than Jack thought it should and he immediately saw why. Instead of a solid chunk of rock, what Harold pried from the boulder was merely a veneer, the underside of the granite polished and lined around the entire edge with a dark magnetic strip, perhaps a centimeter wide and barely as thick as a human hair.

The boulder now looked conspicuously modified. A matching magnetic strip bordered the gaping hole left by Harold and, inside the void, another hollowed-out section contained a single rocker switch. Harold gave it a flick, took the veneer back as Jack watched, and carefully replaced the covering. If Jack hadn't watched the whole sequence with his own eyes, he'd have never believed it.

"Come on, we've got about two minutes," Harold said.

"Two...uhhh, okay. Hey, the boulder, look," Jack

said. He pointed to a blue dot shining on the rock.

"Yep. We follow it. Hurry." Harold stepped between the beam and the rock, and managed to find the direction of the source, mostly because the falling snow made the beam easy to spot. Jack followed Harold as the two walked the diffuse trail in front of them, heading straight into the trees. After about a hundred yards, they could make out a metal cylinder protruding out of the earth, maybe three feet tall, its flat top covered with leaves, needles, branches, and snow. The blue beam's origin was clear.

Harold walked right to the cylinder, flipped up the camouflaged top, and punched a second rocker switch. The cylinder began its return into the ground.

At the same time, a few feet away, a new oddity held Jack's attention. Several younger dead pines, no more than ten or twelve feet tall, began to tilt in unison. Ever so slightly at first, until they eventually listed at nearly thirty degrees. At the bottom of their trunks, an impossibly thick layer of rock, dirt, and snow sat atop a metal plate. Two enormous pistons hoisted the entire fabrication. A faint, dull red light emanated from below, turning the snow crimson.

Jack looked at the whole spectacle and then searched for his friend. He found Harold leaning against a tree, watching the varying emotions play across Jack's face.

"Yeah, that was pretty much my reaction the

first time too," Harold answered the unspoken question. Jack stood there, speechless. "Come on, let's get in. It's perfectly all right, I've been in a dozen times. You'll like it."

"What is it?" Jack pointed at the red glow.

"It's an old bomb shelter, silly. Rigged up quite nicely, I might add. The theatrics were her idea, something about learning about someone through their reactions. Personally, I think she just values her privacy and doesn't want any attention."

"Who is *she*? It all looks so...plain. From up here. How?"

"More later. Come on, let's go."

Harold began descending the spiral stairs beneath the listing pines. Jack followed, the red light guiding his flight down.

Harold tapped a panel on the wall about halfway down, and the portal overhead began to close over them. Before he knew it, Jack found himself cut off from the rest of the world. He peered over the rail to gauge how far he'd have to go to find out what he'd gotten himself into. Not far, as it turned out. The staircase descended perhaps thirty feet in the dim red glow, the spiral steps corkscrewing straight through what was clearly a premade metal cylinder stood on its end and dropped into the ground at some point long ago.

"How old is this...shelter?" Jack asked as they neared the bottom of the shaft.

"From what I've been told, it went in shortly

before the Great Drop. Whoever owned one of the buildings up there owned the land here too, and had some idea of what might happen," Harold said.

They got to the bottom and Harold continued, "So a few things. First, jackets and shoes come off in the first room. Raine is a stickler for that. Also, you might not want to mention your last name. It's up to you, of course, but that stuff has never come up before, and I don't know how she'd react. Third, if she tries to give you the grand tour, be careful. I got us here plenty early, in case she wants to chat before the rest arrive, but I don't want to spend all day here before it gets dark. I've got plans."

"You still haven't told me who this Raine is."

"She's the oldest of the Listeners out here. Been doing it for forty years or so, is what the others told me when I started coming. She's never heard anything, same as everybody else. But her records are meticulous, just like the rest of her home. And she can tell you every part of the sky that's been searched, and when. Not just the general constellations, and not just the stars, but every space between. She's one of the pioneers testing out extra-galactic protocols too."

Jack gave a low whistle. "My parents told me stories about people like this. They hide way far from the ladder cities."

"You would too, if the corporations running the solar system wanted you silenced."

At the bottom of the steps, Harold grabbed a

wheel attached to the center of a giant metal hatchway and gave it a spin. Instead of one smooth motion, however, Harold's body jerked as the wheel resisted. A second attempt failed just as badly. Jack joined, both hands on the wheel, the two of them working together to try and spin the lock.

After a minute of trying with no success, they let go. In Jack's exhaustion, he grabbed the wheel, locked his elbows, and shifted his weight, letting gravity pull for him. He tumbled back. The door swung open, impossibly silent for a structure of several hundred years.

"Work smarter, not harder?" Jack shot a glance towards Harold, who looked surprised.

"That's a first. Raine always keeps it bolted but spinnable on meeting days. I wonder if she just got back or something."

"I didn't see any other tracks in the snow."

Harold paused at that, walking slowly through the hatchway and into the anteroom. A pair of dark blue boots, dry, rested against the wall near an identical hatchway on the opposite end. It lay slightly ajar. A green coat, heavy with a winter core and a fur-lined hood, hung above the boots.

Something feels off. Jack's thought came at the same time Harold walked over to the boots, picked them up, and put one in each hatchway's frame.

"Forget what I said about jackets and shoes. Keep your shoes on. Actually, keep the jacket on too," Harold said. He moved towards the inner hatchway. It opened as silently as its twin, and they both looked inside. One young man wondered what he'd find. The other wondered what he'd see.

Rich yellow light flooded in through the hatchway door as the two peered through. Jack's eyes quickly adjusted to the underground home's illumination. Quietly stepping onto pine floors, he was struck by just how normal everything looked.

Aside from the curved walls, Jack saw and touched nothing remarkable. The parlor near the entrance was complete with end tables and lamps against either wall, along with two old but well-maintained reading chairs. One chair's right arm looked visibly depressed, as though someone sat there often and used the end table as a small desk.

On the opposite wall sat the chair's twin, along with a low bookshelf of pine to its right, purpose-built for the space and hugging the curved wall perfectly as it ran down the length of the hall at waist height. Where the parlor hall forked, the bookshelf continued hugging the right wall, wrapping itself around a tight corner.

Between the diverging passageways, a door led to a well-appointed bathroom, complete with a shower. It was hard to remember this bomb shelter rested three stories below ground. *Does everyone out here live like this? Where does the toilet drain to?* A hundred questions formed in Jack's mind.

Harold stood in the kitchen, which made up the shelter's left-hand fork. Jack peered down its tube of a hallway and saw a door, no doubt leading to a bedroom, judging from the dim, diffuse light coming from under the doorway. Jack guessed the room was carpeted. He looked back at Harold.

"Where's this Raine?" he whispered. Jack felt the hairs on the back of his neck rise.

Harold glanced sidelong at his friend but did not turn his head from the bedroom door. Both eyebrows were raised and Harold's everyman smile was nowhere to be found. For the first time, Jack noticed the distinct lack of noise in the home. Only a faint tick, coming from the bookshelf hallway, pierced the silence. He backtracked past the countertops and the bathroom door, and then walked alongside the bookshelves covered with texts, manuals, and books of all types.

Not what I was expecting when I woke up. Jack glanced at a text titled, "Pentabyte Resolution: The Solar System Camera," followed several steps further down by, "Exploring Exoplanets Using Quantum Entanglement."

The ticking grew louder. Jack came to the end of the shelves and saw the source: a grandfather clock bookending the woodwork, its massive pendulum marking out seconds like a metronome.

Wow. How old is that? How old is all of this?

As he checked out the sides and front of the enormous timepiece, he felt smooth, well-worn wood grain rub against his hands. He touched a piece of history, here in the middle of nowhere, deep underground.

"Hmm, is there a leak?" Jack muttered. He pulled his hand back, wet. He looked up, searching for signs of water dripping down. Then he glanced at his hand.

"Oh, shit."

Jack stood rigid, startled by a palm bright with blood. Adrenaline blasted through him before he realized what was happening. His insides became shattered ice as his ears suddenly heard every sound from the previously silent space. Every faint movement of air, every breath taken, and every gear turning deep within the body of the clock became a siren pinging his mind with the jolt of an electric shock. He felt the air behind him shift and he spun around, fist clenched, legs coiled, arm gathering speed.

Harold rocked back on his heels, feeling the rush of air flow past his neck as the fist flew by, missing him by the barest of margins. He retreated several steps and held out his arms, pleading silently with Jack.

"Jesus, Harold. Look." Jack pointed to his hand and then to the clock, waited for the light to turn on behind his friend's eyes, and started a hurried walk back towards the exit. "Time to go."

"Jack, no. Hold on a minute. We need to find Raine."

"Oh, hell no. Are you kidding me? Empty bomb shelter, bloody clock, raging snowstorm? It's time to leave."

"We haven't checked the greenhouse yet."

"What greenhouse? Is that door number two, over there?" Jack nodded at the door to his left, a mirror image of the door to the earlier carpeted room.

"No, that's the listening room. All of her equipment and logs are in there. The greenhouse is downstairs."

"*What* downstairs?"

"There's a second floor beneath us. It's her farm."

"What if someone is down there?"

"Then they already know we're here. Our footsteps carry through. And they'd either have come up or bolted out the back way."

Harold tried the door to the listening room and found it unlocked. Peeking his head in, he saw nothing unusual. Equipment hummed, and the warm air pushed its way out of the room, into the cooler space behind him. He turned to the final door.

"This is it, let's go," Harold said. He grabbed the final door's latch and pushed.

A strange mix of air greeted Jack as he followed his friend out. Like the initial passageway, he was looking at a spiral stairway inserted into another cylinder buried in the ground. From above, he could feel cold air filtering down in waves, accompanied by the clear scent of fresh snow. That air fought with warm, rising air from below, creating an unpredictable flow.

There must be two open doors. Someone's been in, or out.

They promptly descended the second set of stairs, feeling the air get warmer and more humid as they went. *This must be some farm.* Resisting the urge to take off his coat, Jack remembered his last croissant and his shoes, happy that both were also with him.

As they reached the final step, Jack saw a reddish light coming from a hatchway like the one they'd opened earlier. The air rushed out near the top and rushed in just as fast near the bottom. Another dull hum emanated past the doorway.

Jack let Harold continue to lead the way, following behind into what Jack now understood to be the underground greenhouse.

Row upon row of plants greeted them. They grew under diodes fitted into dozens of fixtures, glowing mostly red, a little blue, and a few occasionally white. The mix of colors combined to light the room—several rooms, by the look of things—a deep red, nearly violet, but somehow appearing brighter than what Jack imagined it should be.

They walked past the many crops, from lettuce to potatoes, from dwarf wheat to dwarf corn, and countless varieties of beans. The greenhouse seemed to go on endlessly, supplying whatever type of food its owner could want for or imagine. Every available space had something. If it wasn't crops, it was fans. If not fans, then irrigation tubing and fertilizer drums and aeroponic supplies. Baskets, gloves, clipboards, scissors, knives, pots, bins, wire screens, and untold other miscellaneous implements lay here and there, everything purposely placed but without rhyme or reason.

"This red light! How are we going to know if there's blood down here?" Jack whispered to Harold.

"Maybe it'll be darker? I have no idea. Let's work our way through these rooms."

Walking quickly through the little farm, the pair noticed nothing obviously amiss in the first chamber, as Jack decided to term it. Through the next hatch, and then another chamber. Still no sign of disturbance greeted the undergraduates. Neither, unfortunately, did Raine. Aside from autonomous bots attending to various duties, the chambers showed no signs of caretaking.

The third and final chamber, which Jack estimated to be under and past the original spiral staircase, had a younger cycle of crops, more greenhouse paraphernalia, and bots in docking stations waiting for their appointed hour to go to work. The two were getting towards the back of the third chamber when the distant echoes of dull footsteps reached the pair.

They hunkered down between greenhouse tables, the foliage and lighting providing spaces to cower from the unknown.

Metallic echoes gave way to more muffled thuds, and Jack guessed that someone was on the floor above, very near the back entrance, based on his still highly sensitive hearing. Glancing over at Harold, he saw his friend tucked between rows of carrots, left hand on a greenhouse table, eyes peering towards the ceiling in the ruddy light.

The two crouched there, at the back of the third chamber of some crazy hidden home out in the wilderness, for what seemed like an eternity. The muffled footsteps began to intertwine with metallic echoes, oscillating and overlapping in fits and starts.

Jack's adrenaline ebbed and he could think again, unconstrained by the fight or flight mentality forced upon him by events.

Whoever is up there has been up there a while now and clearly isn't coming down. It sounds like they're just going up and back again to the main floor. Maybe it's Raine? Seems like they're keeping towards the back of her shelter. Shit, her boots. They're still wedged into the hatches above us.

As the cold pit of anxiety crept back into Jack's gut, his ears registered a change. The footsteps were gone. The air, too, was no longer getting steadily colder. And the draft emanating all the way from the other end of the greenhouse stopped.

Harold stood. Slowly, and with the silence of an owl, he stepped forward, eyes still glancing upwards at the ceiling, as though he could hear better by looking. Or, perhaps, he could see through walls.

Several minutes went by in the continued

stillness. Harold took a total of four steps during that time. Jack stayed crouched, watching his friend in amazement, too frozen to speak, and too attentive to the quiet to contemplate standing.

Eventually, Harold made it to the chamber's hatchway and glanced back at his friend, locking eyes for the first time in what was surely hours. He jerked his head towards the hatch, but he kept his gaze on Jack.

Grabbing the edges of two metal greenhouse grates, Jack pulled himself up, knees creaking audibly as he fully extended his legs. Perhaps it really had been hours. His upper back burned as he stood straight, but his mind quickly shifted focus as Harold headed back towards the start of the long greenhouse. Jack followed at a distance.

They reached the entrance hatchway and saw nothing changed, save for the still air. High above them, the entrance was latched shut.

"Still want to play explorer, Harold?" Jack whispered.

"No. We're leaving. Now. Same way we came. It didn't sound like anyone was using the main entryway, so let's hope they didn't spot the boots. You have everything?"

A quick check confirmed nothing left behind, and the two started ascending the steps. The main floor's hatch stood open, and they stepped in. Immediately, they saw that the door to the equipment room on the right was also open. Harold ran in. Jack looked on from the hallway and found it stripped. Dented carpet, dinged walls, and wet spots were all that Jack noticed.

"It's all gone!" Harold cried. "All of it, it's all gone!"

"You mean the listening equipment?"

"Yeah. It was full of...full of everything she needed to do her work. Anything a Listener could want or use. Even her notes, her journals, it's all cleared out. I can't believe it."

Jack looked around at the empty room. Nothing remained of whatever had been there, aside from a solitary lamp.

"We need to leave," Jack said. He turned around and walked towards the main hatch.

Harold glanced through the room one more time before following his friend.

They reached the mud room's dual hatches to find the first one nearly sealed shut, the massive metal door pressing against the boot Harold had placed after their initial descent. Jack grabbed the hatchway wheel and began to push with his shoulder. Nothing happened. He looked at Harold.

"What the hell is with these doors?" Jack said.

"Crap. Whoever left must have hit the auto-lock sequence on their way out. This door and the next one are trying to seal themselves."

"Why didn't the back doors lock?" Jack asked.

"Because it's the emergency escape, is my guess. Probably a separate circuit. Look, we're gonna have to pry our way out, or use that back entryway, and I'm not sure I want to poke our heads up in the same place as whoever left. Try to find something to wedge the door."

Jack looked at the tiny crack between the hatch and the frame, and had an idea. Walking back towards the bookshelves, he spied what he'd been thinking about: two bookends, both deep green with streaks of white. They were solid marble and shaped like a steeply-pitched roof. He grabbed one and then the other, and hurried back to the hatchway.

"Here, take one and give me a hand."

Together, they wedged the bookends into the gap: Jack's near the top and Harold's near the floor. Each young man pounded on his bookend's flat bottom as the sides worked their way into the space, increasing by millimeters each time the pair took a coordinated swing.

"I think I can get an arm and leg through. Let me try to pry it with my body now. Hold the one on top so it doesn't come down on my head," Jack said to Harold. He wriggled his thin body in between the door and its frame, then placed his back against the door. He heaved to.

Slowly, interminably slowly, the door crept back on its hinges and then gave way with a jolt, as all the fight left it in a rush. Jack toppled back, spilling out into the mudroom where their day began.

Harold pointed to the exit door on the other side of the anteroom, which swung freely away from the other blue boot. "Looks like whatever you just broke opened both doors. Look," he said.

"Good. Get going. I want to leave. Now." Jack was out the final hatchway and taking the spiral stairs two at a time. The panel that closed the outer portal on their way down responded to Jack's outstretched arm as he flew past. A thin, dim band of light began to emerge from overhead as snow fell down around Jack's head.

I guess it's still snowing. He squinted hard against the rapidly brightening light.

Glancing over his shoulder, he saw Harold catching up as they neared the top. Not wasting any time, Jack scrambled up and out the hidden hatch.

Blinding white greeted the pair as they rejoined the topside world, free from the confines of the underground shelter. Harold hit the toggle switch to close the door as Jack looked around.

"Which way is home?"

6

Okay, Harold. I'll keep my shoes on. The memory of the snowy day passed, and the two friends made their way inside the science center. Seven stories of classrooms, laboratories, ancillary rooms, offices, and one museum made up the university's premier building. It was also where Jack spent most of his time nearly every day.

The enormous main atrium greeted him, as it always did, with hard white floors, seventy-foot heights of open air, and glass walls showing either Lake Michigan in front of him to the east, or the dim glow of the city skyline to the south and west, stretching almost endlessly out and up.

At the ground floor, visitors could pivot left off the entrance and find something to eat at the take-and-go, or pivot right and see the dimmed lights in the Great Drop Museum, the building's impetus for existence. Jack was glad to see it closed for the day. He always felt guilty whenever he came to work and saw it bustling with visiting school groups or families, there to learn—or re-learn—the set of precipitous events leading to the modern world.

Aside from these two smaller annexes on the ground floor, the rest of the space was an open atrium. Seven floors of classrooms and assorted accessory spaces all occupied the northern half of the building. Tables, chairs, and sofas stood arranged in clusters for people to gather at and study, or talk, or simply take a break between classes and enjoy the views. Perhaps a dozen cylindrical white podiums stood scattered about the area, each charging a dozen or more personal gadgets.

An enormous holographic sphere floated in midair, suspended in the atrium by an array of projectors. Anyone looking at it from one of the receding balconies on the northern side of the building would instantly recognize it as Earth, spinning on its axis once every five minutes. As the world spun, it gradually phased back and forth between Jack's Earth, with its well-known coastal ports like Memphis and Fresno, and a bygone Earth, the coastlines redrawn to show places that Jack could only relate to through history books or geology classes. Places like Florida, New York City, San Francisco, Louisiana, and Maryland. Places people heard about, or perhaps boarded a boat or a cruise ship to see for themselves. Portions of a sea that once was land, as the rise of the world's oceans crept up and inevitably, inexorably, redrew the coastlines of every continent and sent the most prosperous cities of the early third millennium into a calamitous inundation.

Beneath this orb, a countdown clock of sorts hung, glowing red in lettering and numbers: "123 years, 6 months, 4 weeks."

Jack shook his head, pausing to consider the length of time ticking down to what even the most optimistic models suggested was far too short a span. *If I live to be three hundred, maybe I'll see that world, that Earth. Maybe.*

"Top floor, man," Harold said. Jack snapped out of his reverie.

They made their way to the staircase on the north side of the building. Up they went, each floor above them recessing back further to the north than the level below. The retreating stories continued to overlook the atrium, with furniture found near the edge of each terrace. Each department had its own level, with general sciences on the ground floor. Terrestrial biology, extraterrestrial biology, exopaleoecology, planetary climatology, interstellar cartography, and finally the opaque "solar materials science" made up the successive tiers Jack and Harold ascended.

This final floor held the fewest rooms, being at the top of the "staircase" architecture the designers settled on many years ago, after Jack's great-grandmother passed and some semblance of her contribution to society could be placed in the proper perspective.

Few visitors to the museum or the science building ever made the connection between the architectural design and the history of the Wilson name. Students came to attend their classes, study, or socialize. Museum patrons frequented the center to see the world's past, learn a few new things, or just wear out their young children. The detailed history, the consequences, and the person behind it all faded from public consciousness a little more each year. Only the Wilson name struck a chord, decades and centuries of ingrained dislike imprinted on the populace from an early age.

The view of the lake from the top floor never ceased to impress Jack as he leaned over the railing to look out over the open atrium. Seven floors dedicated to sciences that almost nobody cared about, in a building nobody understood. And Jack's name was plastered on its outside.

As he peered down, he was able to look at Earth's projection and watch the open ocean of the north pole slowly give way to unimaginably massive sheets of sea ice as the globe reverted to what it once was. Always looking backward.

Harold walked over towards his friend and stopped at the railing alongside Jack. "It's a remarkable thing, isn't it? Do you think it was worth the price?" Harold asked. He glanced at the nighttime view of the lake.

Jack sighed. It was not the first time he'd contemplated that question and its answer. "I don't know. Worth the price to who? My great-grandmother? I doubt she'd have cared about the cost. From all the stories she told me as a kid, that woman didn't give a damn what society thought. Everything I've ever read agrees. I think she just wanted society to continue, period. Her humanity be damned, you know?"

"Yeah. I was talking about you, though."

"I mean, this is all well and good here. The building is remarkable, even though I feel like nobody pays attention to it much, except for its views and the museum. The real work we do here goes totally unnoticed," Jack said, then paused for an instant. "I guess sometimes that is a good thing."

"You still didn't answer the question."

"No, I suppose I didn't."

The two stood there, each alone with their thoughts, for several long moments. And then, without a word, Harold turned from the railing and began to walk towards the back of the terrace, turning left down a hallway near the paired elevators. Jack followed down the same narrow hallway at the top of the building. As he did, he looked up and saw faint stars shining down through the long frame of glass seated overhead.

Reminds me of a car ride I once took. Jack's mind crashed back to thoughts of Betty, and the familiar knot in his stomach returned. He took a deep breath, held the inhale, and puffed his cheeks as he blew the air out.

He continued down the corridor. The monotony of cream walls was occasionally broken by portrait lights shining down on some canvas or another, showcasing artistic works from students, professors, and benefactors. He found Harold stopped near the end, past several classrooms, a lecture hall, and the single "solar materials science" laboratory to be found anywhere in the metropolis.

A portrait light shone down on Harold's stark white hair as he stared at the canvas next to the hall's final door.

"Washington, D.C., right?"

"Yep. One of my favorites. One of Betty's favorites too."

Harold glanced at his friend and raised an eyebrow.

"Yeah, well, it was a long time ago."

Lamps and soft light greeted them as they entered their shared office. Two massive wooden desks occupied separate ends of the space, which ran back nearly thirty feet. The open door stopped up against the right side wall, and against the opposite wall sat a sofa long enough for even Harold's lanky frame.

While the hallway outside was covered with

tile, Jack and Harold had somehow arranged for real wooden floors when they'd taken over the office. Bamboo was fine, but Jack wanted something to bring him back in time, when trees weren't planted only as carbon scrubbers or city adornments or mental health adjuvants. The beautiful chestnut attracted a lot of faculty to the seventh floor. For most of them, it was the only reason they had ever ventured all the way up.

"Jack."

"Hmm? Sorry, drifted off there."

"Close the door."

The door closed with a deliberate thud in the late hour. Jack took a few steps towards the couch, with its slightly frayed and dented cushions, and a hastily folded red and black plaid blanket stuffed against the wall along the couch's frame. Memories of waking up underneath the blanket surfaced as Jack pressed himself into the couch's corner. He surveyed the office.

The window at the far end of the room was right behind Harold's desk and between his bookshelves, and the view from seven stories up was a fringe benefit for the man Jack had known now for nearly half his life. During daytime, the city's sprawling network of interconnected skyrises looked like a photographic negative of an ant colony's vast underground maze, except on an unimaginable human scale. Hundreds of feet up, massive bridges spanned many of the enormous rising columns of glass and metal and carbon.

Stretching through the air, it was possible to walk many miles, from one end of the metropolis to the other, and never set foot on an actual ground floor.

Some of these bridges dated back centuries, as a way to connect the fragmented wildlife on Chicago's green roofs. Using the roofs as a jumping-off point, the bridges that spanned the space between buildings moved upwards along with the city's ever-growing skyline. Eventually, the bridges themselves became the center for aerial intraurban ecosystem reconstruction, or simply AIER. Ever-widening buttresses, arches, and bridges filled Chicago's sky with a multi-level maze of pathways.

Starting near midway up, the arches expanded greatly, moving from perhaps ten feet wide before, with little more than a safety railing and long rows of planters, to massive sixty-foot-wide land bridges with multiple feet of dirt piled into a behemoth of twenty-sixth century engineering. Ten-foot-high walls ensconced pedestrians within a narrow open-air tunnel, blocking out views on either side. Only the buildings in front and behind, and the sky overhead, reminded citizens of where they were. Within these islands, microcosms of forests or grasslands grew with no heed of the hundreds of feet of open nothingness beneath them. In addition to providing habitat for untold numbers of plant, bird, and insect species, the oases in the sky meant a quick walk out into nature was never far for any of the hundreds of millions of residents living in one of the most populous cities to ever exist.

This artificial ecosystem greeted Harold whenever the sun set over the city, providing a silhouette of man's attempt at reconciliation with nature. Harold could watch the seasons change at seventy feet up, a remarkable thought that he never grew tired of contemplating.

On this evening, there were no spectacular views to admire through the window, only dark outlines. Instead, Harold walked over and flipped a nearby switch, polarizing the glass and running an interference pattern of electrical activity through hundreds of fine wires enmeshed in the panes, so fine as to be invisible to the unaugmented eye.

"What about the door?" Jack asked.

"Oh, you'll appreciate this. I rigged your sketch on the wall out there to run interference at the other side of the door. Or rather, I attached something to the hollow on the other side of the frame." Harold jerked his thumb back towards the window. "Same switch."

"Ha. Slick! So we're good now?"

"Unless the room's bugged."

That brought Jack up short. *Anyone associated with Listeners gets monitored, Jack. You know that. For all you know, Harold might have just tipped them off about the sketch.*

"Relax, Jack. I swept this morning."

Jack pulled out his cube and took a few steps towards his desk. "Just in case," he said, flipping a few toggles and sliding back a hidden partition. The cube split open down the middle, dividing itself neatly in half.

"Catch," he continued, tossing one part to Harold. He placed the other half on his desk next to him as he sat.

"Are they close enough?" Harold asked. He stared down the short edge of his half, which rested next to him, facing its partner. Harold rotated its direction ever so slightly, and a small light along the interior edge changed from red to green.

"Should be. I've used them further apart before and never had a problem. They're green. We're good. Just don't wander off while you're talking." Jack watched while Harold collected his thoughts. The wooden floorboards creaked beneath Jack's feet as he rocked from side to side at his desk, and the darkened window behind Harold mirrored his ruminations. Silence filled the room for a minute, then two, and then five. Jack was running out of things to look at around the office.

"I got both of your messages, by the way."

"Both?" Harold's brow furrowed for a few seconds, then smoothed again. "Why do you think I sent two?"

"Because I got two. The second one was weird. 'A find like this can't be verified. Must come'? I figured you wrote it." *Let's see how Harold plays this.*

"Ah, no. No, I certainly didn't. Can I see it?"

"Nope."

"Why not?"

"Because the message erased itself."

Harold glanced at the two halves of the cube and saw them both still glowing green. He moved away from the window.

Jack continued, "So something was found, then? Both messages referenced something. What's going on?"

Harold's eyes again flickered over to the cubes.

"One of the mining companies. One of the smaller ones, just a wife and husband operation, working out at the el-four point on one belt rock at a time. Their E.T. contract, it's with Boulder. They found something, Jack. They sent it down."

Jack frowned. "So what? The big boys out past Mars send down stuff all the time. I've got half a dozen samples down the hall. It's always nothing. Cast-off space junk from centuries ago or someone's version of an elaborate prank." *Why did he call me in?*

The E.T. contracts held between the mining companies and a diminishing number of schools were universally regarded as a joke, a legislative placation towards the scientific community meant to mollify their concerns just enough to pass muster with the public relations types. Decades of asteroid miners would derisively send back anything appearing to be artificial, to an institution holding their company's contract, "for scientific investigation."

Little more than an added expense to doing business, every company had to hold a standing contract with one of the few universities equipped to investigate such a discovery. Once sent, the university dutifully investigated the "find" and issued a report. Anything discovered got credited to the institution.

In a century of uncovering, shipping, and investigating, everything ever sent back turned out to be human in origin, either space debris from some forgotten craft, garbage jettisoned surreptitiously, or more recently, cleverly designed and placed hoaxes meant to capture the world's attention.

"Yeah, and that's what Boulder assumed too. They got the sample about a month ago, examined it, did their usual report back to the contracting company saying it was human origin, and everyone went on their way," Harold said.

Jack held Harold's gaze evenly. "Doctor Predmoor, it's been an incredibly long day for me. Whatever you are driving at, I'm not following. Out with it, man."

"Boulder lied, Jack."

"What do you mean, 'Boulder lied'?"

"About the origin. It's not human."

Jack leaned forward. "Oh, get real. I don't believe that for a second. Why lie? Why keep it hidden? It'd be the biggest discovery ever. Where's their proof?"

"The proof is at the university."

"How do you know that? Have you gone out

there?"

"Well, no...But you see, I saw the scans, they were sent to me by..." Harold trailed off.

The jumbled blocks in Jack's mind fell into place.

"By Aramae. She sent you the scans."

"Yes."

"And she's the lead exopaleoecologist out there now?"

"She's the *only* exopaleoecologist out there now."

Jack paused. "There used to be a whole department. What happened?"

"Declining interest, declining funding. Nobody really cares. The money is in the rocks now, face it. The most interesting things ever found in the exo-field are Europa's radiochemotrophs and the cryofossils in its ice. Not exactly sexy."

"So it's Aramae's show in Boulder," Jack said.

"Yep."

"And she really thinks she found something, huh?"

"Yep."

"So why contact us?"

"Come on, Jack. Let the melt run all the way out. You're smart enough."

"Are you crazy? It'd be the single most important scientific discovery since...since the Wilson Method, actually. It would be a transformative event. Everything, everything would change overnight. She'd be famous, she could get funding for a dozen labs. For whatever she wants! She'd lead a renaissance in the field."

Harold slowly shook his head. "You're in fantasy land, man. Try again."

Jack paused. "The contracts all specifically state that the institution gets publishing rights and credit for any returned samples."

"No, Jack. It's not about the contract language. Strike two."

Jack sat back in his chair. Staring for a while at his old friend, his gaze eventually wandered to the window beyond. Looking past the panes, he saw the dim silhouette of skyrises framed by glass, the same ones he'd seen out the same window for many years. *It's too bad that polarizing the glass ruins the view.* His mind continued to wander. *Of course.*

"She's scared," Jack stated.

"She's not the only one."

"She's never been scared. Of anything," Jack said, more to himself than to Harold.

"She's got good reason to be, Jack. Everyone takes the contracts for the money, it's the only way we stay afloat. Not everyone has the Wilson name behind them. Standard funds don't come close to supporting salaries, equipment, travel, and whatnot. Those contracts are guaranteed. The rates are codified! Nobody expects to find anything, though. It's all a sham! The miners know it, the scientists know it. Man, the *public* even knows it. But nobody wants to admit it. Nobody wants to say that there's no one else out there, that we're alone. So we go along! We all pay to play our part in this system. This system that pays people like Aramae to look. And not even she expects to find anything. She uses those contracts to fund the Pluto insertions. Did you know that? This racket turned into a feel-good high a long time ago. A salve for the general populace, the city-dwellers. A way to *tell* ourselves that we're trying, that we're looking. We stopped *actually* trying long before that. Most of us."

Silence refilled the space between the halves of Jack's cube. The floorboards creaked as Harold waited.

"So. She bought herself time with the false report. Smart. People aren't going to transform overnight. Hmm. Her message—and I think we can both agree she sent that second one—gets put in a different light now. 'Can't be verified,' indeed. She'd risk a lot going public right now. You're right. She's right." Jack slumped, dejected. Even the floorboards stopped protesting.

"That's not the whole glacier, Jack. It'd mean chaos. Think about all the institutions that are premised, have their entire foundation, on the idea that we're alone. It's been more than five centuries of looking. Who could blame them? That whole notion that we're it, that we're unlikely to ever find another civilization, that we're one of the first, grandparents of the galaxy, keepers of a flame and all that crap. That all goes away. And imagine what the sinkers, the rewilders, that whole political and economic engine, would do if suddenly their reason for existing—that Earth *is it*—were tossed, just like that. A snap of one person's fingers, poof. Reefed."

Jack hopped in, "People wouldn't throw up their hands at this. If anything, we'd want to learn more! But you're right about the sinkers and the rewilders. The rock miners out past Mars and the ladder groups too. They'd have concerns. They'd worry we'd all start looking beyond the solar system again. Like when *Infinite Wind* launched. Well, maybe not quite like that, but I remember hearing stories. Nobody focused on anything else. It was about building the ship, or its sails, or the orbital lasers, or the solar collectors, or the giant comms lens, or the dozen other critical parts and pieces. That was an entire generation. Everything else stalled out. No new sinking, no new resources for mining, and the ladders only got used for that. Stuff piled up in orbit, or it sat on the moon, waiting for a trip down the gravity well. Either that or the miners risked a re-entry burn going wrong. They'd never want to go back to anything close to that. Ever."

"Aliens would have to ride down a ladder itself to get people to notice. Otherwise it'll get ignored, played off as another hoax, forgotten about in a month," Harold replied.

"Well. Shit. Suddenly I am glad I'm not out in Boulder," Jack said. "You mentioned scans. Can I see them? I still haven't seen this thing."

"I guess we could have started with that.

Gimme a sec," Harold said. He tapped at the pad on his desk and a hologram materialized above it, floating in space. "Here it is. This is what they found."

Jack looked at the slowly rotating hologram from across the room, stood, and walked over. With a finger's flick, he set the hologram in motion, rotating it around its vertical axis.

"It's a pyramid. They found a pyramid? And we're sure it's not a hoax, really?" Jack paused, staring at an impossible image floating before him. "What's the scale of this? What am I looking at, here?"

"It's one to one. That's actual size," Harold said. "I expected it to be bigger, honestly."

"This would fit in the palm of my hand. I wonder how the miners even noticed it."

"I wondered that too, but I didn't get any backstory. I'm sure you'll hear it firsthand from Aramae when you see her," Harold said. He looked up from the hologram.

Jack stared back for several long moments, his mind racing at the thought.

"Shit," was all he managed to say. "Hey, zoom in four times or so, I can't quite make out these images."

Harold smiled at his friend's dodge and dutifully enlarged the hologram until it was several times the original size. Dim light played off the subtle changes in the hologram, revealing small variations.

"Thanks. And, are there any different spectra scans, anything else besides what's right here?"

"This was all I got. You're looking at as much as I've seen."

"All right. Did you look at these much yet? Am I playing catch-up?" Jack hunched over the hologram, prodding its photons with his fingers, spinning it this way and that, occasionally pausing it to get a closer, steadier look.

"I did, yeah. But I couldn't make much sense of it. Seems to me it'd be more useful to you. There's nothing really about its composition from these scans that I can use."

"That's too bad, I'd like to know how old it is. Are we really calling it a pyramid?"

Harold shrugged.

"See these sides?" Jack pointed, and spun the pyramid so Harold was looking at two of the triangular sides, each with circles in the bottom corners.

"Yeah. They didn't look like much, though. Just some erosion of whatever used to be in those circles. Maybe something was attached and fell off?" Harold hazarded a guess.

"Erosion in the vacuum of space would be tough. Maybe possible, who knows. But look at the whole scan. Everything else is pretty smooth. Unless it's an extremely low-res scan and we're just not seeing it, but I don't think so. There's something else.

These two circles here," Jack said. He pointed to the bottom corners of one of the sides again. "These two. See them? These are Earth."

"That's nothing like Earth. No way," Harold said, peering at the ghostly projection emanating from the pad on his desk. He squinted and looked between the two circles, eyes scanning. "Well, maybe a little bit down there, and then perhaps this little bit up here. But that's stretching it. If this is Earth, it's really poorly done."

Jack looked at his friend. He walked back to his desk and grabbed his own pad. With a few fast taps and twirls, he pulled up a hologram of his own, this one spherical and fully colorized, instead of the matrix of light blue lines and dots making up Harold's image.

Jack carried his pad back and placed the two side by side. With a final flourish, his finger gave the ethereal sphere a slow spin.

Harold examined the new image and the old, letting six or seven rotations pass before saying anything.

"They're the same. The contours on your sphere and on the pyramid's little corner circles," Harold said, finally looking up at Jack. "What did you pull up on your pad?"

"I told you. I pulled up Earth."

"No, you didn't. You think I'm crazy?"

"See this here? That's the Panthalassic Sea." Jack pointed to one of the little circles and spun his pad's globe to match. "And this right here is Pangaea. These circles on the pyramid represent Earth's two hemispheres, two hundred and fifty million years ago."

"That's impossible."

"You're looking at it. Unless this really is an elaborate hoax," Jack paused, then spun Harold's floating pyramid a quarter turn. "I am pretty sure this is Mars, at the same time. Although it's trickier. We thought Mars was geologically dead for billions of years, and things look a bit different. But that, there," Jack pointed to a long diagonal streak through the bottom of one of the hemispheres, "is definitely Valles Marineris."

"What about the other two sides of this thing? What are those?"

"I don't know. Neither looks familiar."

"There's nothing on the square bottom, either. I can't imagine leaving a whole side empty. It doesn't make sense." Harold spun the pyramid to show its base, blank and smooth aside from a few small imperfections scattered about.

"Now who's skeptical? A few minutes ago, you seemed ready to believe whatever Aramae said. Now you're having second thoughts."

"It's just so crazy. There's no way this thing is that old. It's outlandish."

"We won't know more from these scans," Jack realized.

"No, we won't. Do you *want* to know more?"

"You bet I do. Threats be damned. I want to know the truth. It's probably some crazy hoax, but what if it's not? That's got to be worth a trip out to Boulder. Come with. We haven't gone out there since...well, before I got married, that's for sure. It's been a long time, Harold. Let's go." Jack surprised himself at how eagerly he wanted to get away.

"Oh, I don't know. There's no way to ladder-climb out there. And it's a really long shuttle trip each way, if it's a hoax. Let me think about it for a few minutes here, huh?"

Jack gave Harold a thumbs up. He grabbed the two pads with their floating models and moved back to his desk with them, setting them side by side and spinning them again with the same slow rotation. Jack studied them as Harold sat and looked out the window at the urban night.

Definitely Earth. And this is Mars too. But, not Mars. Something is different. The third face of the pyramid rotated into view and Jack paused it with a quick tap. *Those look like polar caps. But there's nothing in the middle. If that's a planet, it's not like anything in the solar system. It looks like a water world to me. But who knows. That could be frozen methane or something. Or liquid metal. There's no way to tell from this.*

Jack sighed. With another flick of his wrist, he turned the pyramid on its head and set it spinning like a top, entertained by the simplicity and mesmerized by the whirls. The two friends kept up their silence, lost with their thoughts.

Time's late hour crept up on Jack as the minutes

ticked by, and he felt his mind incrementally slow with each spin of the pyramid. His eyes closed for just a moment and all the events since his morning shower unraveled. *This day has been one for the books, Jack. It can't get much stranger.* He glanced at the small clock on his desk. Both hands pointed straight up. *Actually, this day is done. I need to sleep.*

Harold jostled him out of his spiral. "Jack? Hey. Umm. I can't. I'm sorry. I just can't go out there right now. There's too much going on and I can't get away from it."

"So I'll wait a week or two. Would that be better?" Jack asked. He thought through other alternatives and permutations in his head, whizzing through idea after idea and remembering none of them.

"No. I thought about that too. And it's also, Jack, I do not want to get involved in it. Not like that. Look at how we're acting already, and nobody really knows what we are dealing with. Yeah, maybe it's a hoax. But suppose it isn't. Word will leak out. People are human. At some point, there's going to be *someone* taking notice that maybe doesn't have really lofty intentions. And then where will that leave us? I don't much feel like being disappeared."

Images of a long ago greenhouse with red and blue lights flickered through Jack's mind, sending a chill up the back of his legs. "Yeah, okay. I get it. I get that."

"I'm sorry, man. I can't go with you on this one.

I wish I could."

Jack covered his disappointment and tried to remember his manners. "It's all right. Look, even talking with me, and being as involved as you already are, is a risk. Let's shut this down for the night. I'm tired, I need to go home, and it's late. Or rather, it's early."

"You're not going to crash on the couch?"

Jack sighed. "No…I think I should at least try to go home. It's just a short walk anyhow."

He stood and gathered the halves of his cube, but not before switching off the pads, still spinning their ghostly images side by side on Jack's desk.

Harold reached behind his own desk and flipped the switch by his window, bringing their private conversation to an end.

"Show's over. I'm going to stick around for a few more minutes before I take off. Talk to you tomorrow," Harold said, leaning back in his chair.

"Yep. Have a good night, man." Jack grabbed his bag, tossed his cube inside, and headed to the door.

7

Various ideas, all of them bad, flew into and out of Jack's mind as he shuffled to the end of the hall. Instead of turning right and heading down towards the atrium and the building's front door, Jack took a left. As he approached the rear of the top floor, he passed laboratory classrooms, the fifty-chair lecture hall, and various empty offices scattered about, which most people mistook for bot closets. Just enough light diffused in from the atrium and the skylight above to help guide him to a lonely door, unmarked and simple. He grabbed the handle, his thumb covering where the keyhole would normally be. Jack felt metal slide past itself as the handle engaged and he swung the door open. Another Wilson perk.

Cool night air swept over Jack's face as he stepped out into the city's wee hours. He focused on the skyrise a hundred yards in front of him and craned his neck back as far as it would go. *Almost home.*

At thirty yards across, this AIER bridge was one of the wider ones found at the lower, older tiers. Initially, the science center and Jack's skyrise had gone up separately, but when Jack took the teaching position at his namesake's building and found the property for sale across the street, he'd been able to pull a few strings and spend a little of the family fortune to get this bridge installed. It was a younger bridge, so there still wasn't much in the way of large trees, but a cottonwood Jack planted near the center's door had reached a couple of stories above the walls in the decade since it began life as a scrawny, three-leaved twig. He decided to flop beneath it before heading home. Patches of prairie grass and flowers filled the majority of the space on the bridge and, as Jack settled in against the trunk, he found himself disappearing into the grassy depths deep into the night.

Nobody knows I'm here. Well, that's not really true. I'm sure someone's tracking me, somewhere. But if I'd have left my cube or turned it off, nobody could find me here without really looking.

Heavy flapping from the cottonwood's thick leaves successfully drowned out every other sound of the city, and Jack drifted off to sleep, illuminated by the few visible stars high above Earth, under one of the rarest things: his own tree.

A hazy sky, streaked with very distant light, hung above him. He stood and put a big toe on the nearby dirt path, followed by another toe, and then a whole foot.

Jack, a voice whispered from far off, down the winding dirt path and shrouded by distant trees. He took one step towards the voice, then turned to take a shortcut. The clumps of grass along this new route soaked his pants up to the knee.

Jack. Now the whisper was farther back through the trees. He adjusted course and made for the voice. A narrow path trailed behind him as he went. Jack pushed through the grass for a few more minutes, keeping his head down so he could see where each step would land, anxious to avoid squishing something important or sticking himself with thorns. He glanced up and swore the trees were further away than before.

Jack, go. The calm, insistent voice whispered, again in front of him, although no closer to him than earlier. Ignoring his footsteps now, Jack began to lope over the larger green bunches in his way, refusing to look down, fearful that the trees would again move on him.

After what felt like an hour, Jack reached the trees' dense shade. Before he could check himself for cuts or thorns, a whispered *Jack, leave* came from his left. The dirt path again appeared and he set off along it, landing on the balls of his feet before he sprang up again in earnest.

"Please stop moving around," Jack said. As he bounded, his strides increased their pace whenever the whisper moved itself through the trees or down the dirt lane. A new idea entered Jack's mind and he pinwheeled off to the right, into the forest and out of sight of the trail, before spotting the enormous tree before him. He sat down against the monolithic trunk and surveyed the forest. No sound uttered itself, not even Jack's unlabored breathing. Seconds turned to minutes and Jack strained to hear the voice again. The forest's light dimmed. The sky grew dark. An old leaf sailed motionlessly past Jack. He shivered as the hairs on the back of his neck asserted themselves like the coming of a snow squall. Before he could react, the last of the light went out. He heard a final whisper in the dark, this time directly beneath him, so close that the voice rumbled through his feet, and a single *Leave!* echoed through the forest.

He woke with a violent start. Confusion briefly overtook him as he sorted out where he was. Rough cottonwood bark scraped the back of his head, and goosebumps rose along his neck as he brushed out the little wood bits flecked in his hair. The dream rushed back with a shudder, and the whispering voice reverberated through his mind.

"I'm going to freeze out here," he said to himself. The stars overhead had increased a thousandfold, he noticed, while the city itself was completely dark. Not a single light shone anywhere. *Sometime after two, then.* Feeling for his bag, Jack found one of its straps and stood. His eyes adjusted to the darkness after several moments. *Time to go home. I'll find Harold tomorrow.* The AIER bridge and his bed beyond beckoned, and Jack found the path as his feet fell into their familiar pattern of feeling for the bare earth and avoiding the grasses along either side. Only after reaching the AIER bridge's modest apex did Jack stop.

"Where the hell are my shoes?" Jack searched around in the dark and failed to see much past his drooping, watery eyes. He dragged himself to the other side of the bridge and went home, glad to find an empty condo, drawn shades, and a messy bed. He was out as soon as his head hit the pillow.

An unmemorable sleep passed. The morning arrived, on time as always. Jack, the exhausted lump, slept straight through until almost nine, when a hungry stomach roused him.

"Hello?" Jack called out. Silence answered. He raised an eyebrow, got up, and walked to each room. Nobody.

I need to find Harold. Jack then remembered the whispering voice. He sighed. *I should vid Betty first.* Steeling himself against rising anxiety, Jack dug into his bag for his cube. Toggles, switches, and a projected keyboard later, Jack sat waiting for his wife to answer. After three attempts, the vid connected on the other end, and a dark and shiftless mass appeared before him.

I should have made coffee before I did this. Gradually, the software enhanced the ambient light on the other end so he could make out the shadow of his wife, clearly still in bed and under the covers.

"Oh my god, what time is it?"

"Nearly nine. I'm guessing I woke you?"

"Yes. Oh, the light! Shit. I'm gonna barf." She scrambled out of bed, her barely visible body shuffling off for a few minutes beyond vid range.

Someone's hungover. Shocking. Jack waited while his wife flushed and returned to bed.

"Jack look, listen. You. I don't even know what to say. You just abandoned me yesterday. Without a word, for no reason! And then you didn't vid, didn't contact me, nothing. That is abuse. I am tired of it. It has got to stop. I can't live my life like that. You left me standing there completely alone. Do you know how humiliated I was? Everyone was staring at me! Everyone!"

Jack thought about closing his eyes. *Maybe this'll just go away if I keep them shut long enough.* "Truth be told, Betty, I think they were staring at you because you were screaming."

"And whose fault is that? That's your fault, don't blame me for that. Don't you dare try to turn this around on me. It's not my fault at all. You left.

You. Not me."

"I left because you were screaming at me," Jack replied, voice flat. He screwed his eyes shut and massaged his temples with his fingers as he tried to accurately recall the order of events at the shuttle depot.

"I don't care. You had no right to just leave me like that. That's neglect. That's abuse, and I don't have to deal with it at all. Apologize. Apologize right now or that's it."

Betty's disheveled hair fell across the shadow of her face as Jack looked on at her, bewildered and at a total loss for what to say next. "I, uh. I'm. Look, Betty, I'm really…"

As Jack looked on at his hungover wife, the sheets behind her shifted and rolled from side to side. Betty continued to stare straight at her husband, giving no recognition to the other mass in bed with her.

"Goodbye, Betty," Jack said quietly, before closing the connection. He rolled onto his back and stared at the ceiling. His cube dinged with an incoming vid. He ignored it, instead turning to stare at the series of rotating holograms beside the bed. Clips of parties, vacations, and other happenstance moments displayed themselves on the platform, one after another, switching randomly as a scene played out every ten seconds or so. A wedding scene pixelated in.

Jack, leave. He had no desire to stay in his home

for one more instant. Throwing on the same clothes he had worn the night before, he searched around for his shoes before remembering the AIER bridge. *They have to be there.* He grabbed the cube as he left the condo, barely ten minutes after he'd said goodbye to his wife. The cube had not dinged a second time.

A very different world than the one he left the night before greeted Jack as he stepped out onto the bridge and into the city. The hot, bright, windy, loud morning spilled over the bridge's ten-foot-high side walls. Insects worked their pollinating magic with whatever was in bloom, and birds and small mammals crisscrossed the wholly man-made ground beneath them. Jack walked up to the cottonwood tree on the opposite side, near the Wilson Science Center, and looked around.

Well, here's where I fell asleep. He sat down against the tree trunk. Tall, thick grass obscured most of the ground. *Where the hell did those shoes go?* Jack looked closely for signs of disturbance. *Ah ha.* A big, serrated cup plant leaf, freshly broken, dangled off the plant's square stem a few feet in front and to Jack's left. He stood and walked over, finding his shoes near the base of the large *Silphium.*

It's been a long time since I did that. I'm lucky they didn't go over the wall. Jack put his shoes on, glanced at the bridge's morning scene one final time, and headed for his office. He hoped Harold was there.

He wasn't. An empty office greeted Jack, and he

realized he had no idea what his friend's teaching schedule was for this term. He decided to wing it and meandered down the hall to Harold's usual classroom. Jack was right. The schedule projected next to the door had the current course highlighted in orange. SMS 203: Subterranean Martian Geology. Inside, a dozen or so students sat scattered throughout the lecture hall. One in particular, a fair-haired young woman of perhaps twenty, sat near the glass wall on the far side and looked out over the lake. It was clear she was paying no attention to Harold. Jack smiled to himself and took a seat near the exit. *Tomorrow's leaders.*

He didn't have to wait long. The class usually ended at half past nine and Harold finished a few minutes early. The daydreamer filed out last.

"When's your next class?" Jack asked. He watched as Harold broke down the show at the front of the room.

Harold glanced at the clock and muttered to himself. "Ninety minutes, but it's downstairs and not here. It's the freshman seminar. You look phenomenal. Fun night?"

"Weird night," Jack said, "Very weird night, and the morning wasn't much better. I slept on the bridge for a while, actually. Lost my shoes out there for a bit. Just weird."

Harold glanced up. "You're lucky nobody else really has access to that bridge. Betty, your parents. Or your dad, I suppose. Me. Who else can go out there? I'll bet some vagrant would have loved to find you asleep like that."

"Aramae. I put her in the system. She has no idea, of course. But I added her just, you know, just in case."

"Pretty small group," Harold said. He looked straight at his friend, pressing him in an old line of conversation that never quite wound its way to resolution.

"Yeah, and it's going to get smaller," Jack replied. "Hey, I didn't mean to crash in on you like this while you're packing up. I really just wanted to run an idea past you. Can I close these doors?"

"Yeah, sure. Actually, I'll close them. Nobody's got a class in here until after lunch."

Jack set out the two halves of his cube again, and the two professors began to talk.

8

"All right," Harold said, "I've got to go set up for seminar, but I understand, I think. And I'm in. This is batshit crazy, you know. But I'm in."

"Yep."

"And this starts when?"

"Just as soon as I leave here."

Harold stood after a moment. "Watch my stuff. I'll be right back."

He left the lecture hall and came back three minutes later holding a small, nondescript cartridge. He handed it to Jack. "Here's your first one. It'll be ready by the time you are. I'm good for holding up my end. Don't get killed, Jack." Before

Jack could duck out of the way, Harold gave his friend a great big hug. "And take care of yourself. Nobody else is going to."

Jack nodded. "Thanks. And thanks for helping. See you, see you next time." He gave a wave at Harold's goodbye and started for his AIER bridge again.

Once home, Jack grabbed his previous day's backpack, still mostly packed, and set off again. He made for the elevators, veering towards the express doors before deciding to take the regular ride instead. For fifteen minutes, he wound his way down, stopping and starting as people entered and exited, before finally reaching the shuttle hub. Without a reservation, Jack had to wait in queue for thirty minutes before a shuttle stopped in front of him. He got in.

"Good morning, Doctor Wilson. Destination, please?" the same voice as yesterday intoned through the shuttle cabin.

"Eight two three Dalea Court," Jack replied to the AI. "Thank you."

"Yes, sir. Would you like to put a vid through to there now?"

"No. No, thank you."

"Very well. We should arrive in roughly an hour. Enjoy your trip."

The voice ended as the shuttle lurched forward, building speed before it merged seamlessly with millions of other shuttles, all ferrying their charges to their destinations.

Like yesterday, the trip took Jack through the city's deepest trenches, between vertical farms and skyrises on both sides. The city thinned out as he traveled further west, away from the ladder and the lake.

Eventually, the shuttle passed beyond the farthest superscraper and, for the first time in many months, Jack found himself traveling through streets of homes, on the very cusp of the great city's border. The shuttle slowed at the furthest turn in the furthest road, winding down a short street that turned out to be a dead end. It stopped in front of a small house whose front yard overflowed with wildflowers.

"Destination reached. Would you like to schedule a departure time?"

Jack hesitated. "Yes. This time three, no, four days from now. Four days, please."

"Booking reserved. Have a good day, Doctor Wilson."

"Thank you." He got out of the shuttle, grabbed his bag, and made certain nothing was left behind. The shuttle closed its door as he walked away. It drove off, heading east. That was the only direction available.

9

Blue siding, white trim, and a low-pitched roof greeted Jack as he walked the path to the front of the home. A storm door was closed, but the front door was open, letting Jack look into the house. Everything seemed as he remembered it.

"Dad?" he called through the screen as he opened the storm door and went inside. An old, familiar scent greeted him as he reflexively closed the front door, then opened it again as he realized he'd cut off the breeze passing through.

A coat rack stood off to the right with a single light grey windbreaker hung on it, flecks of dust just beginning to accumulate on its upper surfaces.

Wood floors creaked, not dissimilarly to Jack's office, as he walked through the first floor looking for signs of existence among the mild disorganization pervading the home's tabletops, nooks, and crannies.

On one old bookshelf rested a birdhouse, blue and white to match the home he was in. Alongside it was a short chain, with a clasp so small that only a child could manipulate it. Jack avoided it as he wound his way towards the kitchen near the back.

Here, too, the windows were wide open, with the bright light of noon diffusing through. Jack sat at the kitchen table and looked out into the back yard, focusing on a single tree with one large nail driven into it. Then he noticed the rest of the landscape and the pair of Adirondack chairs pointed towards the whole panorama. Jack sighed and walked out towards them, wondering if he'd made the right decision in coming.

"Hi, Jack. Been here long? You're pretty far from the lake," his father said, turning in his chair.

"Hi, Dad. How are you?"

"I've been better. Still, it's a great day to be here. Are you staying long? What brought you out here? I could have cleaned up the place, if I'd known."

"That's all right, Dad. I wasn't trying to—I came out quietly. This, I wasn't expecting, I don't want you to bother." He stood there with no idea what to say. He never knew what to say. The two looked out at the wilderness for several minutes.

"Let's get something to drink," Jack's dad said, as he rose from his chair and headed inside. Jack followed and wondered if he should tell him about Betty.

"Tea?"

"That sounds great. Please."

The two drank for a moment while Jack searched for words.

"Dad. I'm going to be gone for a while."

"Nothing new there, Jack. You're rarely here."

"I know. I'm sorry. It's hard to visit here with Mom gone."

Jack's dad paused and looked away. "I know. We can keep people alive for centuries and send them to distant stars, but there's things about some folks we can never fix."

"Mom had a lot of trouble being a Wilson, Dad. She tried really hard and she loved us. But history really stacked her deck. I think I can make it better for us in the future."

As soon as Jack spoke the thought, he realized how unlikely that future now seemed. *You're an only child, Jack. With no kids. Going is pointless.* He stumbled back a step. *Tough. I'm going anyway.*

"Do I want to know?" Jack's father asked, looking over his son.

"No, you don't. You really don't. It's better that way. You'll see, you'll understand. I need to grab a few things. Is that okay?"

"What could you possibly need that you can't

buy?"

Jack raised his eyebrows.

"Okay, okay. Grab whatever you need."

Retracing old memories through the house, Jack went room to room, avoiding his parents' bedroom but grabbing something from everywhere else in the process. His backpack soon filled up.

When he finished his scavenger hunt, Jack went searching for his dad again. He finally found him, sitting in the same chair as before.

He stood behind the unoccupied chair for several minutes before slipping off his backpack. Stepping around to the front, he sat.

"This was Mom's view?"

"She loved it. She loved it more when it was trees."

"It's amazing," Jack said, looking out over the endless ocean of green stretching before him. They sat for the next thirty minutes or so, each alone with their thoughts.

Jack heard snoring.

He stood and walked towards his dad.

"I love you," he whispered, kissing his father's forehead as he slept.

Jack slipped on his backpack and looked at the house one more time through blurry eyes.

Then he turned around to face the wilderness before him, and started walking.

10

Jack's childhood forest, with its open understory and well-trodden footpaths, had always been a cool and comfortable place to visit. The vast, impenetrable grassland now stretching for hundreds of miles in front of Jack seemed the polar opposite. Thick, rough grasses bunched and towered over his head as he made his way. There was no footpath, little shade, and even less of a breeze.

He figured the journey would take a couple of months on foot, the roughest part being the initial slog through the eastern plains and its untold hundreds of miles of tall prairie grassland. Jack had never spent any real time trying to hike through them in the past, always preferring the shadier, cooler woodlands. He had never quite forgiven the prairie for destroying his forest, either. As though the plants were directly to blame for the decisions of man. Regardless, that vast green sea now stretched out forever, and he felt a pang of regret for hewing so closely to his beloved trees until now.

Maybe I should just turn around, stay a few days, and take the return shuttle.

Dismissing the idea after a few steps, Jack began a difficult trek through the grass. It was hotter than he imagined, and he found himself quickly reaching for the sturdy old canteen he had grabbed from his parents' house.

After an hour, he took out his cube and brought up its quantum interface, a rarely used feature Jack hadn't played with since college—and even then, only seldom. The interface contained the housing for a cartridge that held one half of a quantum pair. Jack fished out the tiny capsule Harold gave him earlier that morning and placed it in the hole. The cartridge's quantum bit was inexorably linked with its counterpart, which by now hopefully rested where Harold had promised to leave it. The interface projected a blue line west for Jack to follow, with no indication of how far he might have to walk to rejoin the exotic twins.

My arms are going to get cut raw by the grass at this rate. First tree I come to, I'm finding a stick.

Several more hours went by as Jack continued

through the thick grass. The only indication he was headed anywhere at all was the sound of his footsteps, barely audible over the ceaseless and deafening buzz of insect wings all around him.

The air cooled as the sun went down, and in the distance a line of trees stretched out in front of him. *This feels oddly familiar.* The land began a subtle slant downwards and Jack started to wonder where, exactly, he was going to sleep for the night.

"Of all the bad ideas, Jack, this might be your best one yet," he said to himself. "I need to eat."

As he approached the tree line, he realized the ground beneath him had bottomed out, and the trees themselves were all birch, cottonwood, and sycamore. He reached out and felt the furrowed bark of the cottonwood to his left and looked at the tree, which grew straight up forever before radiating outward into an expansive, and loud, canopy of pinwheeling leaves.

"Wow, that's big. This'd never fit on the AIER bridge. The trunk's half as wide as the bridge itself." He looked down and saw enormous roots running along the ground in all directions, some with their own little pockets of life around and beneath them, mosses and other plants, small mazes crisscrossing the ground, puddles of still water filling the odd places.

I bet I could sleep under one of those roots. I've never seen anything like that, even as a kid.

Jack sat against the massive trunk and ate from

his pack while checking his cube. Paranoid that some of the features he had disconnected earlier might spontaneously reconnect themselves, Jack thoroughly examined the cube's intricacies in the fading light. By the time he convinced himself that everything was as it should be, he was exhausted.

This tree is as good as any, I suppose. A reach into his bag withdrew a thin blanket, light yet warm, and he wrapped himself in it. He used his backpack as a pillow.

He figured he had gone perhaps six or eight miles that day. Before he drifted off, he wondered what the next eight hundred would bring.

A snapping stick brought Jack out of his deep slumber and momentary disorientation startled him. His back slammed into the trunk of the tree he'd slept under and fissured bark dug into his skin. The first morning away from Chicago greeted Jack.

Noise filtered into his fuzzy consciousness as his ears took in the cacophony of nature all around him. He saw, off in the distance, most of the city's skyline and felt its dull background noise. But more immediately, the wind, birds, bugs, and trees commanded his attention. Early pre-dawn lightened the overcast sky. A brief calm asserted itself after a minute spent taking everything in.

It didn't last long. Tightness returned to Jack's chest as his mind woke up and zeroed in on one thought. *Nobody has succeeded in this for over a century.*

Everyone fails when they try this. Everyone. You have no idea what you're doing.

Puffed out cheeks, deep breaths, and sharp exhales followed. Jack shut out everything around him as the tightness lifted. He pulled out his cube and got a bearing for where he needed to head. *This'll get easier as you get farther from the city.*

Even though he had hiked about eight miles the day before, the city felt close. Most of the skyline extended well above the horizon. Folks probably ventured out this far reasonably often, for sport or pleasure or misdeed, and there could even be people nearby right now. Running into someone might not be catastrophic, but if they recognized him or even remembered him later, it could turn into a problem. He stuffed the blanket back into his backpack and swapped his shirt for a clean spare—he'd brought several—and put the worn one into a small area of the bag that was studded with hundreds of tiny ultraviolet lights, powered by one of several dozen flexible solar cells sewn into the outside of the backpack. The lights would sanitize the shirt, and Jack hoped it would be enough to keep some semblance of hygiene throughout his journey.

He drained the last of his canteen and looked around, failing to spot what he needed. *It has to be here somewhere.*

Jack looked around again at the trees and searched for the shortest route to the opposite side. It seemed several hundred yards off to his left, and he set out towards it. As he walked he noticed that, on either side of him, the ribbon of trees stretched out as far as he could see.

After a hundred yards or so, he stopped again and closed his eyes. The noises of the woods were all around him. One by one, he turned them off in his mind. The birds were the hardest, as hundreds of them filled the branches overhead with their overlapping songs, calls, arguments, and cries. Eventually, Jack only heard the flapping leaves, and then he turned those off too. In between breaths, he could faintly hear what he'd been hoping for.

Fifty yards to his right, a quiet babble ran over a half-dozen or so rocks. He made for it. The water flowed out of a nearby upslope before vanishing again a few yards past Jack's feet.

Must dive below the surface. Either that or it's really dry right now.

He refilled his canteen and decided to soak his shirt in the spring too. A quick bite to eat, a splash on his face, and he set off again.

Jack neared the opposite edge of the woods. *A stick! Wait, I need a stick.* He ducked back in and looked around for several minutes before finding a suitable branch. It wasn't exactly straight and it wasn't exactly strong, but it would do.

Instead of fighting the dense vegetation with his body, like he had the previous day, Jack's newfound tool helped guide the grasses out of the way as he went, sparing both himself and the plants undue wear and tear. After an hour, Jack turned around and noticed he left hardly a trail behind him.

The morning sun wicked dew from the tall grass and Jack's clothes dried accordingly, only to become wet again as the afternoon heat increased rapidly over the open, exposed plains.

Each stride brought with it a minuscule shift in the balance of power, as the tallest buildings began to set in the very far-off distance and the land began to assert itself in all of its wildness. By the time Jack found relief from the sun under a towering, open-grown oak near the top of a small ridge, the city had disappeared entirely behind the horizon and the high prairie. The hum of civilization droned on in the lull between breezes but it, too, was fading.

Jack faced west and sat under the shadow cast by the ancient tree's extensive canopy. As he ate and drank, he watched the rhythmic motions of what he surmised to be the turbine blades of a wind farm, swinging a few degrees above the distant horizon before diving back beneath it to sweep out their full arcs. A thousand small white blips set and rose over a sea of greens and browns.

The haze from the shimmering heat played with Jack's mind, and he saw a shoreline filled with crashing waves. These ceaseless repetitions overwhelmed his resolve to put further miles behind him. He nodded once too often as sleep emerged and caught him off-guard.

Jack again woke with a start. The shadow of the tree

had long since fled as the sun peeked below its canopy. Sweat soaked his entire shirt. He dug out the canteen as the grogginess wore off, and then searched for a better stick than what he had found at the start of the day. He came up empty. The acorns on the tree, with their big, bushy caps, were still green, immature, and held fast to their parent's stems. It would be a while before they'd consider falling to the ground.

Those windmills cut right through where I need to go. Jack stared off in the distance. He shouldered his pack, which felt unexpectedly light, and sighed. *I don't think going around is an option.*

Leaving the shelter of the oak's crown, Jack set off again much as he had that morning. For a time as he came down off the ridge, the windmills disappeared entirely behind the grass and beneath the horizon, not reappearing for several hours. In the face of the setting sun they were difficult to spot, but gradually the fanning blades crept high enough into the sky that the radiant red light could no longer obscure them. Jack continued his journey while he considered his options. The generator housing for the closest turbines began to appear along the horizon whenever the tall grass teetered around in the early evening breeze.

These go on forever. Jack surveyed the horizon from south to north. *How many days just to reach the edge and swing around?* He dismissed a detour as untenable and considered the two remaining choices. The final frame of the previous morning's vid with Betty flashed uninvited into his mind, and his arms tingled.

I can go through the night or I can go through the day. Pondering various scenarios for both ways forward, Jack eventually concluded there was no good option. Either he would run out of water by day, or badly expose himself to anything with a thermal imager at night.

Before he realized it, his feet made the decision for him. He arrived at the outskirts of the nearest turbines, which rose up and up and up, each topping out well over a thousand feet in the air. The prairie beneath them seemed minuscule, like the fabric of a doormat beneath someone's shoes. Ultralight composites made these towers possible, and their small footprint on the ground meant they wouldn't interfere with the natural carbon sinking beneath Jack's feet. Jack also knew that, within each upright pillar, machinery of a different sort was secretly mining the air, turning gas into solid. Small mountains of graphite filled the voids in those pillars, and they were emptied autonomously every month.

The price for pure, solid carbon still made a clandestine operation like this highly profitable, if of dubious legality. Until the oceans released their stored heat, no longer corroded the shells of sea life, and could support reef building again, it seemed likely that harvesting carbon would remain a part of life.

The longer I'm here, the longer I'm here. Time to go.

Jack made a minor correction to his heading and stalked under the nearly silent blades as the last degree of the sun's arc called it a day. He could just make out the much louder sounds of a fleet of drones off in the distance, flying back to their docking stations for the night. A whole host of mechanized autonomy taking the place of people and all that they would have brought with them.

As the final rays dimmed, Jack saw light of a different kind begin to fill the ground. Hundreds of thousands of points of light filled the prairie's hot expanse, dotting acre after acre in all directions, to every horizon. Some glowed behind thin blades of grass or flower petals, some hovered, and eventually all flew from stem to stem.

The yellow luminescence of the fireflies diffused among the opaque plants. In the time after the sun went down but before the stars appeared, the brief dance of the lightning bugs let the land sparkle with its own light, a nightly reminder that the stars didn't hold sway over everything. The sight of such luminary undulations across the nearly flat landscape stopped Jack in his tracks beneath one of the slowly spinning metal giants. He looked through the approaching darkness and remembered a time long ago, when he'd shared a similar moment with someone able to appreciate it for what it was. His hand warmed at the thought, although he didn't notice.

He waded through the firefly dance. The turbines fell past Jack's slow, careful steps. First one, then another, and a third. The towering stacks began to fill the dim in every direction. Jack struggled to maintain his proper course, and soon everything around him began to look the same. The grass, the fireflies, the windmills overhead, all of it repeating endlessly.

Crap, I'm lost.

He reflexively grabbed at his cube, muscle memory working quicker than he could think. He'd already begun queuing up his blue line when he caught himself and powered it down.

Just go with it. Maybe in the morning, Jack.

The fireflies and their dances waned with the dusk, and Jack lost sight of the horizon. Night exerted itself fully over the land. As he neared another small ridge, the tall grasses thinned and fell away, leaving a low profile at the crest that let Jack see for many miles. He stopped and sat. The silhouettes of the windmills obscured some of the nearly imperceptible shift of light from ground to sky.

He looked to where he guessed east should be and hoped to see some cityglow from Chicago, but almost nothing revealed itself to Jack's eyes aside from a thin shadow extending into space. Exhausted, he lay down and felt warmth from the ground radiate into his back, inching through his arms and neck and doing battle with the cool night breeze for control.

Pinpricks of light flooded the sky as the fireflies

surrendered the stage. Ten thousand distant suns shone overhead, with the faintest outline of the Milky Way visible in the background.

Every once in a while, a star would traverse Jack's view at an odd angle, drawing a line across the sky in invisible ink and angling always for the single thin beam of darkness extending up from the horizon in the east. *Ladder shuttles. Or deep-space shipments hitching down. I wonder what comes in late at night, under cover of darkness.*

Oh look, north. Jack stared at a familiar constellation.

His absentmindedness fled as he found his bearings. With north and east both mapped out in his mind, he could roughly find his path again and put some ground behind him overnight.

Jack continued to lie there, though, staring up at the stars.

Time passed and the sky turned. Some dots of light dipped below the horizon while others rose to take their place. Jack found himself staring up at Proxima Centauri, wondering whether anyone there was staring right back at him at the same moment. A very old song sprang to mind, one his mother sang to herself when she thought no one else was around:

One little star
Shining out through the night
Are you looking way out there?

They Left One Tree

Can you carry the light?
One little star
In that massive sky town
Have you found your lost brother?
Are you on your way down?
One little star
Will you some day arrive
Can you shine on some other?
Will we know you're alive?
One little star
Keep up your hope
To Night.

Tears ran around his ears and wet his hair as he finished, and the lump in his throat grew four sizes. The pulse in his temples pounded as his ears burned, hot and wet and both in the same moment. *I miss you, Mom.*

11

Ten minutes passed. So did another ten, followed by ten more after that. The wind stopped, the lingering breeze died, and the windmill blades fell silent. *I could just lay here forever. Nobody needs me to get up. I could just stop. Like Mom did.* Ten more minutes went by. *Why, why am I doing this?* Cool nighttime air began to sink down around him as the last heat of the day bled out into space. One single hand stayed warm.

After a while, Jack stood. He brushed the imagined dirt off of himself and looked up again. As he found north and east, he set off roughly in the proper direction. So long as Polaris and the star ladder stayed where they were supposed to, Jack couldn't get too lost. Behind him, he overlooked a subtle blinking of several stars, out of sight and out of mind. He held course for the rest of the night, putting half the wind farm behind him before the first glimmer of the earliest morning light struck the tops of the spinning blades.

It was the flattest expanse he had seen yet on his brief journey. So far, no place looked to offer any better chance for rest or provide shelter than another. The only thing Jack noticed, aside from the brightening morning, was its creeping brilliant redness.

What a pretty sky.

A small open patch in the endlessly thick prairie appeared before Jack, no bigger than himself. *Deer bed.* Jack remembered seeing them in the forest with his father when he was very young. He could feel the heat of the day begin, sunbeams searching for the lowest path through the sky. *This will have to do.*

He shoveled down some high calorie bars he'd tossed in his bag earlier and chased it with quite a bit of canteen water. The thin blanket came out and he gave it a sniff.

Smells almost like rain. He turned on the cooling lines and thousands of thin, solar-powered strands sewn into the blanket began working to keep the blanket cold to the touch. Jack stuffed himself underneath the blanket and again used his pack to rest his head on.

I hope nobody sees me. Exhausted from a nearly full day of walking, Jack fell asleep before he could think another word.

"What is he doing out there?" a woman asked. She sat in an unremarkable conference room as a hologram projected out from the center of a huge white table. Blue contour lines stitched together a panorama of the landscape Jack had just spent a night wading through.

"I have no idea. We can't even figure out who he is. This AI that's out there following him isn't a really capable one," a second, younger woman replied.

"Well, tell it to stay out there and keep following. Could we ID whoever it is with just that AI?"

"Probably not, ma'am. The AI was built to survey mammal populations. It just doesn't have the equipment needed, even if it got right up in his face."

"Why don't we just ping his lenses?"

"I already tried that, ma'am. He's not wearing any. Or at least, he's not wearing any we can get into. He's also right near the edge of our customary range. Nobody usually makes it out much further than this, because of the storms, especially this time of year."

"Shit. I was hoping I wouldn't have to ask for another AI. Tell me if anything changes, and I'll work on what comes next. I'll be back in a bit." The first woman stood and walked out, leaving the second woman to watch the soundly sleeping man's projection on the table before her.

The raindrop landed squarely on top of Jack's closed eye and crept through the crevice between his eyelids. The cold burning woke him, and the red dawn that greeted him earlier was gone, replaced by a nauseous shade of green. He stood, looked around the edges of the deer bed, and saw the tall grass bend halfway over in fits before shooting up straight again, only to be blown back down in the next instant.

That's probably not good.

After packing away his meager sleeping quarters, he realized he had no idea of the time. Jack checked both it and his bearings with the cube, which hadn't been taken out for nearly a day. He drank nearly the last of his water, turned back to his quantum interface's westerly path, and took a few steps forward as the grasses continued alternating above and below him with the wind. A dark grey line of clouds played peek-a-boo with Jack, hiding behind the vegetation between the gusts.

That's definitely not good.

Jack caught the briefest of glimpses of one batch of clouds that hung far lower than the rest. They grew closer every time the grasses bent.

Jack frantically looked around and saw open prairie as far as he could see, which wasn't very far. He stopped, frozen in place, unsure of where to go.

This must be what animals feel like. Run, Jack. Maybe you can beat it.

And so he ran. Two quick pulls tightened the shoulder straps on his pack. He clipped a third strap across his chest and made it as tight as he could while still being able to take a breath. Gone was the stick he had found by the spring, forgotten back in the deer bed, which now was far to the east behind him and retreating further with each step. He crashed forward, oblivious to the trail he left in his wake, running with adrenaline and instinct but little else. Ten minutes, then ten minutes more. Small ridges became short mountains as his exhausted legs caught fire. All the while, the wind slapped blades of coarse grass across his face, nicking exposed skin here and there until his whole face stung. The cold rain mixed with hot blood and stained his shirt pink in rivulets and drips and drops.

Now that cloud is really, really low.

A chill started at the small of Jack's sweat-soaked back and ran straight up his spine as he looked up and into the cloud's underbelly. The green sky was at its deepest there, and the rain somehow stung even more. One of the raindrops hit his shoulder with surprising force and Jack staggered to his knees. Another drop struck him in the back of the head, and Jack saw stars while he looked straight at the ground. A third grazed his ear and landed on the back of his hand, the white sphere disintegrating on impact and spreading itself everywhere.

What the hell?

Jack ripped off his pack and threw it under him, groping inside half-blindly for the blanket he'd slept under only thirty minutes before. He covered himself with it and reached back into his pack to palm his cube, working from both muscle memory and fear-induced clarity in equal parts. The blanket went instantly rigid around him and the pelting stopped. Jack could think again.

This'll fly away at any moment.

Tensing himself, he thumbed the cube again and the body blows recommenced. He grabbed a corner of the cloth in one fist and smeared a muddy footstep on another. He pressed a knee into a third and hunkered down. Jack thumbed the cube yet once more. The pelting again faded.

This time, noise began building around Jack and his ears popped in rapid succession. A moan crept under the blanket, and Jack held on with such force that he feared he'd snap the bones in his fingers. He was reminded of an emergency shuttle roaring down a Chicago street. The howl overtook everything else around him until he heard nothing at all. The hail tapered off, but the blanket continued to be hit with all manner of debris, buffeting him but protecting him from serious harm.

Minutes passed. The buffeting slowed, then ceased. The noise subsided and the hail did not return. Jack waited a while longer before he dared release the blanket to peer out from under it. He was not prepared for what greeted him when he did.

The first thing Jack noticed was the horizon, and how much farther away it now appeared. The star ladder, hardly visible last evening, now stretched impossibly off in the distance. He'd somehow spun around in the storm.

The space where he'd come crashing through in a run some time before—those two or three miles now in front of him to the east—were simply gone. Only the wind turbines, most of which were listing or missing a blade, remained. Bent grasses, twisted flower patches, bare earth, and the naked contours of the land started perhaps thirty yards from where he sat.

Jack tried to stand but stumbled badly. His shaking body decided on its own to wait just a second longer before regaining its balance. He looked down, saw his shoes were still on, and laughed. An instant later his legs quit and Jack returned to the ground.

Would anyone have even found me?

The emptiness surrounding him overwhelmed his shell-shocked psyche as he surveyed the storm's aftermath. Without thought or reason, he cried. Images flashed in his mind as he lay huddled. A lost family, a lost wife, a lost love. A lost future saved only by five earlier seconds of running. A past behind him utterly destroyed, to the roots. No structure and no recognition. Only twisted pictures of what was, with only a vague sense of where to go.

Jack cried himself to sleep in the mud.

"Ma'am!" The woman shouted from the table.

"Yes?"

"We've lost our surveillance. A storm came through and ripped the AI right out of the air. It's gone."

"Crap. Did we ID whoever that was?"

"No. But ma'am, there's a very good chance he was killed in the storm too. Right before the relay died, there was tornado coming down on top of him."

A palm covered the older woman's mouth for a moment while she thought about that. "Well in that case, let's forget about it. And make no notes about the activities of the AI right before it went dark. Just mention the storms." *I'm glad I never put in that request.* "We're just going to sink this into the ground and move on. Understood?"

"Completely, ma'am."

More rain fell on Jack several hours later. He scrambled to his feet as water again crept into his eyes, and he scanned the clouds expecting a repeat of earlier events. Nothing. Just rain. Jack put his head back and yawned, raindrops moistening an otherwise parched mouth.

He grabbed the blanket and spread it on the ground, folding the ends up into a shallow box before freezing it in place with his cube. *That should gather a bunch.*

Jack stood for a while, staring off, looking at his surroundings and wondering where the day had gone. The rain increased. Jack could see mud running off of himself and onto the ground. *I must look a sight.*

The small pool he'd created to catch water had perhaps half an inch sloshing around its bottom, enough for Jack to stick his mouth into and drink from. He filled his canteen next. The rain continued, drowning out all other noise, and Jack was grateful the wind hadn't joined in the afternoon fun.

Thirty minutes more, and the deluge continued, the blanket-pool filling deeply enough for Jack to dunk his full face into. He laughed to himself. *Well, why not?* Jack stripped off his soaked clothes, revealing enormous welts where the hailstones had struck earlier. He threw all the clothes into the water and then he, too, got in. His toes went white, as did the rest of both feet up to his ankles, but he couldn't tell. The water went from clear to muddy in an instant. Working fast, he rinsed off as best he could, grime and sweat adding themselves to the darkening pool of water. The welt on his head made Jack recoil with shock as he rinsed and scrubbed his hair. *No wonder I slept. I hope I don't have a concussion.* As the rain tapered off, Jack finally felt clean, and he emptied the water from the blanket all at once with the tap of a finger. The last of the water washed over his feet in a final cool wave, just as his toes started to tingle and burn with the return of blood. Jack turned on the blanket's heating elements to help dry it out, and folded his wet clothes into it as well, putting the whole mess into the UV part of his pack. He got dressed and turned west. Rays of sunlight bounced off the clouds far beyond him, and a breeze ran through his fresh clothing as he sighted his heading and set off again, slightly damp but scrubbed clean of the grime from before.

He wished he'd remembered his walking stick. There wasn't a tree in sight, just wind turbines. And the grass was soaked.

"I'm tired of these stupid windmills," he said, seeing them out to the horizon in every direction. Several nearby looked much worse for wear than they had at the start of the day. "I'll bet every one of them is full of graphene and nanoribbons too. Great-grandma would be so proud."

As the day drew to an end, the fireflies again made their presence known, in the fleeting moments between the day and night shifts of the sun and the stars. The ground lit up once more for a time, and then patchy clouds obscured the stars from Jack as he pressed forward, ever onward, a quantum tether guiding his path to an unsure destination.

The next morning Jack saw, in the distance, the end of the windmills and pushed himself to be well clear of them before he stopped to sleep. *At least the sky isn't deep red again.* No deer beds announced themselves this time around, so Jack made do as he could in the prairie, cocooning himself and his pack in a blanket, which thankfully had dried itself well during the night. He ate nearly the last of his rations. Gnawing worry bothered Jack's thoughts for the brief period before he fell fast asleep.

The sun would have been well past its peak, were it not for the overcast clouds greeting Jack when he woke that afternoon. Another day, another hike through the bluestems and the gramas and the sedges and the echinaceas. Even the thin black line in the sky behind him hid above the clouds, and with the departure of the windmills, Jack's man-made reference points were well and truly gone. So too was his food. He went another night through the grass with his pack light, wondering when he'd get to where he needed to be. The clouds remained through the night and on into the following morning, and the occasional tree began to pop up here and there in the landscape. Always an oak, the gnarled branches broke up the monotonous skyline from miles away. Each one occupied an impossible form as he passed it. Branches ran inches off the ground, massive in diameter and length, like a child running their fingers over the ripples of a pond, daring them to get wet. Each tree bent a little under the weight of massive green acorns, with their rough and fuzzy acorn caps still clinging tightly to the trees.

Beneath one of these watchmen, Jack stopped mid-morning to sleep, pressed up against a huge, cool, granite boulder resting next to the tree's trunk. Shade, and something that wasn't grass, helped ease his mind. An uneventful snooze followed, although the previous day's hunger was now more than a simple nuisance.

He woke late and packed again, wondering how much farther he needed to walk. Without checking his cube first, he got underway in the same approximate direction as before.

After several minutes, he checked his path to fine-tune his direction and saw he had become turned around. His cube was, in fact, pointing him back the opposite way, to the oak he'd just slept under.

Oh no, it's broken.

Jack reinitialized it, hoping it was just a glitch, but the line still took him towards the tree. He trudged back, the hunger momentarily forgotten as his stomach tied itself in knots far tighter than they'd been a few minutes ago.

He sat down on the rock next to the tree trunk and stared west, the horizon stretching out far before him. No other trees were in sight. No landmarks, no anything. Just gently rolling plains and a slowly reddening sun sinking lower along the horizon.

Shit.

Frozen to the rock as though he were carved

from it, Jack sat as the sun continued to slip further in the sky. The breeze began to cool.

I need water. Like, soon.

Jack took out the blanket and set it up like he had several days before, edges up, ready to catch anything that might fall. *Even if it's just the morning dew. I guess I'm going to be cold tonight.* The sun continued down and the familiar rhythm of an ending day began again. Jack dug through his pack on the rock and put on every piece of clothing, which wasn't much. Everything was so snug against him that by the end, he needed to put his cube on the rock because it otherwise dug into his thigh.

"Can I eat a firefly?" he asked aloud. The thought of crunching down on the lowly insect roiled Jack's innards. *I guess I'm not that hungry yet.*

Several acorns lay by the rock and Jack picked one up. He popped off the large, fuzzy cap. The green shell gave way next, after a couple of solid thwacks against the rock. The creamy nut sat intact in Jack's hand.

Its bitterness was palatable only because Jack's hunger made it so. Still, this was better than nothing, and there were several more around the rock. From the looks of it, some were also crushed underneath the rock, their shells splintered and jammed up against the space between the rock and the ground. The grass looked like it had recently been flattened beneath the stone.

Jack grabbed one of the acorn shards and gave it a tug. The end popped out from the edge of the rock. It had, indeed, been trapped.

In the fading light, Jack examined the shard. The thin, sharp edges rolled between his fingers as he flexed the fragment back and forth between his thumb and index finger, its corners digging into his skin and serving to focus his thoughts as he pumped it slowly, in and out.

He paused. The shard snapped in two.

Jack stood and looked at his cube atop the rock. Toggling it, a faint blue line bore straight into the perch he'd been sitting against for some time.

"Harold, you wily, sly little..."

Jack found the hairline border, just like Harold had so very many years ago, and opened the access console. He pushed the single, solitary button down, which took a good deal of force, and was rewarded with a solid, satisfying *thunk* as some internal latch gave way. The entire top of the rock rose up ever so slightly, hinged around a single point near the tree. Jack swung the lid up, revealing a hollowed-out rock before him, loaded with supplies.

Harold, I wish you were here. Food and water stood out initially to Jack, being as hungry as he was. There seemed to be plenty and then some. He decided to eat and drink to his stomach's content before delving any further. Only after he was full did he start to inventory everything else inside the rock. A spare water bladder. Some more food underneath a second thin blanket. Two small print books, both detailing edible plants and fungi. *These look ancient. Where did he find them?* Another shirt and two pairs of socks. A Chicago Cubs baseball cap.

Jack took the opportunity to put his garbage into the rock, and he repacked his supplies to better reflect his newfound trove of stuff. He figured he could carry about two days' worth of water with him now, which would tie him down less and hopefully let him cover ground faster.

Lastly, he went back to the console. Next to the single button were two cylinders, each a little fatter than a cigarette, but only half as long. The one on the left was lit with a blue ring around it, while the other one was dark. Jack pulled his cube out and ejected an identical cylinder from its quantum interface, and then took the unlit cylinder out of its hole and slammed it home into the cube's vacated void. *There. Now I'll know where I'm going again.* As Jack put the ejected cylinder into the rock console's now-open hole, the blue ring dimmed and went out, leaving no light but the stars.

Time to go, Jack.

Before he left, Jack looked around the tree for any fallen branches roughly his height but, in the dark, saw only small twigs and other kindling. He found his new heading with the cube and set off walking for another night under the stars. The constellations spun into view one after the other, and with nobody else to talk to, he told himself stories of the heavens.

12

Betty got home a little after three o'clock and dumped her bag on the floor. More than a week away and she hadn't missed the place until yesterday, when she began to wonder if her husband was ever going to vid her back. Clearly, he didn't care about her enough, or he would have called the day after her drunken morning, or the day after that, or the day following. Each day of silence made Betty brood even more, until she decided that when she got back from vacation, she'd really put Jack in his place.

Except, Jack wasn't there. No bags, no cube, no toothbrush. It was as if he'd never returned at all.

No note explaining how sorry he was, no message in the kitchen saying he had gone to Harold's. Nothing.

Betty looked at the clock. *I bet he's still at work. Probably sleeping in his office, hiding from me.* She turned around and left again, taking the express elevator all the way to the ground floor. A quick walk across the street to the science center and then she stormed up, up, and up the steps, heading straight towards her husband's office. She paused to catch her breath.

"Jack!"

The door swept open with such a start that Harold nearly toppled back over and out of his chair, coffee flying every which way all over his half of the office.

"All right, where is he?" Betty took several steps towards Harold, who was trying to recover his balance while holding his mug and whatever coffee might remain. He took several seconds to compose himself before looking up from his chair.

"Betty, hello. What do you want?" he asked, raising a single eyebrow her way while peering down at the empty mug.

"You know damn well why I'm here, asshole. Where's Jack?"

"Definitely not at the bottom of this mug. And now I'm all out of coffee. It's mid-afternoon, and I have a night class to teach, so I need a fresh cup. Walk with me?" Harold stood and made towards the door, sidestepping his friend's wife along the way. Out and down the hall he went, before Betty realized he wasn't coming back. She rushed to catch up, not wanting to lose Harold in the vast depths of the science center. *I never remember where anything is around here except for their office. I wish it was easier to reach, I hate taking all those stairs.*

Harold made his way down to the ground floor in no great hurry, being careful to seem calm and composed. He rehearsed what he planned to say once his mug was refilled and he had his prop.

"So where is he?" Betty tried again as she caught him midway down to the café.

"Do you really want to have this discussion here, in public, with all of these people around? I won't ask again." Harold maintained a slow walk. He could smell a fresh pot brewing as he neared the café.

"Where. Is. He." Students studying nearby looked up at the pair and tiny indicator lights on their lenses flickered to life.

Harold stopped, steps from the coffee counter.

"Jack? I don't know, Betty. I haven't seen him in more than a week. I haven't seen him since he came back from your vacation the same day it began. I have not seen him since he told me he saw you in bed with someone else!" Harold yelled. More heads swiveled. More people looked down from above. More lens lights came on. "Why don't *you* know where he is? He is *your* husband, Betty. Not mine. Why did it take you this long to find me and ask? I figured he was with you, trying to patch things up *again*! How could you do that to him? Hey, don't walk away. I want to know where he is too! Where's Jack Wilson? Where is your husband?"

By now hundreds of eyes watched them and at the mention of Jack's surname, the murmurs began in earnest. Lens lights flickered off and people began that distant stare, present but not present. After Betty fled out of sight, Harold refilled his coffee. Only when he raised the mug to cover his face did he allow himself to smile. He held the mug up a long time.

That evening, his normally sparse lecture hall was filled to capacity.

13

Trees were becoming more common for Jack as he walked, and not just oaks. Lines of mixed hardwoods increasingly filled the horizon, and small creeks and streams made the second leg of his journey shadier and easier to stay hydrated. It had been two days since he'd come across Harold's cache, and so far this second leg felt about the same as the first.

More importantly, after walking under an especially large cottonwood, Jack found a particularly well-shaped walking stick, which he promptly appropriated for himself.

As the second leg's second night drew to a close,

he found himself in the thickest forest he had come across yet. After a solid mile of hiking between mossy trees, the woods thinned out and opened up before him all at once, revealing a wide river. It stretched out everywhere and moved a substantial amount of water downstream. From what Jack could see in the early dawn, it was at least several hundred yards across.

The narrow shoreline intermingled sand and mud and rocks, and Jack decided to wait for more light before venturing out any farther. With the tall trees close behind him, the sun took a little longer to show up, and Jack took some time to consider what was next.

This must be the Mississippi. He wracked his brain and tried to remember his geography. *How am I gonna get across this?*

As the sun came up over the trees, Jack's face fell. *That's not the other side. That's an island in the middle of the river. I can't even see the opposite shore with all this mist. Fording is out.*

Jack also knew that bridges and roads were out. The single, solitary bridge was connected to the single, solitary east-west highway that remained on the continent, and it was heavily monitored. Every other major road, and almost all of the minor ones, had long since been chewed up and sprinkled back over the world's oceans, either as rubble zones or as powder to soak up carbonic acid. Drops of food coloring in a pool, perhaps, but the roads didn't serve any other purpose, and it couldn't hurt.

That lone highway was several hundred miles to the south, anyhow, and Jack knew he didn't have the supplies for that sort of detour. He sat there, unmoving, and watched the morning fog burn off. By the time it was all gone, Jack could barely see the opposite shore, and his teeth hurt. He unclenched his jaw.

People must have crossed it millennia ago. Before bridges. But those people could probably swim. Maybe I could build a boat? Or a canoe? Jack laughed. Softly at first, but then louder and louder, until he couldn't help himself. *Jack, listen, look around you. Aside from this pack on your back, you have nothing. How would you hollow out a canoe? Get a grip.*

He walked the shoreline and made his way south, noticing for the first time the thousands and thousands of mussel and clam shells lining the shore. Looking out into the shallow water, he could make out even more clam beds, clams of all shapes and sizes, probably millions in all, stretching out across the water. A family of otters floated by, several with rocks on their bellies, which they used to smash clams and snails to pieces.

They're eating well. One of them glanced over at Jack for a moment, sized him up, and then turned away, uninterested. Breakfast was far more important.

Soon after, Jack began to notice all of the birds. Small ones, big ones, raptors, waterfowl. They were everywhere: huge flocks on the water, roosting in trees, or flying overhead. Several massive birds with giant white heads perched at the top of some of the dead trees on the island a few hundred yards away. One of them took flight, soaring for a second before diving straight towards the water. It pulled out of the head-first dive at the last moment, enormous yellow feet stretching out beneath it, clasping, grasping, talons going beneath the surface for an instant before re-emerging with a watery meal, still wriggling. Its fins twitched as it gasped in the air.

Maybe I could fly across. Jack continued his slow walk down the shoreline and considered his options, which were few.

You could go home, Jack. Look how far you've gone already. You can bet nobody has seen this part of the river in a hundred years, maybe more. Most people have probably forgotten that it even exists. And here you are. You could go back. Fix things up. Harold would be thrilled to see you.

"To what end? Back to the university? What about Aramae? And her find? I know I don't owe her anything. She's an adult and she takes care of herself. But she asked me to come."

Do I really know that, though? One weird message sent to me. It could be anything. And it's not like we've seen each other in years. Who even knows what's going on in her life. She could be married, for all I know. Like me, ha. Do I really want to open myself up to all of that? Turning around would just be so much simpler, so much easier, and so much faster.

Jack sat down on another rock, his head in his hands.

If I go home, I'll hate it. I know I'll hate it. I'll always regret it. There's just no way. I have to get across.

As he stared out again, another brown lump floated by before breaking apart. Another family of otters enjoyed the morning sun. He watched them until they vanished downstream.

That's a crazy idea, Jack. No.

Turning around, Jack walked back into the woods, looking everywhere on the forest floor. For the next few hours, exhausted as he was, Jack found every fallen log, every branch, every wooden anything that looked like it would float. By the end, he had a pile so mismatched and haphazard that he wondered what he'd ever do with it all.

Make a big enough pile of something, Jack, and someone will find a use for it. Look at great-grandma's work. Piles of carbon now soar from the ground into space.

He separated out the mess one piece at a time. Organization brought order to his chaos and let the idea grow in his mind. *It only has to work once.* Heading back into the forest to search again, Jack ripped apart every vine he could find. He dragged them and all of the wood back to the shore, then paused for lunch and went back to work. The beginnings of what would charitably be called a raft began to form.

Four logs of varying length and diameter, all large enough for Jack to stand on individually, formed the base of the raft, lashed together with the collected vines. He sorted the other sticks and placed most of them loosely on top. One of the logs stuck out quite a bit more than the other three, but Jack could lay down without getting wet, and he used some of the sticks to wrap extra vines around, should he need them. Exhausted, Jack stepped back to survey his work.

This thing's going to kill you if anything goes wrong. There's no way it survives a storm intact. This is a terrible idea. Probably best to stop thinking about it and just get on with it.

The water stung as Jack shoved off, his hands quite raw from the day's labors. He used them as paddles, working to get away from the shore and into the main channel. A sickening feeling overtook him as he floated away from the shoreline: first ten, then twenty, then fifty feet away. Jack leaned off to the side and threw up.

Initially, Jack's plan was to skirt the end of the island he had seen that morning and then make for the opposite shore, but it became clear after only a few minutes that the current wouldn't allow for that, not without proper oars and some way to rudder the craft. Instead, the island slipped away as the current carried him downstream, further and further from where he wanted to go. Jack knew if he dared to take out his cube and sight where he was supposed to be heading, it'd tell him he was south and getting more south every minute, floating off course. The raft seemed river-worthy, but he was at the mercy of the main channel. Soon, he had more than a thousand feet of water on either side of him, and the sun was beginning to set. Every time Jack tried to paddle, the current would fight him, keeping the raft where it wanted it, unwilling to give up its first human passenger in generations.

Jack sat back in the middle of the raft, such as it was, and watched the land slip by, bit by bit. The island he had initially wanted to skirt was now long gone upriver, no longer visible after several bends in the waterway, and he was no closer to the opposite shore than he'd been an hour ago. The setting sun reminded him that he had again not slept in almost a day, and Jack feared he'd soon be too exhausted to think straight. The bump on the back of his head began to throb as he tired.

I should nap. This thing seems stable. The sky's clear, and my head's not.

Adjusting his pack so it would rest on his chest instead of his back, Jack settled down on four half-submerged logs floating uncontrollably down the biggest river on the continent, and tried to sleep. It didn't take long. Even Jack's fear of water couldn't override his wearied fatigue. Exhaustion worked its magic and he drifted off while drifting downriver.

When Jack opened his eyes again, millions of stars and a radiant band of dust overhead greeted him, as it had now for days. Jack found north quickly in the stars, got his bearings, and still found himself in the middle of the river. A cool breeze blew across his face as he sat up.

"That breeze could be enough to push this thing to the other side, but I've got to catch it." Jack knelt with his arms outstretched, looking so much like a biblical figure praying to some long-ago god. He faced east and felt the wind press against his body.

That's not going to be enough. Jack fished around in his pack and pulled out one of the blankets. Clouds began to shroud the stars from view.

The blanket unfurled, flapping in the air as Jack tried to think of a way to turn it into a sail.

That...might work. He grabbed four of the smaller sticks he'd brought on the raft, spread them out, and jammed them into the narrow crack between the two center logs so they'd stand upright. He weaved the blanket between the unstraight posts and wrapped one of the longer vines around the whole thing, like a ribbon around a package. The wind fought him the entire time and everything took twice as long as it should have. Gusts constantly threatened to push the blanket through the wooden anchors and nearly ripped the blanket from Jack's grasp more than once.

Finally, Jack figured he had it as good as he'd get it, given the dark, and he reached back into his bag and thumbed his cube with one hand while holding the blanket tightly with the other.

The raft lurched as the blanket went rigid, and Jack could feel the wind push hard against his makeshift sail.

If this wind gets any stronger, I'm going to have a new

problem.

Slowly, imperceptibly slowly in the nearly pitch dark, the raft moved across the main channel, pushed by the easterly wind. Several times during the night, Jack felt the raft slow down and speed up. One strong gust blew the Chicago Cubs hat right off his head and into the river. As he held the blanket tight, he hoped the little raft wouldn't run aground on some unseen impediment and for the wind to continue. He still couldn't make out the western shore, and he couldn't tell how fast downstream he was continuing to move, either.

14

That is not a good sky.

An eerie red dawn greeted Jack several hours later. The raft continued its journey across the river as he sat with every part of himself pressed up against the makeshift masts while they protested against the increasing wind.

Jack figured he had about another five hundred feet to go until he reached the shore, but with the wind blowing the way it was, he wasn't confident he'd get there before the masts failed. *I can always try to wade at this point. Let's see what happens.*

Fifty feet, and then another fifty. Jack saw the shoreline now, looking like a mirror image of the one he'd left some twelve hours ago. Fifty feet again, and the clam beds became visible under Jack's tiny raft. Some shells stuck almost out of the water, with razor-sharp edges ready to slice anything brushing by. Perhaps even the little vines holding together four disjointed logs.

By now the wind was pushing Jack west at about ten feet a minute. Several hundred yards to the south, a sandbar jutted out in front of the raft's path like a hook.

Let the wind carry it further.

It seemed as though the sandbar, barely an inch or so above the water, connected back to the main shore. By the time Jack toggled his cube to make the sail go limp, the raft was firmly in the middle of the oncoming outcrop. Jack stowed the blanket and got the gear ready to disembark, and wondered what to do about the raft.

It'll break up during this incoming storm. And besides, there's no time. I've got to find shelter.

Soft scrapes along the bottom meant Jack's ride was at its end. He hopped off and hurried along the sandbar's hundred feet or so, past the muddy, rocky shoreline and into the forest beyond.

The wind now threw small waves across the river, inundating the sandbar. Jack looked back just in time to see one lapping wave crest over the sandbar and carry the sad little raft away, no longer carrying a passenger but simply adrift, alone and untended.

The woods shielded Jack somewhat from the whipping winds but he knew he still needed to find shelter, and quick. The forest floor was open; the trees themselves massive, ancient, foreboding. Years —perhaps decades—of leafy debris carpeted the ground, muffling Jack's footsteps as he searched for something to ride out the storm in.

For once, luck was on Jack's side as he found an enormous standing tree trunk, forty feet tall and blasted off at its top by what looked like lightning. Jack noticed the top half of the tree nearby, lying on the ground, its leaves long since withered away.

The upright trunk was almost entirely stripped of bark, such that Jack couldn't even tell what sort of tree it had been in its prime, but right now all Jack cared about was the hollow at its base, maybe five feet wide and about as tall, extending up into the dead wood.

Jack crawled in on his knees. He found the hollow a bit tight, but spacious enough for him. Looking up, he saw nothing. No shred of light peeked down through, and he knew he'd fared better than he had any right to with this find. The wind outside howled, and a morning sky had once again gone from ruddy to pale green. Jack decided to use one of the blankets to wall off the entrance and wrapped himself in the second.

Thank you, Harold.

By the time the worst of the storm hit, Jack was fast

asleep, curled up, oblivious to all things. Meanwhile, his little raft continued along its own voyage.

At first, the slapdash little craft bumped against sandbars and shoreline rocks, getting stuck here and there. Sometimes for hours, sometimes for days, but the craft remained miraculously durable. Had anyone been around to watch its journey, they'd have remarked at how well the logs held up as they were jostled in the various eddies and currents of the massive river.

Over time, the raft found its way back into the main channel where it floated along, passing by millions of clams and fish. Occasionally, an eagle would perch on it for a time, or land with its latest catch to be eaten during a leisurely midday cruise. If not eagles, then otters climbed aboard the platform to wrestle or play, or just sun themselves on this odd little mess of logs. Through all of this, for days upon days, the raft floated by no people. Not a single human eye watched its journey. No mind pierced its meaning or wondered at its story. Nothing thought anything of the drifting little island, floating and barely visible from the far distant shorelines. Alone and rudderless, Jack's raft passed this way unseen and unlooked for, even after a hundred miles.

The one single bridge across the river, far down south, was actually much closer to the ocean than to Chicago. It saw very little traffic, usually just students heading to college or automated haulers moving captured graphite to and fro. The crossing was monitored because of its unique status. Occasional miscreants or self-styled adventurers would try to cross it and inevitably be noticed, caught, moved away from the rewilded spaces, and back to the ladder cities where people belonged.

A woman sat in a conference room. Some weeks ago, she had purposely forgotten about a hailstorm and a tornado and a man who wore no lenses. Now, she found herself watching a live holostream of the bridge, thrust upon her without warning while she worked on something else. After orienting to the scene on her display, she spied the reason for the intrusion. Floating slowly, adrift, and covered in bird droppings, the little raft passed under the bridge and came out the other side.

Surprise and curiosity mixed with urgency as she tried to get the raft picked up by whatever nearby AI she could muster. Once she found a hoverbot large enough to haul it out of the water, she'd had enough time to think through all of her possible actions.

She did not seek out anyone, like she had weeks ago. The man from that storm would remain dead. He had to. She had assured her boss of his demise. If this wasn't his raft, that meant someone else had gotten out even farther without being noticed. Either way, it didn't bode well for her career, and she really wanted to keep this job. Carbon sinking wasn't going away any time soon, and her company controlled every sinkable acre east of the river she was staring at, plus quite a few west of it. Sinking was big business and people were the antithesis of sinking. When one came, more followed. If it became common knowledge that it was possible to get out this far without being picked up, the illusion of control would vanish. Only permitted researchers from the few remaining science schools entered the landscape, and they didn't go on foot. Or build slipshod driftwood rafts.

No, this raft had to disappear. If it got much further south, it would be noticed by the port, and then she'd be in real trouble.

Without wasting another moment, she flicked her lenses and took control of the AI, landing it squarely on the raft. She swiveled her head, engaged the drone's small saw, and reached out with her arm, cutting the vines that still held the tiny craft together. In seconds, the job was done. The logs separated and spread out in the water.

The immediate crisis was over. At the next opportunity, the AI would wipe its memory, per her instructions. She took her lenses off to rub her eyes and, for the first time, noticed how much her hands were shaking. She wondered if she had seen the last of her mystery traveler and if she should even try to search for him.

What reason could she possibly use to explain scouring millions of acres of carbon sink?

<h1 style="text-align:center">15</h1>

Jack woke up to a sharp pain at the small of his back, right at the point where he was curled up tightest. A ragged line of grey light poked into the hollow from the dim edges of the blanket, and struggled to wake the tree's one and only guest.

Dirt crusted the right side of Jack's face, and he sensed the pulverized leaves drop from his tangled beard as he sat up. He felt around in the leaf litter for his cube, initially coming up empty as he tried to get his bearings. Through one squinted eye, he found its dull glimmer and reached out to thumb the blanket into limp submission.

The squinted eye closed as the light found its

way inside after being shut out through the long hours Jack had slept.

"I wonder how long I've been in here." He crawled out and began organizing his pack. The clouds made it difficult to judge where the sun was, so Jack did the only sensible thing he could: he illuminated his path in pale blue light, sighted a rough line, and set off, eating into his rations as he went.

The forest, littered with downed branches and the occasional snapped trunk, challenged Jack's eagerness to put the woods behind him. What should have taken only a few minutes to cross turned into an hours-long exercise in wayfinding and keeping his bearings, as the circuitous route through the trees made Jack wonder, if only for a moment, whether the forest wasn't quite ready to give up its human guest.

The trees gradually thinned as Jack felt himself ascend from the floodplain. As he finally cleared the woods, he turned around to look where he had been.

The river seemed much wider from the western side than he'd remembered. From the vantage point staked out on the small hill he was on, he could see the easterly bend to the north. It turned again as he followed the line of the trees, giving him a rough idea of the water's flow. A dawning realization crept over Jack.

I'm a lot farther south than I was yesterday.

A low rumble drew Jack away from the river

and spun him around. His eyes shot up to the clouds, expecting to see another storm on the horizon. Instead, he saw a glimpse of pale blue peek out and a dozen rays of yellow pour down, illuminating the plains in the distance. The rumbling continued far, far off. Jack strained to make out its source as he started back on his journey through the grass that now wrapped around him waist-high, with occasional thickets burying him up past his head. For the most part, though, Jack could finally see where he was going.

Minutes again stretched into hours. Several small creeks and streams coursed over the landscape for Jack to ford or replenish himself. Or, when the sun finally began to dim, to wash himself. A clear sandy creek bottom turned noticeably muddier after a bath. This latest creek was no wider than three strides and only as deep as Jack's knees.

Clean and somewhat refreshed, he searched for a new walking stick, hoping he'd finally find one that would last more than a day or so. He did not.

As he left the creek, the same low rumble again caught his ear. For the first time, the ground beneath him *felt* like it was rumbling too.

The breeze, still until now, also picked up. On it was a stench that stopped Jack where he stood. *That is foul. What am I heading towards?*

The noise, the vibrations, and the smell did not stop or cease, but intensified as Jack kept hiking his cube's blue northwesterly line. Rolling hills and plains limited how far he could see, keeping the horizon nearby for the next hour as the clouds thinned. The sun continued to set just a little to the left of where he was headed. The successive series of ups and downs made his legs burn, but one final hill beckoned him forward nonetheless.

The grasses mixed with purple and yellow coneflowers and dropped off in height as he neared the top, with an array of understory plants that changed in both color and shape with every step.

He crested the top of the last hill on what felt like the longest of long days. The land in front of him opened up wide, and it stretched out to a distant point without so much as the ripple of a hill or the dip of a creek.

Unlike all the panoramas across the plains until now, the landscape before him was on the move. A sinuous streak of brown flowed from north to south.

Huge clouds of dust rose from the ground, partly obscuring the view from the hilltop, but Jack now knew the origin of the noise he had heard all afternoon.

From horizon to horizon, looking nearly like the river he'd rafted across, a million bison thundered past. Huge, hairy, and with horns, the herd moved with a single purpose, traveling to a destination only it knew.

Calves ran beside their mothers, their tiny hoofs

taking twice as many steps to keep up. The herd crushed everything in a quarter-mile swath. No vegetation was spared: not a single blade of grass stood unbent.

I guess I'm staying here for the night. There are worse places. I just wish the smell was better.

Jack sat atop the hill mesmerized by the sight as the herd continued on undeterred and unbothered by his presence. The bison's ancestors' ancestors had never seen a human, and until now, neither had they.

Nobody would believe this if I told them.

Jack fished out his cube and set it to record everything, much like he'd done alongside the road an eternity ago, in a different life.

The sun fully set behind the plains, and after Jack had a bite of food, the dull monotonous roar of millions of hoofbeats put him to sleep.

Fireflies filled the grass around him and the stars spun up overhead, one for each of the huge animals he'd just seen. As he slept, Jack dreamt of the bison stampeding from horizon to horizon, kicking up dust and obscuring a band of stars in their wake.

When Jack woke up to the howls, the Milky Way shone straight down on him, a dusty bison path stretching across the sky.

16

The howls replaced the rumbles he'd fallen asleep to, although the hum coming from the ground told Jack the herd wasn't far past earshot. The hair on the back of his neck stood as he tried to recall everything he had ever learned or heard about wolves. Stray thoughts flitted through his mind. *Packs…social structure…avoid humans…*

The howls continued as he sat frozen, although each new cry seemed further away to the south, in the direction the bison had trampled. After a while, Jack began to dream again.

Early the next morning, more low rumbles from the

north roused Jack from a sound sleep.

Stragglers, huh?

The plains before him had been utterly flattened, the bison having left a ruinous, mottled brown scar across the land. The stragglers' hoofbeats got louder as Jack sat on his hill, eating and drinking from his stores while he watched for any sign of movement.

Maybe I'll go see what sort of damage the main herd did.

Jack closed his pack and waded downhill through the short grass and clumps of white wild indigo in bloom, their racemes reaching past the top of his head.

A quarter mile further, the land opened up to reveal its bison scar. The ground vibrated ever stronger as the even-toed ungulates drew near.

They sure are taking their time.

He looked north. Brown heads just barely crested the horizon in the distance, above the taller grass of the lower elevation.

The small group ambled towards Jack. Each thud of a hoof set the ground quivering. Their bodies hid in the tall grass to either side of the mangled earth.

At a little more than a few hundred yards away, Jack got a clearer picture of what approached.

He squinted, rubbed his eyes, and squinted again.

Jack stood transfixed in the middle of the trodden ground as the massive creatures loomed. The tallest stood nearly thirteen feet high. Several others measured well over ten feet. They were all as hairy as yesterday's herd. Coarse brown fuzz covered every inch from head to toe. Unlike the bison, what lumbered toward Jack had two highly curved tusks, each at least nine or ten feet long. A trunk swayed between them.

"There's no way. Mammoths. Columbian mammoths," Jack spoke aloud, oblivious to everything except the herd. Or perhaps it was a family. As if to confirm, out of the grass came the smallest of them, previously overlooked and hidden behind the thick tufts of vegetation. It stood perhaps five feet tall and headed straight for Jack, curious about the never-before-heard sound and the funny creature standing on two feet.

Jack remained rooted. *I thought this experiment failed generations ago.*

The youngster was close now, maybe ten yards or so, and the ground finally stopped shaking as the rest of the family paused to watch. All eyes turned to Jack and their "tiny" family member. The largest of them spread its hairy ears wide.

A trunk reached out to sniff and prod Jack here and there, ruffling his hair as the calf took in the novelty of it all. Human eyes locked with the mammoth's as the calf came ever closer.

"You're a curious little guy, aren't you? Or girl?" Jack said. He reached out to scratch the calf's trunk. "You are unbelievable."

Several minutes went past as introductions

continued.

"So how many of you are out here?" he asked to the rest of the family. "Are you it? You can't be it. You all look healthy and mostly young. There's got to be more of you out there somewhere, right? I mean, what are the odds?" It felt good to talk to something after a couple weeks of solitude, even if these unlikeliest of creatures had no idea what he was saying.

The curious calf's trunk continued to explore Jack and his belongings. After a tentative minute, it made its way into Jack's pack and smelled food. It tried to pull the pack off Jack, who was spun around and dragged backwards with no warning. As his balance tipped, he stepped to steady himself and felt his foot land on something not quite firm.

A high-pitched trumpet blast rang Jack's ears as he realized what happened. The small trunk let go as the calf quickly retreated towards its family.

"No, nooooononononono! I'm sorry, little guy!" Jack said. He stepped towards the calf, which was now back behind the largest mammoth. Its ears were still out, and its enormous head swayed back and forth while it continued to stare down Jack.

"Oh, shit."

The family formed a half-ring around the calf while facing Jack, and the big mammoth took a step forward, its head held high.

Jack turned and ran.

The mammoth lowered its head and followed.

The top of the hill he'd spent the night on was perhaps fifty yards in front of him. Jack looked up at it and frantically hoped mammoths preferred flat ground. Just as he got to the base of the hill, his foot caught an outcropped rock hidden among the plants and he tripped, going down with barely enough time to get his arms out in front of him. He felt the ground shake as the mammoth thundered right behind him, and then the enormous creature caught up and trapped Jack between its huge, curved tusks. It batted him back and forth like two hockey players passing a puck as its head rocked with fury. After half a dozen or so blows to both sides of Jack's chest and arms, the mammoth stood high and let out a wail that put him nearly unconscious. He played dead as the mammoth backed up and rejoined the others. The family moved away and resumed following the bison trail.

Lie still until you can't feel the footsteps, Jack.

That took an hour. The whole time, a vulture made lazy circles overhead.

The omen was not lost on Jack.

It's hard to believe humans killed those things off. Jack chuckled despite himself. Instant regret followed the pain in his ribs, where the decidedly un-extinct mammoth's tusks had landed blow upon blow.

The vulture still circled overhead, joined by several of its friends as the light from the sun occasionally silhouetted them. Jack reached up to examine his chest and gingerly poked and prodded his sides. Huge red welts lanced their way from his armpits to down past his ribs, each the imprint of the broadside of a mammoth tusk. Painful breaths kept Jack from passing out.

I don't think anything is broken, but this is going to bruise like hell. Can someone even get bib contusions? Rib. Rib contusions. What am I saying? Jack moved the self-exam to his head and checked for bleeding. His hands returned with only dirt.

It took another fifteen minutes to stand and look around. Grass. Endless grass and rolling plains, with only a single tree and the long brown scar to break up endless swaying monotony.

Maybe there will be something over the next rise.

It took a few more minutes to shoulder his pack, which brought fresh ripples of agony as Jack tried to get underway. He wondered how far along his faint blue line he'd have to walk until he reached the next supply cache Harold had hidden, somewhere out in the wilderness.

For once, Jack was thankful for the tall grass. It hid him completely from sight as he focused on putting one foot in front of the other, somewhat along his path. A dip in elevation meant he fought much of the mid-morning march through mud and muck, mired in ankle-deep water, which soaked his feet and the bottom of his pants, and slowed down his progress even further.

By mid-afternoon Jack estimated he'd gotten no

further than perhaps five miles, and every breath brought new, ragged pain. The ground angled up again and the grass thinned. Jack could see beyond a few feet for the first time since morning.

More grass. Miles and miles of every shade of green and brown stretched out in front of him everywhere. Patches of yellow or purple or pink or white interspersed the landscape, but the waves of green that swept across everything overwhelmed him. No trees or landmarks, no vibrations on the ground or drones up above. No small shadows able to cast dim oases. Only the wind, the grass, and himself. Everything rose and fell with a land shaped eons ago by glaciers and man. Now growing unnoticed and ignored.

The quiet rivulet of a stream trickled through the landscape and brought Jack to a halt as night fell. He sat down along a narrow bank and peeled off his wet shoes, wet socks, sweaty backpack, and damp shirt. Not knowing what else to do, he threw the clothes into the backpack, turned on its UV light, put his head against the ground, and fell instantly asleep.

17

The reporter bot hovered outside Betty's front door all evening. It had smuggled itself into the elevator storage and made a mad dash for it when a maintenance AI took a ride to the very top of the building. Nothing else had gotten this far in the weeks since Harold and Betty's very public argument went global. Not only was it unheard of for someone to disappear, but for a Wilson—one of the last Wilsons—on top of that was simply too much for the world's cities to ignore. Hundreds of bots and even a few intrepid reporters in the flesh descended on Chicago, each pursuing their own story, their own supposed leads, their own sources and leaks. Nobody, though, knew much more than they had when the news first broke. Harold, Betty, Jack's father, students, old classmates, and random people looking for their quick shot at fame were all in orbit around a story that was going nowhere.

When Betty finally opened her door to head off to work, the bot sprang to life and peppered her with question after question as she headed to the express elevator. It continued to get in her face, right at eye level, until the moment her ride began and the bot crashed first into the ceiling and then the elevator floor, where it rolled around until it came to rest at Betty's feet. As she slipped out, she gave it a final kick for good measure and dodged the dozen or so more that waited for her just beyond the elevator doors.

The entrance to the clinic was no better, as computer-generated voices again peppered her with shouted questions. More bots tried to hover their way in past the admittance desk, only to fall flat on the floor once they got too far inside the building's walls. Children used them as makeshift kickballs while their impatient parents watched and waited for a nurse to call their child's name. Betty strode past all of them on the way to her office. She closed the door.

Hundreds of inbox messages all asked the same thing: where was her husband? She didn't know. That's what she had told Harold the day after their spat. It had been what she told the police, the lawyers, and the university administrators too. If she had dared to venture out to her father-in-law's house, she would have told him the same, but Betty's courage failed her each time she thought of summoning a shuttle to take her to the very outskirts of Chicago.

And she still had no idea where Jack could have gone for so long without being found.

At the end of her day she trekked back home, past the bots and the faces, up the express elevator, and into her penthouse condominium. As she absentmindedly walked from room to room, she ran a hand over every item and made her way to Jack's study. For a moment, she did not recognize it and wondered why it felt strange.

There's no holoprojections. It's just the furniture and his things.

She thought of all the times she'd walked in to see some great forest or plateau stretching from wall to wall, and she smiled.

And then the smile disappeared. Just like Jack.

18

Jack's progress remained slow, days after his brush with death. The welts along his chest swelled and turned from red to purple to yellow as his body healed. The vultures left, and aside from the steady hum of a million bees and other insects, he saw no other creatures along his path. The pale blue line took him unerringly northwest, and after a long, painful rest that first day, he decided to switch back to a nighttime routine and slept while the sun shone. In his exhausted state, it was much easier to follow the blue line's path at night too.

After five days of this, provisions became a concern again, and Jack estimated he had about two more days of food at his current rate of consumption.

I wonder how far I've gone.

Dawn broke. He decided to stop along the north side of the latest hill he had crossed, and found a tall thicket of sumac to bed down under for the day. Getting out of the sun would be nice for a change. He wrapped himself in one blanket to stay cool and shaped the other to try to collect any dew or rain that might fall while he slept. Thus ended another night on the high prairie alone, with only a pale blue line for company.

"Kym! Over here!" a man's voice shouted through the grass. Jack jerked awake at the noise and sat bolt upright under the sumac canopy.

"Where are you?" a woman's voice replied.

Jack heard a body crash through the grass somewhere in front of him but couldn't make out any forms. The prairie obscured everything more than a few feet from his small sumac grove.

"Morgan, for crying out loud, where are you?" the woman called out again. Her voice had moved away from Jack, towards the bottom of the hill.

Jack ever so quietly turned off both blankets and slowly rolled them up.

"Down at the very bottom. You've got to see this. Get ready to count," Morgan yelled.

"There's so much of it! But how'd it get here? Well, never mind that for now, I guess. I don't think anybody's recorded it this far out, ever. There must be ten thousand of them," Kym said.

"It could take all day to survey, too, but the team doesn't expect us back until tonight, right?" Morgan asked.

"This won't take all day to count. Two hours. Three, tops."

Jack heard Kym reply, still unable to see either of them.

"I guess we'll have to find a way to fill the time."

The voices were next to each other now.

"What, here? Are you crazy?"

"Why not? There's no one else around for miles, and we've never done it in a field of orchids before. I'd bet nobody has in centuries. Don't you want to add it to the list?"

Jack didn't need to hear any more to guess where this was headed, and he smiled to himself. *So much for my nap. They must be a part of the census teams permitted to study the prairie. I wonder which school they're from.*

An hour later, everyone was asleep. Jack woke first, still under the sumac. He drank a few silent gulps of water, guessed at roughly where the eager couple had bedded down, and considered his options.

He left his pack behind, slipped out from his hiding spot, and headed downhill. The hot, windy afternoon blew the tall grass every which way. From his crouch, he couldn't see anything past a few feet, and he took great pains to not bend any clumps of big bluestem or indian grass on his way down. Only after several minutes did Jack momentarily panic, when he looked back and realized he could not see the sumacs, nor any discernible trail that would lead back to them and his gear.

He sucked in a deep breath, exhaled, and stood on his tiptoes. He turned in place and could just barely make out a few sumac leaves through the grass. He turned again to look back down the hill and thought he saw the shape of a breast through the swaying grass.

The wind drowned out any noise he made as he crept back to his supplies. He waited.

Hours passed and the couple finally began to stir. They murmured to themselves as their voices carried back to Jack.

"Let's get dressed, come on. We should be able to make it back to the camp before it gets dark. It's only what, how far out are we?"

"Ten miles? I don't know. I just hold on for the ride."

"Funny, I thought that was my job."

A slow exhale. "Are they all charged up?"

"Let me check...yep. About five more minutes. Want to go again?"

"You're the worst. Fine, but be quick about it. Then we're outta here. We're going to need to return tomorrow, you know. We never actually did get a population count for those prairie orchids."

Jack heard round two. Fifteen minutes later, two fully clothed people rose up and out of the grass. Each held, over their head, an enormous pair of propellers encased in what looked like an open briefcase. The helicopters-in-a-box each rotated and whisked the pair away. They flew just above the grasses and aimed directly towards the setting sun.

Jack watched their two small dots zip along the horizon as he gave chase. Eventually, he lost sight of them. He hoped they were flying a straight line back to their destination.

The sun set. Jack continued in what he thought was the right direction.

If I'm lucky, this might not be too far off my blue line. I just hope it's easy to stay hidden.

Stars again spun up. After weeks out beneath them, Jack had no trouble using them to navigate. Cool night air dried and chilled his clothes as he slid between the grass bunches with a practiced ease. Hours passed and Jack looked to find Polaris for the hundredth time, keeping it to his right as he forged ahead.

Night, Jack noticed, was a time of silence. No birds called out. Insects clung to their plant stems or found their tiny burrows. The occasional raccoon or opossum rumbled through, but Jack found that he heard mostly the wind, gurgling streams, or himself. It was a world alone, between days. He could lose himself to idle ruminations with no distractions or worries, and just slip noiselessly across the land, unseen and unhurried.

Tonight, he wondered what he would find when he eventually got to Boulder. Would Aramae be there? Would anyone? He wanted to touch, see, and examine the little pyramid with his own hands and eyes. How would he even know what to look for? And what was he going to do after that? Summon a shuttle and go back home? Teach, again? Simply living off his family's fortune did not appeal to him. And the press would no doubt be all over him.

Fear of an uncertain future threatened to paralyze him where he stood, and he realized he was going to have to deal with his marriage. Loping off on some crazy quest was going to delay things for a while still, but it wouldn't solve his problems, just postpone them. He wasn't entirely certain what would await him when he did decide to confront the whole mess. Hopefully, he'd have a plan by then. He left his future self to figure out what that would be.

A high-pitched whine ended Jack's brooding, and he crouched. The whine dropped in tone as it flew further away, more or less following the direction he was headed.

He stayed put for a few more minutes and strained to hear anything. Stillness reigned, but right before he was about to move again, he heard a faint carry of laughter off in the distance.

Jack edged closer for the next half hour, thankful there was no shrubbery or dead growth from last year to make much noise.

Maybe some firebots burned this a few months ago.

The laughter grew louder and Jack counted more than a few distinct voices. His mind flashed back to Ember and Hannah and the cool autumn evenings spent outside with that small group of friends. Were these people similar?

At last, Jack saw dim lights illuminating a little camp in the middle of nowhere. Five people were busy taking down sections of a tent, constructed from bolts of the same shape-shifting wonder fabric Jack had utilized with great success on his own journey. As he watched, the last of the tent came down, and three smaller tents went up in its place, the fabric repurposed for a new need, similar to how Jack molded his blankets to suit his varied demands. Jack was also now close enough to hear some of the voices, two of which sounded rather familiar.

"Hey Morgan, help me pitch this tent, will you?" said a recognizable female voice.

"That's what she said!"

"Grow up, Ethan," Morgan's voice echoed.

"Aren't you sleeping alone again tonight, Ethan?" said a fourth voice.

"Fuck you, Cassie."

"In your dreams!"

Roars of laughter from the rest of the group

ensued and Ethan ducked into his tent before he shouted a final, terse, "good night!"

Everyone else laughed again and quieted down as they finished with their own shelters. Gradually, they drifted off until only Kym and Morgan still made noise. Eventually they, too, were still.

Boy, those two really have a good time. Jack traversed the final distance to the campsite. He avoided the two lights and clung to the shadows, and wondered if this was a long-term site or if the group was just there temporarily. Jack hadn't worried about bears much, but he had seen a few tracks and knew there were some around. The area felt pretty freshly trampled on, so he figured the researchers probably didn't have anything permanent set up. He started to look around for anything that might store supplies.

Incoming clouds slowed the search for a while, and Jack's faint starlight came and went.

"I'm telling you, there's Listeners out here, Morgan."

A distinct whisper traveled on a breeze. Jack stopped cold and inched a little closer to the couple's tent.

"No way. We'd see evidence of them. Everyone's gotta eat, and if what I've heard is true, their equipment uses a lot of power too. Where would that come from?"

"I've always heard they were well-financed. They could have outside help. Or a small fusion reactor underground."

"Oh come on, Kym. That's really a stretch, don't you think? I mean, we are really in the middle of nowhere out here. How would it all get here, unnoticed? Without being tracked or seen?"

"Look. I'm telling you, this afternoon, I could have sworn there was someone else out there besides just us."

"You always do like to put on a show..."

"Shut up, Morgan. I'm serious. I didn't see anyone but...there was this feeling. Haven't you ever felt the hair on the back of your neck stand up?"

"That's just an old survivor's tale from when everyone nearly froze to death, to scare people into staying in the cities. And for the record, no. On the other hand, I can feel something else start to stand up..."

"Feel it! Feel my neck! There it goes again!" Kym whispered.

Jack sensed he had begun to overstay his welcome and slunk away from the encampment. A deer trail, fresh and narrow, helped him get out of immediate earshot. After a minute, Jack slowed down long enough to catch his breath.

As he started moving again, he nearly tripped over a hard, low-slung box that he'd missed earlier. He cursed his stubbed toe, picked up the box, and ran. He stopped only after the rest of him hurt just as much.

The next morning, when the researchers went

to break camp, Ethan noticed their supply box gone
and a trail leading away. Still sulking, he chalked it
up to bears and wrote it off as lost before leaving the
grassy expanse for Chicago and the Wilson Science
Center.

19

Bears were far from Jack's mind when he woke up the next afternoon underneath the shade of a huge oak tree near the top of another nameless hill. He walked up to where he'd dropped the supply box the night before. The box was metal, grey, and dented all along its top and body. There was no lock: only latches, and a cylinder to turn.

"Bingo," Jack said.

He took whatever he could fit and replenished his supplies. Another sterilization bag, more food, some filters attached to water bladders, and best of all, a wide-brimmed hat.

He tried it on. "Real leather? Someone will miss

this dearly. Maybe I'll be able to get a proper nap tomorrow." For the first time since he'd crossed the Mississippi River, he didn't need to squint.

Jack looked through the metal case one more time to see if anything else could be salvaged. He peered at the top's underside and read a small line stamped into the metal.

"Property of Wilson Science Center, Chicago. If found please leave as-is, automated drone pickup," he read. "Shit."

Jack re-latched the case, threw it as far back towards the research camp as he could, and took off down the opposite side of the hill. He stuffed and zippered his supplies as he went, but completely forgot the perfect walking stick he'd found near the base of the oak. Only hours later, long after the sun fell and the stars rose to dance their path through the sky, did he remember it.

He cursed again and pressed on.

For the first time in days, his chest didn't feel like it'd been pounded on by mammoths, which of course it had. At least something was getting better.

Harold snuck into his office early on a Saturday morning, before the building opened to the public but after the nighttime custodial staff finished their work. The sun still hid behind the lake's perfectly flat horizon and a sliver of moonlight peeped from behind a solitary cloud. His wooden desk felt smooth and cool as he ran a hand along its edge. He pulled up an inventory of all the research teams and perfunctorily scrolled through routine reports, logs, and requests. *The joys of administration. I hate it. I hate this crap. It feels so meaningless. A monkey could do most of this.*

Towards the bottom of the requests list was a system-generated line from the farthest-out team. They were over two hundred miles from the city's outskirts and nearly three hundred from the lake itself. "Drone Pickup" was all the top line said.

Harold stared bleary-eyed at the blinking entry line without comprehending the words. He wondered where Jack was and what he was up to, or if he was even still alive, somewhere out in the middle of the vast, empty continent.

The line sat there, demanding attention.

Harold rolled his neck and stood. He grabbed his full, steaming coffee mug and held it while he looked out the window at the city and its empyrean engineering. It stretched for as far as he could see. Five minutes passed, then ten. The earliness waned as distant sounds of life echoed and vibrated and unstilled the building and its inhabitants. Soon people would arrive, the day's cycle would begin anew, and Harold's solitude would pause until tomorrow.

He sighed. *Let's read it.*

Harold sat back at his desk and opened up the report about the drone pickup. The air in front of him changed to project a hologram, obviously shot by the drone that had ventured out from Chicago to retrieve the wayward supply case. Harold sat and watched for several minutes, the system's AI able to truncate down the trip to only the relevant times.

"How did it get closed again?" Harold muttered aloud, a few seconds after the drone got near the case. He sat up and backtracked the footage, watching it a second time, then a third, and a fourth. "This wasn't a bear," he said.

"Computer, overlay footage with regional map, and zoom out to put Chicago on the eastern edge."

Where was this survey team again?

Several seconds of rendering put the location into proper context for Harold, as the region zoomed out and merged with the now-tiny recording.

"Put it on the wall, please, and flatten."

The hologram flew from the middle of his desk to a nearby wall, and the gradual undulations of the terrain flattened until Harold was left looking at a map, one eerily familiar to what he'd looked at weeks ago with his friend.

With two fingers, he plucked the drone's video footage from the map and expanded it until it was larger than life. Harold played it for a fifth time, at half speed.

"That trail is way too narrow for a bear. And there's no debris anywhere, no eaten food, no scratched metal. And that case is *closed.*"

Harold put a minute of the footage on endless loop and stared at the wall for a long time. When he sipped his coffee, it was cold.

"Computer, trace."

His pointer finger traced a light green line through the trail on the most zoomed out frame of footage available. It took time and wasn't perfectly straight, but neither of those things mattered to him.

"Computer, straighten and extrapolate my line across the entire map on this wall."

His pulse climbed.

Harold's light green tracing was joined by a bit of red at both ends. The red lines grew until each stopped at the edge of the wall map. One line stopped when it reached Lake Michigan. The other line passed just north of Boulder and kept on going.

"Oh, no." Several seconds of silence ensued, followed by a much louder, "Shit!"

"Computer, erase," Harold said, even though he knew the damage was done. Anyone interested in Jack's disappearance would certainly have him under surveillance, and while he could evade them, he had to know ahead of time, not after the fact.

The room at once felt a lot smaller to Harold, and he became possessed of an overwhelming urge to leave as fast as possible.

His feet carried him without thought until he arrived at a door, seldom used, that required a thumbscan to activate. Pre-dawn light filled the door frame as Harold stepped out onto Jack's AIER bridge. He walked over to the big cottonwood, sat beneath it, and tried to get his thoughts in order.

After a while, his nerves unfrayed, his head cleared, and he began to devise a way forward. The rest of the city continued to awaken around him as the sun finally came up across the lake.

20

Several uneventful days passed for Jack. A thousand types of flowers bloomed among hundreds of stiff grasses over dozens of endless rolling hills, and Jack knew only a handful of them. The heat stifled everything during the day, so he continued to walk at night. His appropriated broad-rimmed hat made life on the treeless expanse bearable, and he made good progress, aside from one very long detour around one very large marsh that took the better part of an evening to navigate. That night, the darkness conspired with the muck in an attempt to suck away his shoes and entomb them for a millennium.

As he worked his way around the marsh that night, his mind wandered and questioned the basic tenants of society's relationship with nature. Would the land—this land or any other outside the cities—ever again know a human's stride? Or would the land stay wild as people slowly migrated off-world, clustered around the star ladders that took them to the solar system and beyond? A century from now, two centuries, three? What about a thousand years out, long after he died, long after other planets were settled, other solar systems. What shape would humanity's legacy take? And what about his? Jack ruminated along this line of thought for many miles, until he came across another oddly placed granite boulder.

The second resupply rock looked much like the first, hidden in plain sight. To the casual eye—if one had been available—it looked like it had been there forever. Jack stopped at it and opined to himself that he'd traveled much farther than two hundred miles, on account of his river raft adventure.

Harold had really packed in the food this time. Jack spent a whole day eating and resting before he set off again on a new path. A new cartridge in his cube directed him to another cache, a hundred miles off somewhere in the distance, still in the middle of nowhere. Just before he got underway, he captured the scene on his cube. Maybe someday he'd have a chance to show it to someone else, and that person would also get to see what almost no one had seen for centuries: the high prairie at midsummer, stretching forever. Riotous floods of color broken only by occasional waterways and the lines of trees that clung to them like the vanguard of a failed invasion. As the sun set, Jack took off again and wondered what this leg of his journey had in store for him.

Still more uneventful days followed, mostly because Jack avoided the bison herds, and he definitely avoided the mammoths that inevitably seemed to follow a herd's wake. This far out, there were no wind turbines, no solar farms, no anything. People had erased themselves from the land, pulling back, and back, and back again from every small- and mid-sized city that had once existed. Every road was gone. Those spaces now stored carbon under the ground instead of ferrying tens of millions of cars and trucks over it.

In fact, Jack hadn't seen a paved surface, nor anything close to one, since he'd left his father's house. Now, on this third leg of the journey west, he understood why.

"Nobody would willingly make this trip. Nobody has the knowledge to do this. Hell, I'm struggling, and I've got help and only have to go a hundred miles at a stretch. Someone without help would, what, hunt? Nobody hunts. And it is brutally hot out here."

Little aches and pains, blisters at the ends of sore feet, scratches over peeling and sunburnt skin, legions of insect bites, and dry, cracked dirt on his shins were also beginning to get old. The only water Jack had run across for a week was from small creeks and streams, in some cases reduced to a muddy trickle. It hadn't rained for a while, and even the air was dry. There hadn't been shade for two days, not even a glade of sumac to crawl under. Jack thanked the survey crew for the hat and Harold for the blankets. He'd have otherwise succumbed to exposure.

One night, after he scaled a particularly large hill that rose up from nowhere, Jack stopped at the top to look around. At first, he noticed the hill's unusually short vegetation, almost like it was mowed. A giant mowed hill surrounded by tall prairie. It was also dotted with rusted metal tubes that stuck straight up out of it from a dozen points. Then he looked down the other side in the full moonlight. He expected to see unbroken prairie brightly lit by the moon, but instead immediately saw a break in the grass. Even at night, the laser-straight line was obvious. Nothing remotely like it had appeared anywhere along his journey. Adjacent grasses outlined the break clear to the horizon: a little gap where something should have been.

Jack consulted his cube and projected his blue line out into the night.

Not quite right. It'd take me a little too far north.

He continued downhill. Ankle-high grass muffled most of his footsteps until his shoe caught something solid and stuck to the ground. He tumbled, disturbing the night but little else. The ground was hard, packed, and firm under his palms. No spongy-softness like everywhere else. This hill felt foreign, alien. It didn't belong. Jack scrambled to leave it.

Once at the bottom, he turned around to look at the hill. The night sky formed a picturesque silhouette around its edge.

It's symmetrical. Like a bell curve.

He considered it for several moments before he turned and headed to the border of the short grass. He glanced at the narrow path to his right. In front of him stood hundreds more miles of impenetrable wild. He stopped at its edge.

Every nick and scrape burned. His toes throbbed, his legs would have ached if he could feel them, and his skin stretched over him like a too-tight drum. He wavered and wobbled in the night air.

He turned right and made for the narrow opening.

The short grass from the oddly symmetrical hill ended abruptly and changed over to gravel. Not fresh, dusty gravel with sharp edges, but gravel that was smooth, layered, caked with dirt and moss and time. It felt strange. The semblance of something nearly normal, yet still utterly out of place. His normal had become entirely different since he left Chicago to head west. West, along an imaginary line, to an imaginary woman, to find an imaginary relic at some nearly forgotten oasis before the mountains.

Was it all imaginary? Or real? Who could tell? Jack wondered if there was any truth to his plans or if he would simply wander forever, down a broken path, to pursue this unattainable dream.

Much of the path, it turned out, was covered with the thick moss, and Jack could only vaguely feel the contours of the gravel beneath his feet as he went. The vegetation on either side enveloped him overhead in the night breeze but he was able to march, unimpeded, for many miles. The straight line erred neither right nor left, but kept its course true long after the odd hill sunk far beneath the horizon behind him. As night wore on, Jack became curious about the trail, but exhaustion merged into delirium before daybreak, and he found the soft moss much too inviting and comfortable to resist. He set his blankets up to condense and collect as much water as he could coax from the air, and then lay down on the strange path. He fell immediately asleep.

Dawn came. Exhaustion followed.

"Just get the water and go back to sleep, Jack," he said to himself.

Both blankets had collected enough water to fill one bladder, but little else. Anxiety crept in with the morning sun, red with despair. Jack took no notice. He changed into some UV-sterilized clothes and fell back asleep on a fresh patch of moss a few feet down from his previous bed. The world, in kind, paid Jack no heed as he slept on.

He woke some time later in a cold sweat. The blanket and even the moss beneath him were soaked through, damp and cool.

Why am I so thirsty if I sweat through all this?

Jack looked around for his bladder and put down nearly half of it in seconds. It was then that the water droplet hit him square in the back of the head and echoed across what was surely miles and miles of ground.

Another one landed on his eyelid, a third on his foot, and then a clap of thunder in the distance reminded Jack of what had jerked him awake in the first place.

Relief and water took turns running off him, mixed in with more than a little dirt and mud. For the second time on his journey, Jack stripped, kept blankets shaped to pool the rainwater, and got clean. For two hours, a crazy naked man danced in the pounding rain, rubbed clothes against a rigid blanket, drank as much as his belly would allow, and filled every conceivable container to their brims with water. By the time the deluge subsided, he'd peed twice.

The clouds gradually cleared and the sun was lower in the sky than he realized. Jack flicked on his cube's blue line. The narrow path was a good fifteen degrees off course. If he followed it farther, he'd only err more.

I can't. Not yet. This is easier.

Jack packed away his supplies, stood, and began again down the mossy, gravel-covered path. He was both lighter and heavier than the day before.

He made it nearly twenty miles that night, unencumbered by vegetation, refreshed and fully hydrated for the first time in many days. The path continued on. Jack began to wonder why it was there at all. It hadn't forked or turned or intersected with anything. Just one straight line that went forever.

At the end of the second night on the trail, the level horizon broke and the sea of grass became less. In the distance, it was no longer the tallest thing around.

A metal sign rose high above the still-forming heads of indian grass and big bluestem. It listed hard and the rust was obvious in the early morning light, even from a great distance. Another oddity to go with the moss-covered path he had trod so much distance over. The miles between Jack and the sign closed quickly, and he was determined to reach it before he bedded down for the day. Warmth crept up the back of his neck as the sky went from black, to grey, and then to pink, orange, and yellow. For a brief minute, the high clouds took on a shimmering radiance: the low sun graced their bottoms and revealed mottled underbellies, visible only to a careful watcher during the same few quick moments of every morning.

Jack found himself at the old sign. He craned his neck and looked at it from all sides. There was as much rust on the metal pole as on the sign itself, and Jack wondered how it still stood in one piece. Flecks of yellow hinted at an original color of the pole, but that could have been a rust-eating fungus just as much as a paint color. Jack didn't care to investigate.

The sign itself was actually three signs: all rectangles welded to each other along their long ends, like one of those giant ancient candy boxes Jack remembered seeing once at some cultural museum when he was a child.

Only some of the words were still legible on each of the three signs, and Jack struggled to make out most of them.

"Dang…at…dig," Jack said as he looked at the first side.

"an…er…ural," was all that was visible from the second.

The third side was completely eroded away, with nothing legible left to puzzle out.

The sun continued to warm and Jack decided to call it a day. He cast his meager quarters over himself before spending another stretch of time asleep on the moss.

He woke at sunset, the day again uneventful. Again he ate, and again he packed, and again switched on his cube, and again found himself off course, even more so than yesterday. Again, he considered leaving the trail to head towards his next rendezvous. Again, he looked at the rusted sign, and again decided to continue down the trail.

By now, Jack had seen enough night skies to know that they were getting longer as the stars slowly shifted their tracks across the celestial sphere. Every morning for about a week, Hercules had chased him near dawn and gained a little bit every day. This chase urged him on more each night, and he knew that an extra mile or two, every day, would add up as the days inevitably shortened. At no point in Jack's life had time ever been less visible, and yet more important, than at that moment.

More signs appeared regularly that night, every mile or so. Their long form and distinctive shape marred an otherwise pristine horizon. Jack passed a dozen of them before dawn. Hercules was hard-pressed to catch him that night.

Jack did not expect the river. One moment, the grasses passed along either side as they had for miles. The next, they thinned out rapidly along his right and came to an end as the path veered left, the first turn since its origin many miles back. The river simply appeared. Starlight reflected across its slow surface almost perfectly.

He peered over the edge of the path as he walked, surprised at how far down the water seemed. Maybe it was the darkness playing tricks on him. He squinted and hoped for some clarity. At that same moment, one of the bits of moss-covered gravel caught Jack's foot just right and sent him flying out into the night.

His outstretched arms missed the path's edge. So did his head and half his chest. Momentum flipped him end over end, and his feet and legs found themselves trying to slow his descent towards the river valley below. Jack felt his dad's canteen hurtle away, but in the confusion he couldn't make out a direction. Not knowing what else to do, he brought his arms and shoulders up and dug his fingers into whatever was in front of him, in a desperate attempt to slow down and let his legs find a purchase against something, anything. An outcropped rock pressed under his right foot and he instinctively flexed every muscle, from his hip to his little toe, and demanded gravity grant him a reprieve. He felt the strain on his knee and heard the fascia around his foot's arch tear a little. His involuntary scream bounced off the river valley's walls for several seconds, rebounding back to his ears as clearly as if someone else had yelled it.

He stopped.

He looked down, and he looked up. Both seemed far away in the night. For a moment, Jack thought he heard hooves nearby. When they didn't slow down or diminish, he realized he was hearing his own heart.

21

"I told you, I don't know. Stop asking me. No, he hasn't contacted me. Yes, I know how long it's been."

Betty sat, and stood, and sat again, and stood again as she walked around, three or four steps at a time, aimlessly. In the hour she'd waited to be seen, she had fielded questions from two different journalists about her husband's continued disappearance. Before a third could contact her, a little roverbot scooted in front of her and rose to eye level.

"Doctor Wilson? They're ready for you," the artificial voice said.

She stood and followed as the bot toddled off.

Both passed through two sets of doors. After a long hallway, Betty found herself outside a final door, tall and round and white. It opened as she neared.

She saw the other woman approach from a large conference table. A blue hologram projected up from the center of it. Betty smiled and took the woman's outstretched arm to give it a firm shake. As she looked at the other woman, a chill ran straight through her. Although the other woman smiled, Betty somehow doubted she was happy.

"Good morning, Betty. Or do you prefer Mrs. Wilson?" the cold woman asked.

"It's Doctor Wilson, but Betty is fine."

"Wonderful. Come over and have a seat." The other woman held the back of a chair.

"Ah. Thank you. And for seeing me today, Miss…?"

"Why don't you call me Jane? I think that should do."

"Jane." Betty took the offered chair and looked at the blue hologram for the first time. It was easy to recognize the outline of North America, from Concord to Memphis to the great western port of Fresno.

Jane took the seat opposite Betty. She filled the chair's full height but only half of its width. Betty noticed Jane's lenses and wondered if she was being watched from afar, even though there was no indication the headgear was recording.

"So let me get right to it. You think you know

where your husband might be," Jane said. She looked straight at Betty.

"Y-yes. Yes. At least, I think, I believe so. I think he left the city."

Jane's smile diminished but remained. "Mrs. Wilson, if he left Chicago, he'd be known. A person can't simply disappear. You must know this."

"Well, yes. I know that. I mean, if he were in a shuttle or heading up the ladder. Then he'd be easy to find. But that's not what he's done, or someone would have tracked him down weeks ago."

"Betty, the few roads beyond the city are monitored. If he'd walked instead of taken transport, he'd be picked up. The fact is, the last time he turned up on a manifest, he was headed to your father-in-law's house. And we've talked to the man several times, with the same story each time. The man was asleep and doesn't remember your husband having ever been there when the shuttle dropped him off. The last time there's an eyewitness at all was his colleague Harold, who says Jack came to him distraught."

Betty thought back to the argument she'd had with Harold. *I'm sure he said that.*

Jane saw Betty flush and shift in her seat. She waited patiently for a reply.

"That was...that was not a great day," Betty finally said.

"Mrs. Wilson, has it occurred to you that Jack may have hurt himself? There is precedent in his family. I'm sorry. Your family. Your in-laws. It wouldn't be the first time."

Now Betty turned so pale that Jane thought the poor woman might pass out. Instead, she vomited. The white table turned bright green with streaks of yellow.

Jane stood and backed away, summoning a nearby servbot to clean up the mess.

Betty crouched beside the table, a hand to the ground and her head down, as the bot did its work. After several minutes, she found her way back to the chair.

Jane continued, "I'm sorry, I wasn't trying to upset you. Truth be told, the only reason this is garnering so much attention is because he's the last Wilson, aside from his father. You have no children, correct?"

An involuntary hand fell towards Betty's lap before she pulled it away. "No, no children."

"Betty, are you all right? Can I get you something, perhaps a glass of wine for your nerves?" Jane asked. She motioned for the servbot to come back.

"No! No. No, thank you. No. Just water, please," Betty replied. She looked up at Jane with wide eyes.

Jane's smile grew again.

"He's not dead! He's not. I think he's heading west. It was the last thing he said before, ah, before he came back to Chicago. Look into Harold, he'd tell Harold anything. He'd know. Just, please, he's not dead. I know him, he isn't suicidal, just upset. Very upset."

"But again, Doctor Wilson. The roads, the shuttles, they show nothing."

"I already said he would try to walk. But not on the roads."

Jane no longer smiled. All the animation fled her body in a rush, like she'd spied Medusa. Her gaze now riveted on the hologram between the two women. It was her turn to be the pale one.

Between the nausea and the suggestion that Jack might have hurt himself, Betty took no notice of her host's new demeanor. She kept her face buried behind her palms while cold sweat dried against pallid skin.

Two people walked by in the huge room but neither dared approach. Fascinating distractions sprang up out of the ground or the opposite wall, and feet picked up their pace as they passed.

After several minutes, Jane's gaze shifted back to Betty, still with her face in her hands, who wished she had stayed in bed that morning, and maybe every other morning too.

"Betty, thank you for coming in. I can assure you, we'll look into what you've given us. If we find out anything, someone will be in contact with you. Can I send you off with a servbot, to make sure you get home all right? You still look rather pale, and I would feel so much better. I can even make sure it keeps the reporter bots at bay."

Betty was ready to decline the help, until Jane's last sentence.

"Yes. Please. That would be such a relief."

"Absolutely, no problem at all. Give me one minute." Jane tapped her lenses on one side. Eyes flickered rapidly around a screen that only she could see, as if that mattered. Betty looked a little green again.

Poor girl. I wonder if she'll get better.

Jane readied the bot to travel with Betty. As she finished the requests and tapped her glasses again, she realized she wouldn't have to wonder.

With Betty on her way home and a bot in tow, Jane glanced back again at the hologram of North America. She had inquiries to make, very quiet inquiries. Her mind jumped to the face of a young analyst many weeks back. Jane tried to remember her name.

22

Long and short bursts of light pulsed from a small, opaque half-dome in the middle of Harold's office desk. Several sheets of paper lay next to it.

Harold set down his pencil, leaned back in his chair, and took off his glasses so he could rub his forehead. Rain hit the window. It had hit the window all day and on into the evening, but by now it largely went unnoticed.

"This had better be the final one, Aramae," he said to the empty room. He studied the papers for a minute and nodded.

"See you in a couple days," he muttered. Harold tapped out a reply on his half-dome and then grabbed his part of the entangled pair. He tossed it in a desk drawer. Even if someone found it, the worst they could do was shatter the housing and its interface. Setting up a new pair with Aramae would be easy: just bury one half in asteroid samples and send them on their way, and wait while the unmanned shuttles slowly moved the cargo. Nobody paid attention to the E.T. program.

Harold stopped by the supply room and went to the part reserved for resupplying the survey teams. He grabbed enough entangled pairs and basic supplies to finish what he'd started.

It took three carts to load everything, including several large rocks all labeled "specimen." He made his way downstairs, past the students and the slowly spinning holographic globe, and into the darkened museum through the staff door. From there, it was a quick trip to the museum's service entrance and into the large, long-range shuttle that waited for him. He made sure everything was neatly stowed, looking like any other ordinary rock shipment, paperwork and all.

Nobody knows their ass from their elbow with this stuff anyway. If I got searched, I could say the rocks came from freaking Neptune *and nobody would know enough to challenge me on it.*

Once he got into the shuttle, it whisked him away. Before he fell asleep under the city lights, Harold thought about what he'd find in Boulder and wished he'd gone with his friend in the first place.

I wonder what he's seen out there.

* * *

Utter fatigue almost put Jack to sleep. A myoclonic jerk saved him, and he heard more hoofbeats before he realized they were, again, from himself. A deep breath cut itself short as he took in dirt and coughed ferociously. The paroxysms threatened to dislodge him from his precarious perch.

A throbbing pain in his right foot pulsed in the background of his mind, beyond thought but not forgotten. The tumble down the embankment replayed itself and Jack wondered if his yell had found any ears. Surely, they would be here soon if anyone had heard.

Where did this even come from? I didn't cross anything major recently. Jack tried to remember what he had seen before taking a tumble. *It was the western bank. I'm certain of that. The eastern bank...maybe the river turned. Am I at the bend? Maybe it runs east from here for a while. Shit, that means I can't go south.*

Without thought, Jack shifted more weight to his left leg and took some of the pressure off his painful side. The shift pushed his exhausted muscles past their breaking point and the leg buckled. Dirt and gravel tumbled downhill or blew into the air, swirling around Jack's head and sending him into another round of coughs as he fell. The whole thing was entirely too much to handle, and the ground continued to disintegrate as the spasms wracked his body. More dirt flew. Adrenaline did nothing to help, his muscles long past any point of usefulness. All he could think to do as he picked up speed was cover his face and curl into a ball. Ten seconds felt like an hour. The ride down threw him harder with each bump. On the final lurch he went airborne, flying through foggy air so thick he couldn't tell which way was up. He stopped just as fast, plunging into muddy water, back first.

His pack absorbed most of the impact against the shallow river bottom, flattened and sucked into the mud in the same instant. Jack found himself face up, the tip of his nose just above the surface, but not far enough out to breathe. The backpack stayed stuck as he thrashed about in the shallow water. Every new movement seemed to pull him further into the murk. The tip of Jack's nose went below the surface.

It was a battle to see which hurt more: his lungs or his legs. He acted on instinct and slipped one arm, followed by a second, out of the backpack's straps. He sat up and drew a deep, ragged breath. It felt like the mammoth had returned to sit atop his chest as he tried to take in air, his body working against him in the attempt to expel river water and replace it with something useful. Finally, the urgent need to breathe subsided, and the coughing started once more. Each spasm reached to the very bottom of his lungs and sprayed out a fine mist to mix with the morning fog. Jack pitched onto all fours. Mud from the shoreline got under his fingernails. He crawled forward, heard a faint splash as he hauled out of the water, and collapsed.

Some time passed before Jack could move or do

anything besides cough. By the time he thought about his pack, the fog had mostly burned off.

He summoned whatever strength he could manage and took three steps to the water's edge. There sat the pack, still sucked into the river mud. He grabbed the straps, crouched, and bore down. He knew he only had the strength for one try. The mud was reluctant to give up its hold, but its grasp slipped as Jack swung his weight from side to side: first near the top and then cascading down to the bottom of the pack, until it rocketed up and out of the water. Jack fell into the shallows on his butt and clutched his pack as water streamed out of it.

He dug through his pack and sifted past the ruined food, the sopping blankets, the soaked little antique books, and the muddy clothes. He pulled out the cube and popped open the chamber where the entangled bit was housed. It glowed blue. He flipped the toggles and pulled back a flap, and a familiar blue line shot outwards through the mist, pointing west. His shoulders slumped.

Jack dragged all of his supplies to the edge of the valley wall and sat against it. He stared into the last of the fog and began to sob. This time, not even a shuttle's AI could hear him.

The sun revealed the full valley to Jack as it journeyed towards the sky's meridian line. The water was wider than he thought, and the fifty-foot walls along either side shorter, but still not scalable. At least from where he sat.

I tumbled down the least-vegetated part too. Ten feet right or left and I could have grabbed something higher up. Or been impaled.

"This isn't a natural valley. This is some leftover relic," Jack said to himself. He came to his senses and took stock of his inventory. He washed the blankets at the water's edge and got out a lot of the mud, which flowed down an otherwise clear river. The books were a lost cause. Of the roughly six days of food he thought he'd had, perhaps two days were salvageable. The canteen was also gone.

Sorry, Dad. I know that canteen saw a lot of use when I was a kid. At least I've got the stuff Harold cached, and there's water nearby for now.

He saw no way to get out of the steep valley, so Jack reluctantly hugged the river's western bank and started walking north, but not before leaving all the broken and useless junk behind. He couldn't afford to haul the extra weight, not on a bad foot.

The journey north was mostly cool that afternoon, the sun first behind clouds and then behind the valley wall as the afternoon wore on. As Jack dried out, the river water evaporated, and a crust formed over everything from his hair to his shoes to the straps of his backpack: a thin, brown, dusty film.

With the dirt came a smell too. One Jack hadn't encountered in the many miles he'd journeyed. It stank of mold and methane, and mixed with his sweat to feed legions of bacteria on him and his belongings. Whenever the breeze died down for a moment, the stench reached up to swirl around his head.

This'll reach miles downwind. Jack looked around. *Maybe at nightfall…no, it'll be too cold by then. It's got to be now.*

He stopped at the river's edge, stripped, and walked out from the shoreline. As he waded further, he noted how utterly clear the water stayed. Clear to the bottom, clear as far out as he could wade. A sharp poke beneath his big toe told him why.

The poke didn't cut him. Nothing bled, but it did stop him short and he looked down. Two grey shells sat upright, slightly open. Numerous faint, parallel lines etched their outsides, each one marking a year of growth. He stopped mid-river and looked around. They were ubiquitous. He was amazed he hadn't stepped on one before now. The river bottom stacked them two, three deep in some places. Clams. Everywhere, clams. Some grey, some brown, some white, still others purple or green. Either the water was playing tricks on Jack's mind, or some of them were the size of his head.

He scrubbed his hair and face with his hands and, as he thought about it, grabbed an empty shell and used the rough exterior to scrub the rest of himself as well. For the second time that day, he muddied otherwise perfectly clear water.

Afterwards, he felt less crusty and smelly. The shell got tossed in his bag and he walked north again. His foot throbbed, but his hunger overrode it and everything else. At least he wasn't thirsty. He was, however, far off the line he should have been walking.

That night, he ate a quarter of what was left in his bag, threw the wrappers aside, and again slept between the river and the valley wall. Only one of his blankets felt like working, and it finally dawned on him that the wide-brimmed hat was gone.

Morning came. Just as before, for weeks now on end, morning came. Last night's hunger persisted.

I can't continue to eat through my food.

He stared at his grey cube, remembering how every single nick, scratch, particle, mark, and chip on it happened. Years of use. The cube went everywhere with Jack, a hallmark of sorts. One lifetime etched into its six sides, now silent and unlit.

One practiced set of moves could take him away from all of his struggles. He'd be home in an hour. Two, at the most. His last name would keep him out of trouble, even get him some free publicity. The Man Who Crossed the Mississippi. He had captured some scenes to add to his holography collection. He could revisit these places any time he chose. Just one moment with his cube, and it'd all go back to normal. He grabbed the cube, pressed its corners into his fingers, and began to squeeze. His eyes closed.

A warm smile. A dry, slightly smaller hand. Laughter.

He let go. The cube fell, silent.

Jack stood and looked east. The star ladder wasn't visible but he knew it was out there, far past the horizon. He looked down at the river, once more amazed at the sheer volume of shells that dotted the water. His stomach growled, and a pin dropped in his mind.

He waded back out into the shallows and looked down. Thousands upon thousands of clams looked back up. Stories of history, told by great-grandma Becky, played through his mind.

He pulled up a clam. Or was it a mollusk? He didn't care. The shells split apart with one sharp tug. A pang of guilt coursed through him as he scooped out the meat. It flinched.

"I'm sorry, little guy. I'm really, truly sorry about this."

It wasn't delicious, not by any means. But it wasn't bad, either. He went back for more, feeling guilty each time but going back all the same. After fifteen minutes, he was full and again started to head north through the steep valley. The clams were with him the whole way.

Lunch and dinner were much the same as breakfast, and Jack slept again by the side of the river, unable to climb the valley wall and unwilling to cross back to the opposite bank. His foot still throbbed, and every time he checked his course on his cube, the line pointed more and more to the south.

How many days have I been off course? Three? Four?

Jack pushed on again through the night, powered by a mix of worry and clams. The valley widened unexpectedly as he got further north, and at daybreak he understood why.

Ahead of him lay massive concrete slabs, each the size of his AIER bridge back in Chicago. They jutted out of the river at odd angles. Some were cracked in half, some pressed against each other, and several smashed up flush against the valley wall, blocking his path.

These were supposed to be cleaned up more than century ago. At least that explains everything downstream. When this breached, the water must have scoured the valley walls for miles.

Jack walked up to the slabs stuck across his path. He waded out past the shore a few feet and tried to look around the edge of one, to see how far it went. The other end of it rested in the water more than a hundred yards upstream.

Great, I've got to climb over these.

Jack turned around to look south and wondered how long it would take to backtrack all the miles he had walked along the edge of the river. Days.

And I'll bet I can scramble out of this valley once I get past the debris from this dam.

Jack figured that if he jumped while standing next to the enormous slab, he'd be able to get a fingertip grip on its top, but barely. The only problem was, he couldn't jump. His foot throbbed even thinking about it, and he knew if he injured it more, he would be in real trouble. He backed away from the water, went to where the edge of the slab had ground itself into the valley wall, and looked for anything he could use to boulder himself up and over, so he could walk the hundred yards on top of the concrete to its far side.

The first few routes up were failures. Either the valley wall's dirt crumbled as he tried to step up, or his bad foot couldn't hold his weight underneath him. He sat and caught his breath, and again looked at the corner in front of him. Concrete on the right, dirt on the left, at nearly right angles.

Ten minutes passed, then twenty. Jack looked around as an idea formed. A fist-sized piece of concrete lay nearby. He picked it up, walked to the corner, and began to pummel the dirt right next to the concrete, ripping out deep chunks. First down low, then higher, and eventually as high up as his arms would reach. More than a little anger and frustration helped power his excavations.

Once finished, he sat again to rest before using his newly-made handholds to anchor his climb. His bad foot stayed off to the side and rested on the concrete face. This stabilized his body while keeping weight off the foot. Using his one good foot and both arms, he shimmied up, swung his bad foot over the ledge at the top, and hauled the rest of himself onto the flat surface.

"All of that work for maybe ten feet," Jack said, peering behind him.

Jack spat on the concrete slab as he stood, ran

his hands through sweat-soaked hair, and rubbed them against his pants to get rid of some of the grease.

After that it was easier, the hundred yards of flat concrete a simple walk. He could see a bit further too. The valley walls did, indeed, get less steep past the decaying remnants of the ancient dam. He had been right, although he still couldn't puzzle out why the debris remained in the first place.

They could crush this and add it to a reef somewhere, or re-buffer another infinitesimally small percent of seawater.

At the end of the hundred yards of concrete, he scrambled over the edge and let himself dangle and drop, falling the final four feet and flexing his good leg to absorb the weight of landing.

Twenty minutes later, he passed the face of what was once a dam and walked through to the other side. That cleared the way for him to, at long last, leave the valley. Before he scrambled up and out, he stopped once more and ate his utter fill of clams and mussels, and took as much water with him as he could.

No more paths that look easy.

His cube's blue line pointed him almost due southwest. He had moved north at great cost to his time, supplies, and health.

The next two days were a blur to Jack. He didn't deviate from his thin blue line again, not for any reason. He walked the first day for nearly twenty hours straight, ate as he went, and stopped only for a four hour break during the heat of midday. The day after was the same. By the end, he had gone through nearly all of his remaining food.

That little detour was a mistake. I went almost half again as far as I needed to. And I lost Dad's canteen.

The third resupply cache sat in the middle of the high prairie. Hundreds of striations over its top disguised it as a glacier-deposited erratic, but by now Jack knew the routine. A little more than two days after he escaped the river valley, he finally felt a cloud of worry lift from his mind. He would be okay, at least for now.

"Harold, you are wise beyond your years," Jack said as he rooted through the supplies. The usual: a new blanket, water bladder, hat, food. But this time a bar of soap, a small square of a mirror, and a razor blade were buried in the supplies, along with a note.

Jack laughed at the meager shaving kit and his friend's foresight, and smiled as he unfolded the paper and began reading.

"Jack- I saw the metal case and the footage from the drone picking it up. I figured it was you when I mapped it out. I'm sorry. I might have accidentally blown your cover. And Betty seems to be starting to get an idea of things. I'm getting out to Boulder just as soon as this cache and the next one are dropped. With luck, I'll be there when you read this. Keep moving.

-H

P.S.- Keep those shoes on."

Jack looked up from the note and forgot all about the wild around him. He turned to the sky, scanning it for signs of anything that didn't belong. That evening and the following morning, he didn't stop to rest.

23

Aramae looked across the room at her old friend, head cocked slightly to the side, with one eyebrow raised.

"I'm telling you Aramae, he's fine. He's got blankets, food, water pouches, odds and ends. By now he should even have shaving gear," Harold said.

"But no communicating? No maps? You could have told me before now. We could have done something. He's just out there all alone. For what, over a month at this point? Close to two?"

"Honestly Aramae, I think that's what he wanted. He didn't leave Chicago on great terms. I got the feeling he *wanted* to be inaccessible and unreachable."

"Then he's certainly getting that wish. It's just so dangerous. Being alone *and* going dark. There's so much that can go wrong. It's crazy and you signed off on it, supported it even."

"It was either that or let him truly solo it. I think he'd have struck out on his own regardless of what I did."

"The two of you somehow always end up in trouble. If you'd told me, I could have helped. I know this part of the continent better than either of you ever will. You pick up a lot in ten years."

"So help me. What do I need to do? Tell me. I want to go find him out there. I should have gone with him in the first place."

"You? No. None of us are college kids anymore, but Harold, you're in no way fit to go out there. I'm going. I'm better than either of you ever will be in the rewilded lands. I'll make better time than you. And besides, I need you here to keep up the supply drops. Without those, this never works."

Harold stared dumbly back at her for several moments before she continued.

"I can see you running through every counterargument in that head of yours. None of them are going to work. I'm going, this isn't a debate, and I'm taking the pyramid with me. It'll probably be safer out there anyhow. Especially if people back east are starting to wonder. Jack's about the only untouchable person in all of this. If you or I vanished, nobody would notice. But look at what Jack's disappearance has done. Even his *wife* is famous now."

Harold glanced at Aramae's face. There was a flash of something. And then it was gone, just as fast as it had appeared.

"I'm leaving before dusk. What do you need me to do before then?" Aramae stood and moved to leave her basement office.

"Well for starters...those lenses. How much do you need them?"

"I use them for everything. Why?"

"Because you'll get tracked with them. They have to stay behind. You need a way to follow the entangled pairs too. Jack's using that archaic cube of his, the one that does everything. I don't suppose you have anything like that?"

"He still has that thing?" Aramae paused and pursed her lips. "Come on, let's get out of here."

The two walked out of her office on the lowest subterranean floor of the school building, past laboratories and assembly rooms, testing centers and launch simulators. After many upward flights of stairs, they finally reached the surface and stepped out into the sunlight. Low rooftops, no more than a few stories tall, scattered themselves around the campus. Harold was still surprised at how little had changed out here since he had attended. A few chipped sidewalks, some faded paint, another wind turbine off in the distance. There also seemed to be fewer bodies milling about than he remembered. The two walked down a sidewalk, Aramae half a step out front.

"Aramae, how's enrollment?"

She lost her half-step lead before she answered. "It's down. By about a third."

"Since we were here? That's a lot."

"No, since last year. You don't want to know by how much since you were here."

"Are you...how much pressure is there to close the doors?"

She looked at him and squinted in the sun, as always. "We've increased our asteroid contracts a lot. That's what's keeping us afloat. If those go, we're reefed."

Harold nodded and they kept walking. Aramae took back her half-step lead.

They walked for fifteen minutes until they got to the edge of campus near the historical section, with the real farm and the other relic structures.

Harold pointed at a building that looked less worn than the rest of the historical section. "That house is new. I don't remember it being here before."

"Yeah, I had it built. It used to just be that lecture hall over there that looked out over everything. When I took the position out here, I negotiated a period house into my contract. Now I have this great view whenever I want. Come on in."

They arrived at her front door and entered.

There were wood floors, quiet walls without any displays, and cords. Cords everywhere. Lamps, appliances, everything was plugged into the wall. Harold noticed it immediately and wondered what life had once been like, so dependent on large, centralized power and tethered to literal streams of electrons that stretched for dozens of miles.

After the cords, the biggest thing he noted was the silence. The whole house was still. He couldn't get over it. Not a single screen anywhere. No inducers and nothing hummed, aside from some kitchen appliances.

Aramae noticed Harold's expression and smiled.

"I love it here. I don't think I could survive living anywhere else for very long. It took living in this house to make me realize just how loud everything else is. I can't imagine what a ladder city would be like anymore. I'd just die if I ever had to move back."

"Jack would like this. You should see the AIER bridge he had built back in Chicago. It's massive. It connects his skyrise building straight to the Wilson Center, and there's exactly five people in the world that can get out onto it."

Four quick fingers popped up from Aramae's hand, and a fifth waggled back and forth.

"Who's the fifth?"

Harold looked at her waggling finger and then at her.

"Oh," she said. "Wait here a sec."

Aramae left the room and Harold found a comfortable chair. He admired the artwork, the space, the light. Mostly the quiet, though. Aramae was right. Chicago was loud compared to this, although this much silence might become a little unnerving.

Maybe it takes time.

She came back down with what looked like two oversized pens, light grey with metallic housing.

"Here. I can use these. At least for the entangled pairs," she said as she unscrewed one at its center. "See? There's a spot for a cartridge in each one."

Harold furrowed his eyebrows and tightened one corner of his mouth. "Why two? The other half of each pair goes in the rock cache that I drop. You have to exchange them, pop them in and out along the way."

"I made these in applied quantum mechanics lab, with my lab partner. When they left after graduation, they gave me theirs."

"I still don't understand. You'd only need to take one with you, the pairs let you find the caches."

Aramae stared back. "I know how they work. I get it. I'll take one with me. Put the other one in the last cache, okay?"

"But there won't be anything to pair it with."

"Harold. I know what I am doing. Trust me. Put it in the last cache, please?"

Harold caved. "Okay." He took one of the pens from Aramae. *I wonder if it writes.*

"How long until my first one is out there?"

"The rock cache?" Harold looked around. "Can I work from here?"

"Sure. Go anywhere you want."

"In that case, by the time you get yourself ready to go, it'll be set."

Harold got to work and Aramae left him alone, gathering her own supplies much like Jack had, many weeks ago.

"I'm going out. I'll be back in two hours."

True to her word, Aramae arrived just as Harold watched a drone drop the first cache. He told it to return and closed down his screen.

"How will I know how you're doing?" he asked. He handed her the first of her entangled pair cartridges. She loaded it into her oversized pen and tapped one end. A little green beam pierced out from the other end. As she moved the pen back and forth, the ball bearing at the lit end swiveled to keep the green line in its fixed position until the angle of the pen prevented the bearing from swiveling any further.

Harold remarked to himself that he'd never engineered so elegantly simple of a device in college. Or ever.

"Watch the news. You'll know. Otherwise, just get those caches out there ASAP. Someone will notice that I'm gone, soon enough. Can you stay here? Watch things?"

Harold looked around, the house familiar yet

alien, comforting and uncomfortable all at once.

"Yes. I'll figure things out. Good luck, Aramae."

"No luck needed. Just a good plan, supplies, and know-how. And we've got all three." She stood and hugged him, and slipped out the door. Harold saw the pen flash green as Aramae adjusted her heading. She walked off into the trees, never looking back.

24

Jack's discovery that he could eat off the land proved critical. Every brook, creek, stream, and river he forded became a chance for a meal and some real protein, something his battered body desperately needed after hundreds of miles of wear and tear. The grasses shortened as he continued farther west, until one day he spent his entire journey with his head above the botanical datum, able to see for many miles the whole time.

The landscape rose in unnoticed increments and the streams became fewer and smaller. Still always full of mussels and clams, but they began to ebb away, much like the season. The constellation

Hercules continued to catch him a little more each night. Rain showers started to feel cold, and they seemed fewer and farther between.

Ironically, the land felt less wild the more he walked. Perhaps it was his familiarity with the terrain and its monotonous sight and feel, the grass just as harsh and abrasive today as yesterday, and last week, and last month. The repetition of things wore on him. Each footfall was an attempt to leave no path, crease no blade, crush no stem. But the land also became more barren. Jack could see the scars better, this far out. A long, straight flat of short prairie blanketed what was certainly an old highway that drones had scooped up, crushed, and deposited in some ocean shelf. Another vain attempt to scrub acid from the seas at any cost.

Maybe the coral could regrow. And maybe staring at the stump of an amputated limb could make a new one sprout.

The scars from old roads weren't the only oddly flat terrain in the otherwise rolling hills. Giant flat sections, a mile or so in length and width, popped up with regularity. So did pieces of wood, obviously milled, exposed and standing straight up out of the earth. Slowly worn down by the elements, these cedar fenceposts wrote a story of land history unread for centuries.

Odd lakes, strangely geometric, with bedrock sides. Trees along waterways, only half as tall as they should be. Herds of bison, mammoth, and pronghorn, but few wolves and fewer bears. Flocks of birds, but so few eagles. One day, he was blessed with the flyover of millions of passenger pigeons. He bathed at dusk that evening. Several more mossy gravel paths looked inviting. Jack resisted.

His foot gradually hurt less. More days passed. The only trees he saw were near creeks. None were oaks. He slept under them during the day and heard only the gurgle of a slow brook. At night, only the wind. And some nights, nothing at all.

The next cache was identical to the previous one. Harold's predictability incorporated itself into the rest of Jack's journey. He rubbed his face and felt the stubble of several days.

Maybe I'll shave tomorrow.

And then another path appeared. It started along the latest unnamed creek, clear and cool and shady. Jack woke from a nap and the path was simply *there,* along the opposite bank, where none had been before. Crushed grass, snapped shrubbery, and disheveled river rocks disturbed an otherwise bucolic scene. Jack grabbed his pack and idled in the middle of the water as it trickled past his ankles. Nothing else moved upstream or downstream, behind or in front of him.

He hesitated, crossed the creek, and stood in the middle of this curious path. Perhaps three feet of crushed ground was on either side of him, smooth and parallel. As if an enormous rolling pin had fallen from the sky and rolled into the creek while he slept.

Days of boredom got the better of Jack. *Eh, what the hell. It's not man-made, that's for sure.* He kept walking down the fresh path's center: out of the tiny floodplain, past the small tree line, and back into the dusky sunlight.

The rolling pin landscape continued and ran over the short hill beyond. A sundown breeze started to pick up as things cooled off. It felt good against Jack's face.

The short hill came and went but yielded no new clues about the mystery path's creator, just a continued ribbon that meandered off towards the west through the prairie.

There was no gravel, no rusty sign, no anything this time around. A brief turn into a patch of purple prairie clover put Jack in the middle of a quick detour. The delicate clovers were all clipped, their tallest stems cut back by some invisible scythe that mowed through the field. A smattering of other flowers and grasses stood bent but were otherwise unmolested. More deviations in the path appeared, and Jack noticed each led into another patch laden with purple prairie clover, only to then turn unerringly back to the west. Jack was off his blue line again, headed too far south, but the grass was barely knee high and this oddity, out of place here in the middle of nowhere, demanded an investigation.

Hours passed. Jack continued in the full moonlight and had no trouble seeing the edges of this strange flat path, but he could never reach the front of it. Dawn came and he forced himself to rest.

No sense being exhausted when I get to wherever this leads.

The second day of tracking followed much like the first. Jack decided that whatever made the path moved just about as fast as him, because the trail meandered as far as he could see, but he never caught a glimpse of its creator. He also deduced that, whatever it was, it must have come to that creek soon after he dozed off and had quite a head start on him. Jack only hoped that his quarry needed to sleep at some point too.

At dawn after the second night, he caught a glimmer of movement just at the horizon. He was tired, though, and the shape of the thing was indecipherable at a distance. Jack weighed the pros and cons of continuing as he reached another high point and the sun began to cast long shadows from behind.

Another minute passed and the sun rose a little higher. Just enough to let Jack see his quarry and ask a whole new question.

Harold put a cache on wheels?

For the first time in his life, Jack wished he had lenses, so he could zoom in and see exactly what he had followed for two days. His cube's magnification suite worked wonders for small, up-close items, but lacked what he needed now.

It looked like a huge, gliding lump. One that flattened everything underneath it as it went, oblivious to its own destruction. It dipped down the backside of another hill and Jack lost sight of it.

Harold, you make no sense. Why make me chase my supplies? Are you worried someone will spot it? A rock that moves on its own isn't exactly inconspicuous.

Jack sped up his pace and now understood why he'd had such a hard time catching this mystery rock. It simply had not stopped moving. He crested the hill and spotted it again, still heading west. Now Jack jogged. He was very close.

Behind the rock, some of his supplies were trailing out a foot or so, caught up on the underside of whatever crazy device Harold rigged up for this cross-country trek.

I hope that's nothing important.

Jack ran, not wanting to lose whatever it was that hung off the back of his supply cache. He ate up a downslope in big strides and let the weight of his pack, and the hundreds of miles he'd come, guide his feet. As he sped towards his supplies, he flushed a pair of prairie chickens, their fat bodies and stubby wings nearly colliding with Jack's head as they tried to gain altitude and get away.

The cache stopped moving and Jack closed in. His quads burned from the trip down the hill, and his knees and one foot protested the harsh treatment too.

Then, the cache began to turn around. First one, and then two, eyes looked straight at him. An armored head stuck out from the front of the "cache," and Jack realized just how wrong he'd been about the last two days.

The enormous rock he pursued was no rock at all. It was a living, armor-plated carapace, huge beyond reckoning, even in Jack's world. Until now. The creature stared at him, its head nearly waist-high to Jack. The top of the carapace stood level with Jack's gaze.

Memories of a certain angry mammoth surfaced somewhere in Jack's mind, and he took several quick steps back.

"They said glyptodonts were impossible." He looked at the massive armadillo in front of him. "But here you are. How?"

The glyptodont stared back, giving no indication that it cared to answer Jack's question. Jack started to reach out to touch the hard, domed carapace on the creature's back. Before he could, he found his hand intercepted by the top of the glyptodont's head. It pushed up and moved Jack's hand around to one spot with practiced ease, then froze and stared at Jack. It pushed against his hand again.

Jack blinked and looked back. No fear. No curiosity, even. Only a patient gaze and the gentle pressure on his hand.

Jack scratched. Slowly at first, and then with increasing speed. The pressure stopped and Jack's newfound companion closed his eyes. Its tail, similarly armored, smacked the ground repeatedly and sent dirt everywhere. Jack laughed.

"Okay, then. How are you doing, big fella?" Jack continued to scratch. "You are so far away from where you're supposed to roam, aren't you? I thought you all were a more southern species. I guess that was wrong too. How are you even here? How were you even born?"

The glyptodont looked at Jack again, this time with its head slightly tilted. The enormous tail again flew to the earth, creating a small trench in the ground as it battered through roots and topsoil. One of the clods landed squarely on top of its head, much to its own surprise, and Jack saw it flinch for the first time. Jack brushed off the dirt.

"I'm going to call you Clod. Clod, it was very nice to meet you, but I have to be going. I'm sure you can relate."

Clod stared back, unmoving.

Jack gave Clod one final scratch on the head and took out his cube. The familiar blue line pointed to his next supply cache: due north.

"Let's hope that one doesn't have to be chased all over the place like you, huh?"

Jack got back to his line and continued on it for a while before he looked for a place to rest. For the first time in many days, a tree appeared along his path. An oak. And an old oak by the looks of it, sprawled out with massive low branches in all directions, like a welcoming set of benches for weary travelers. Jack stopped under it, set himself up to sleep, and got to it.

Fitful dreams filled Jack's rest. Pings and flashes of faces, never there for long, crowded his mind. Brooks and trees and rain and grass, and an unending blue line, coursed through a maze of a world. Jack found himself lost at every juncture. Every choice he made led to a dead end. No matter what he did or where he turned, he could not find a viable route. He swore he visited the same parts of the maze over and over, so he put a shoe at each of two dead ends, certain that he would come back to them after just a few short turns. When he got back to the spots where he thought they'd be, he stared only at empty space. He tried again, and again, and again to come back to those shoes, only to fail with each attempt. Shoeless and lost, he continued to wander, the whole time hearing thunder move closer and closer, the thumping rumbles getting louder until they were right overhead and pounding into his chest.

He woke up.

The stars overhead were partly blocked by an enormous head that had laid itself against Jack's chest, weighing him down considerably. The head snored.

"Uh. Clod? Is that you?"

No, it's the other roaming glyptodont that you ran across earlier, genius.

One eye opened halfway to look at Jack and then closed again. The snoring resumed. Jack put one arm on Clod's head and tucked the other behind his own, and looked up at the stars filtering through the tree's leaves. A single tear rolled down the side of his face and he fell back asleep, this time soundly.

Aramae reached her first cache in half the time Jack had needed to reach his. The land was still familiar to her at this point, a hundred or so miles out. She hiked between alternate stands of pine, fir, and spruce, or scrubby shortgrass openings intermixed among the high conifers. Sharp reliefs of the land popped up several times a day to challenge Aramae, but she had gone over similar rugged outcroppings many hundreds of times in her past. The ones she crossed now barely slowed her down. Her oversized pen flashed its green line only twice along this initial leg. Just the occasional double-check to see that yes, indeed, she was still headed in the right direction.

Long ago, shortly after she moved into the quiet house currently occupied by Harold, Aramae learned that she could do her job from anywhere. The special view from the lecture hall that she chose to share with Jack during her biogeology class was only the initial germ of an idea which tugged at her the way a bit of thread teases the wearer of a favorite sweater. Unable to resist the impulse, at first she worked outside near the old farm, or in her home's yard, such as it was. The steady drum of passersby during the semester got old after less than a month, though. Other faculty would drop by with questions. Students, either curious or needy, sought out the oddball professor who lived in a house. Accomplishing anything while outside became an anxious struggle as she wondered how much time she'd have until she was interrupted again.

So the sojourns began. At first as a way to get some distance and not be in some office cage, the trips started during the mornings when she didn't teach, or on days off. The surrounding five miles became like the back of her hand. The old neighborhood visited by Jack and Harold—oh yes, she had heard about that, on a night long ago when it was just Jack and her—still held an air of disquieted movement, and she avoided it at all times. The remaining wilderness was totally wild, without even a trail, aside from transient animal paths.

Her roams gradually increased and her stays became true escapes. Communication was easy enough, and she got permission from the university's chancellor to hold lectures remotely. This required Aramae to holographically project herself back into the same lecture hall she had once spent so much time staring out of.

The crazy professor who lectured from nowhere, as she became known. Her classes were always full, the students more curious about their teacher's habits than about the course's content much of the time. But it drove interest, and enrollment, and tuition dollars. Of course the chancellor had said yes.

Other people would occasionally venture out with her. Nobody lasted long, though. Either too chatty or too clueless, too loud or too questioning. Second trips were rare, thirds unheard of. This included the men. Their capacity for stillness was never quite what she needed, even the ones that didn't try to explain everything. Eventually, she gave up trying altogether.

She did everything remotely: her research of Pluto, her grants, collaborating with engineers, and signing off on the asteroid contracts that kept her fully funded and free to pursue her work and her goals. At her longest, she went away for two weeks and ranged out past the century mile mark. Her students, able to follow her journey from campus, remarked at how she went about her daily life without any of the care and comforts they all enjoyed back at school. Most thought she was lonely. In truth, she was happy. And so she was similarly happy when she ran into Harold's first supply drop.

"Not bad, Harold. Not bad at all." She removed the foodstuffs and other supplies from the rock supply cache like she imagined Jack had done several times from the other end of the line they both walked. Then, she popped out the entangled bit from her pen and swapped in the daisy chain's next cartridge. The pen flashed its green beam to guide her to the next hollow rock.

This'll be farther out than I've ever been. What fun. I

Her new route pushed her ever so slightly northeast as she set off. Aramae marveled at the new land and wondered how long it would take to come face-to-face with the only person she could imagine being with, out in the wilderness.

25

Soon after the meeting between Jane and Betty ended in Chicago, a discreet flash lit up one corner of Jane's lenses. She flicked her eyes towards it and found herself in a condominium, high above the city streets. She could hear Betty in a bathroom, still dealing with the same nausea she'd gone home with earlier.

Nothing to be done about that.

The bot she'd dispatched home with Betty had done a superb job. Every room showed at least two views. The microcameras had attached themselves firmly to the corners of the wall by the ceiling before turning on their holographic camouflage. With their little rotors tucked firmly away, they were completely invisible to human eyes. Even if she'd gotten up to dust cobwebs, Betty wouldn't see the little devices. Only knocking into one could reveal its presence. Each one had enough power to hide itself and still transmit for two months. After that, Jane hoped this would all be over. Besides, in two months, Betty should be getting out regularly, and there'd be plenty of times for the little insect-like devices to fly out the front door with her.

"Nice place," Jane said to herself as she looked from view to view. The kitchen was almost spotless. No pans in the sink, and a sheen of dust covered the countertops everywhere but near the coffeemaker, which was spattered and full of old coffee stains and stuck-on grounds. The living space and bedrooms were similarly neat as a button and looked as though someone had put on a fresh coat of paint. None of this prepared her for the last room.

Enormous trees and ankle-high grasses greeted her as she switched to the last two cameras, and she wondered how the little spy bots had figured out what to do with themselves to stay hidden.

Whoever created those AIs should be promoted. Where is this?

There were no hints of physical walls or a door. Only a desk, set in the middle of two pine trees and surrounded by bunches of grasses, gave away the illusion.

This is some of the best holography I think I've ever seen. It must be her husband's study.

"Computer, identify the trees." The little AI program living in her lenses found the trees and outlined them, hashing out the rest of the image.

"Ponderosa pine," a quiet voice spoke.

"What the hell is that?" Jane replied.

"This is a member of the pinea family, found primarily in western North America. It is one of the primary trees making up the Front Range of the Rocky Mountains."

"Show me a map of where they're found."

A map of the continent appeared in her lenses and a broad north-south line emerged, hundreds of miles into the continent's carbon sink.

Jane sat back in her chair and put her arms up and over her, until her elbows rested on the top of her head. She scratched her back.

Seems as though Betty might have been onto something, after all.

Jane set off to learn more about the man she now pursued and what or who might have driven him so far away. Something tickled the back of her mind, something forgotten and undone.

I've got work to do.

Betty rose from the toilet as strands of hair, coated with little bits of breakfast, fell in front of her face. "I hope I didn't look this bad when I was out," Betty said to the mirror.

She dragged herself into the shower, determined to scrub away the nausea that had plagued her for days.

I still can't believe I'm pregnant. I don't even know that guy's name or how to find him again. She stepped out, dried her hair, and got ready, the nausea replaced by heartburn. *There's no way to explain this to Jack if he turns up alive. It's not possible for him to be the father and he knows it.*

If he's dead, though, people would just assume it's his and nobody would ever know. And I'd be his beneficiary alongside the Wilson Foundation. I think I'd get two-thirds with this child.

Later that night, she fell asleep after several tortuous hours of alternately hoping that her husband was either alive or dead. Neither option appealed to her.

The following morning provided no further clarity, only another trip to the toilet.

26

Jack and Clod became the oddest of odd couples after only a couple of days out on the open flatlands. Jack headed towards his fifth cache with the lumbering beast alternately by his side or off on some distant tangent, looking for something to eat throughout the day while Jack hiked as straight of a path as he could. The hat from the last supply cache was all the shade that could be found as the landscape conspired to grow ever-shorter plants across an increasingly dry terrain. The only water Jack could count on now came from the condensing power of his blankets, which had to be deployed in the wee hours of the day.

Other than the ruptured dam, there had been no indication of humanity of any sort for quite some time. Except for Clod, the un-extinct glyptodont, product of a mad scientist working at some far-distant lab. The big creature's odd antics kept Jack entertained. Without fail, Clod would wander off without reason or warning, only to somehow find his way back to Jack at an equally unexpected time, the big boulder of a creature able to materialize out of the odd patch of high grass or low trees that popped up here and there.

"You must have one hell of a sniffer," Jack said once, after Clod reappeared at the end of a particularly long day.

The grasses themselves were now almost always knee-high at best and seemed to Jack to be even rougher against his clothing and skin than before. Seed heads, beginning to mature at the top of all the stalks, reminded Jack about the passing of days as mile upon mile meant more of the same. Even the bison herds grew scarce as the wind-swept landscape rose a little more with each turn of the stars.

A week after meeting Clod, they found the fifth cache together. Three days after that, they were walking west when Clod froze in place.

Not for the first time, a line of clouds stretched as far north and south as the horizon allowed, which was considerably farther than when Jack had stood in the tall grasses back east. All morning long, the two happenstance companions walked along Jack's line to his sixth cache. They'd both seen the line of grey clouds that marched towards them. Jack hoped for rain. Clod thought nothing of the changes in the sky. The wind had blown with warm gusts out of the south for several days, making things pleasant for Jack. The humidity it brought was also welcome: he had been able to collect a lot of condensed water.

Now the coming front changed all of that in only minutes. The thunderstorms were evident from sixty miles out. Jack stopped to collect rainwater directly in his blankets as he had so many times already. Clod took the barest of interest.

"It's going to be great, Clod! Just watch, I'll be clean again in no time. And I'll get a few days of water out of it, at least! Harold's sent a lot of water bladders. I guess he's figuring that I would break a lot of stuff by now. But we'll show him, won't we?"

Clod sat and stared back impassively. His huge shell rested flush with the ground.

Storms washed over the land with sheets of new life. The darkest and lowest line of clouds passed first. The south wind shifted in seconds as the warm, humid air gave way to something much colder and out of the west.

Clod stood at almost the same instant. His massive tail, which usually dragged behind, went on point, its armored and articulated joints curling back and forth only once. Two tiny ears pointed straight out front. Nothing else moved, as though he were made of stone itself. Only the condensed breath that poured from his nostrils in slow tempo showed otherwise.

At first Jack noticed none of this, preoccupied as he was with collecting rainwater and cleaning anything he could think of. After several minutes, though, something pinged in the back of his mind and he, too, stopped moving. Wet hairs on his neck tried to stand.

The noise was faint and carried on the wind. Buffets of rain drowned it out in fits and starts, as droplets lashed Jack's ears and muffled anything that wasn't precipitation or gale. Gradually, the front passed. As the clouds rose and the sky lightened, the rain tapered off and the thunder became distant in the east behind them. The buzzing from far off to the west now became louder and easier to pick out.

Clod could be heard sniffing the air, as well.

"What is that?" Jack asked Clod. He squinted.

Little geometric bumps marred an otherwise straight landscape. The rain's shadow moved and revealed the unmistakable signs of human settlement. Tiny black dots zipped and scurried through the air around the bumps, and the occasional low cloud of dust escaped from the surface past the horizon.

I thought all those old towns were dismantled long ago.

Gear and water were temporarily forgotten about as Jack stood amidst his supplies and looked at the tiny flea circus playing out far beyond him.

He thought back to a time many years ago, when he'd asked his dad about the limits of their great city.

"You're right, Jack. It does end all of the sudden, doesn't it?" Jack's dad said. "It wasn't always like this. Chicago, and every other ladder city on Earth, used to have dozens or hundreds of smaller towns attached to them. Towns stretched everywhere you could lay your eyes on. Big towns, small ones, some an experience just to try and reach. People lived everywhere, Jack. That had to change, though. Do you remember why?"

"Because the ocean swallowed up all the world's beaches. That's what my teacher told us last year," Jack said.

"Very good! Yes, Jack. All the places on the map that touch the ocean today used to be much, much farther from the sea. But that changed. Eventually, people needed all..." he paused, "All those towns we just talked about—remember them? Well, people needed that land to help the oceans go back to the way they used to be. Your great-grandma Becky was a big part of that."

"Why couldn't the towns just stay? What happened to them?"

"That's a good question. So if the towns had stayed, then it would have cost more carbon to support them than the world could afford. Travel, food, supplies. It might be small amounts, but there were lots and lots and lots of towns. It would add up. And all of that land is really, really important to the world and the oceans."

"Where'd they go?"

"The towns? Well, a lot of them were already mostly empty. The few people left in each town got to choose where they wanted to live, and other people helped move them and all of their stuff. Once the whole town was empty, the erasing drones would come in and do their work. Those drones do pretty much the same thing as that eraser there." Jack's dad pointed to the end of a pencil on the desk next to Jack's bed.

"And they take the town away?"

"Slowly, yes. Every building gets taken apart, every sidewalk and road crushed up. Every single pipe, wire, lamppost, sign, playground, pool, and anything else you can think of gets dismantled. The drones sort it, huge drones fly in—or drive in if there's still a road—and take it away. Then, once the town is gone, they remove all of the roads leading into it."

"Why? Why not just leave it empty? It sounds like a lot of work."

"You're a very smart boy. I knew your kindergarten teacher was onto something last year."

"Daaaaad, you didn't answer the question."

"Oh ho ho! No, I didn't! It turns out, if the town stayed empty, people wandered back and tried living there. Ghosts in a ghost town. And that created all sorts of problems. But equally important, once the town and all of its roads got erased, then the fun could begin. Everyone loves building ecosystems from nothing. Trees, grasses, flowers. Re-meandering streams. Covering up old scars. Can't do that with all of the people stuff still there."

"What about the stuff? Where does it all go?"

"Most of that work is all done, finished many, many years ago. But all the stuff got re-used, and companies paid for it. Wood became especially valuable since trees stopped being cut. Your forest was a special case, but generally. Even the crushed concrete got bought, mostly to dump into the ocean. Sometimes near the coast, sometimes not. Anyways all the money got divided up and returned equally to anyone that still lived in the town when it was taken apart. It wasn't perfect. It mostly worked."

"Why mostly?" Jack tilted his head.

"Oh, some people thought they'd get rich by sneaking from town to town. They pretended to live in a long-empty home, so they'd get a share of the money once the town was erased and everything sold. That's when the carbon sink companies started watching the roads. The people hopping from town to town got caught then, and the problem went away. They kept watching the roads after that, though. They didn't want anyone sneaking out again."

* * *

Jack remembered all of this as he and Clod looked off in the distance. He wondered about his next move. Jack still stood there, pondering, when Clod set off and wandered north. The glyptodont decided to detour around the hustle and artificial bustle. Jack followed.

A pair of narrow streams and their thin tree lines kept the drones and their work out of view most of the afternoon, but the wind continued to carry the noise. Several times, Jack heard the air protest in giant *wup-wup-wups* as transport drones took off and flew southeast towards Memphis.

I wonder if the concrete's headed for the Gulf of Amazonia.

Afternoon gave way to dusk and dusk to night as the pair reached a spot due north of the town and turned back southwest again, to line up with Jack's ever-present thin blue line. The sounds of the drones diminished, too, as the wind no longer carried the noise toward the two travelers.

Jack imagined the town and what it may have once looked like. Was it like the great coastal cities he had sketched? What had the world looked like so long ago, here in the middle of nowhere, surrounded by a flat nothingness of grass, stunted trees, sparse animals, and fast weather?

Another day ended and another evening began. Jack's mind still churned with thoughts and images of old buildings, like the ones he and Harold walked past many years ago in the snow. Was that what this town had looked like too? By the time the Milky

Way spun up overhead, Jack decided to find out.

Clod slept several feet away. The silhouette of the gentle beast smoothed over the moonlit horizon, much like the huge rock Jack had climbed many weeks ago along the side of one of the few roads still around. Jack stood and headed back east.

He'll never know I'm gone. I wonder if the drones work through the night.

Two hours later, a hard knock of concrete beneath his feet was the first clue that he was close. The broken road felt so odd and alien after weeks of prairie earth. Jack walked alongside it and kept his footsteps muffled as he approached.

Dull hums began low in volume. The road bent around a short hill which blocked his view. As he rounded it, he stopped. Thousands of drones covered the roadway in front of him, going back hundreds of yards, every single one of them docked and charging.

Maybe they go back to work right before sunrise.

Jack looked at the little hill, no more than twenty feet high, to his right. *That's perfect.* He retraced his steps for a couple hundred yards and then made for the top of the hill. It felt like forever, but Hercules hardly moved overhead as Jack ascended through the short grass.

Once there, Jack sat more still than the breeze and more quiet than the stars.

How am I going to see anything?

Fortunately, the moon had an answer. Tucked

behind some clouds, it peeked through just enough after several minutes. Jack could see the remains of the town.

It had never been a big town. Maybe, centuries before, it would have been four blocks long and four blocks wide. In the moonlight, Jack could mostly make out what was left. Lumps of brick, roughly geometric. Some taller than others. Places where a few of the roads had been. Sporadic streetlights standing at nearly straight angles. And one giant sphere, far taller than anything else, resting high on five spindly legs.

What was that for?

Jack looked at everything in the dim light and itemized as he went.

If that's limestone brick, it'll get pulverized and dropped into the ocean. Actually, if that big whatever-it-is has any iron in it, it's headed for the same place. How ironic. All those coastal cities people tried so hard to save from the sea, and now this place is purposely being taken apart. And most everything's probably going to the same destination.

Jack ruminated on that thought as he lay there and watched the little town. Nothing happened. Sooner or later, the drone army would finish its task and this place, too, would cease. All memory of it forgotten. Whatever lives transited through history here would fade. Events, too. Parades, festivals, concerts. Dances and great romances. Bitter endings. The first brisk fall day of kindergarten. Baseball games and block parties, barbeques and anniversaries. All gone. Across the continent, this same scene had unfolded thousands of times before at other towns, the traces of history purposely erased from the land forever, passing first out of memory, and finally out of time altogether.

In another century, some future adventurer standing right where I am now would never know this place, nor any place like it.

Dusty books or yellowed scans, collected and stored in some museum's basement, may shed a candle's light onto what was once a roaring sun of humanity that stretched across every horizon but ultimately scorched everything it touched.

There could be no more sprawl. There could barely be people. Only the magnificent ladder cities dotting the globe made society possible.

Our future is ahead, out, up. Not down here. Not in the dirt.

As he continued to watch the partially dismantled town, he recognized it for what it was: Earth's past. A derelict thing, no more belonging in the modern day than anything else that's been dead for many years. Just an empty husk.

He felt a hand warm. Just one. He looked up at a night sky that continued to clear and traced out the constellations without conscious thought. His gaze wandered until it finally settled on a star, ordinary in its dimness and nearly lost among all the rest. He stared at it for a long time. No pattern of thought, or clear idea, broke free from the froth of his mind until he saw a blue steel mug. A small circle of friends from long ago. Two chatty girls, and one other very quiet one. He wondered what the people of Proxima Centauri were doing tonight, up there in the sky. Thoughts flew back to an evening in Boulder, and he asked himself why he had ever left.

27

"Believe me, Aramae. You'd love Chicago," Jack said.

"You know I've been there before! It's too much for me. And besides, I've got a great offer to stay out here. What's there in Chicago?" Aramae replied.

"There's a university with a great science program! You could take any position you want. There's nobody there with your talents. You could write your own ticket. You're a lock, and I might know someone that could put in a good word too."

"I don't want to get hired because of someone else's last name, Jack."

"I didn't mean it that way, I just was…"

"I know. But Jack, there's more to life than a

university. Why should I move to Chicago, what's waiting for me there?" Aramae replied, softly. "I don't feel like being in a ladder city all alone. I did that before. I don't want to do it again. I'd rather stay out here, where it's quiet. Why don't you stay here?"

"I would, really. But my dad's all alone now since my mom…left. And someone has to oversee the foundation. I mean, he's doing that now, but I don't think he wants to do it much longer."

The two sat silently for a while as the sun dipped. Cool spring air carried a mix of fresh rain and lilacs. The back corner of the school, near the farm, had been their spot for three and a half years. After a while, Aramae spoke again.

"Jack, how come you've never asked me out?"

Just then, the puddles nearby became the most interesting things in the world to Jack. He sat there and traced their shape in his mind, wondering how deep they each were.

"Jack…"

"I, uh. I mean, you know, there were times when you weren't single. And there were times when I wasn't. And then for a while there, I was a mess after my mom. And…and I don't know. I wanted to. I should have."

Aramae took Jack's hand and held it.

"And now here we are. You leave in a month. I'm not going to try to talk you out of going back. But I know I can't go out there, either. I'm staying here."

"Maybe I'll visit," Jack said, still holding her hand.

"I can't promise what my life will look like if you do. And I suppose the same is true for you. But if you do visit, I'll be exactly where we are right now. Right here, on this spot. And Jack, I would have said yes."

A month later, the long-range shuttle dropped Jack off at a familiar cul-de-sac on the far outskirts of Chicago. He walked up to the screen door as his luggage towed itself along behind.

"Dad?" Jack yelled through the screen.

"Upstairs! I'll be right there," a voice called down.

Jack went in and looked around. Nothing had changed. Every bit of furniture and every hologram was exactly as Jack remembered it. There was not a trace of dust on anything, anywhere. The place looked like it belonged in a museum.

Jack wandered about. He looked at the holograms and saw their smiles and memories. In one quiet corner rested a birdhouse, faded and a bit battered, but otherwise unchanged after almost twenty years. The chain it once hung from rested next to it on the end table. Jack traced the links with a slow finger.

"I do that too. Once in a while," his dad said from behind him.

"I remember this like it was yesterday."

"She loved going in there with you. We both did. But I think for her, it was a part of what kept her going. Once they cut it down, she was never quite as happy. She was sick a long time, you know. It's not anyone's fault, what happened."

"I know, Dad."

"She hung on a long, long time after that."

"Dad. Let it be."

They both stood there and stared at the birdhouse a while longer.

Several hours later, over a dinner of quinoa, black beans, and salad, Jack brought up his plan.

"Ah, hey Dad. So I was thinking, now that I'm back and done with school: I want to be closer to the science center. I'm going to be working out of there a lot, either teaching or doing foundation things, and I don't want to plan a shuttle every day. I'd like to walk."

Jack's dad studied his son. "I can imagine that you don't really want to live here with me."

"It's not that, it's just…"

"Relax, Jack. I get it. I was your age once. Near the science center, you say? I think I have an idea. Did you know they just put another fifty stories on one of the adjacent skyrises?"

"No, I didn't. I haven't really paid much attention."

"Well, they did. And a few weeks ago, they

opened them up to be shown. How about you go and look, see what you think?"

"Don't you want to come?"

"No, I think you should do this on your own. I know with the Wilson money we aren't exactly normal, but you should still check it out by yourself."

"What if I don't like it?"

"Then you've still got your room upstairs. I bet the dinosaur sheets are around here somewhere."

Jack got an early start the next morning. His shuttle dropped him close to the huge freshwater lake that had drawn so many people to the city over the centuries. He got out near the science center's tree-lined entrance.

Red buds and pale green leaves dotted the path, with new bird nests still visible in the branches. Flowers and dark green grass carpeted the ground beneath the still-open tree canopy. He looked up, past the AIER bridges connecting the nearby skyrises.

Near the top of one building, he could barely see the tiny silhouettes of construction cranes thousands of feet in the air. They stood just a little higher than the rest of the surrounding buildings.

That must be it.

Jack walked around the outskirts of the science center's grounds and towards the skyrise's entrance.

Up a few steps, through a revolving door, and into an open air lobby, Jack spotted a lone figure behind a nearby counter.

"Excuse me, is there a realtorbot available? I'd like to ask some questions," Jack said.

"Actually, we have a live sales associate on site. The owners felt they'd get a better response from potential buyers if they put a real person here."

"Even better. Are they available?"

"Let me check. One moment."

The concierge turned away and Jack focused his attention on the view from the lobby, which mostly consisted of the north face of the Wilson Science Center where he would be working, and open water and shoreline beyond.

Not bad.

"Sir? She'll be down in a few minutes. If you would have a seat, she'll find you."

"Great, thanks a bunch."

Jack turned and walked towards the lobby windows. He stopped in front of them and looked up, pressing his head against the glass. He could see the very top of the science center's seven stories.

"I know it's not a great view from down here, but I promise you it gets better," a bright, feminine voice said from behind Jack.

He turned. "Can't wait to check it out," Jack replied, offering his hand. "I'm Jack."

The associate accepted the hand and shook it. "Hi Jack, I'm Betty. Nice to meet you."

"Likewise."

"So what are you looking for? Studio, one-bedroom? There's some for sale about halfway up that I could show you."

"Actually, I wanted to ask about the new construction at the top."

"Oh, yes. Those units certainly have a lot still open. They only became available recently. Not many people know about them yet. How'd you hear about those?"

"Ah, a family member mentioned it. They knew I was looking and thought I might like the location."

"Well, as you've already figured out, it is an unrivaled field of vision. Especially the south and east faces. Having that little school right next to us really helps limit the obstructed views," Betty said, gesturing towards the science center.

Jack smiled. "Imagine if the school weren't there, how much more the lower levels would be worth."

"Exactly! It's such a waste of space anyhow. Whoever heard of a seven-story building in this city, and right next to the lake! It's almost as criminal as those one-family houses that are on the far outskirts of the city, next to the sink."

"Both places would be worth so much more as a skyrise or a vertical farm, wouldn't they?" Jack answered.

"They sure would. Then, I could make more off commission and pay for med school a lot quicker."

"Med school, huh? I'd have thought this was

your full-time job."

"No, this is just to pay the tuition. I go to night classes right now and do this by day. It's my first year."

"How's it been going? It must be close to exam season."

"That was last week. I'm done for now. Let's hope for a busy summer here. It'd be nice to focus less on this in the fall, and more on studying."

Jack crinkled his brow. "Which school do you go to? Rush?"

"No, Benedictine. I know it's a little further from the lake, but not much. The shuttles usually only take me twenty minutes and I can study on the way."

"I know that place. Great school. They also do pre-med there, right?"

"Yep. I'll be there for the entire stint, start to finish. When I'm done, I'll be Doctor Martin. You've been there?"

"A long time ago. My parents went to a building dedication and dragged me along. I must have been like four or five. I don't remember most of it, other than the little lake and that cemetery."

"What was a little kid doing at a cemetery?"

"Oh, my mom got bored and took me exploring."

"It probably looks about the same now as it did then. Would you like to view some units? I shouldn't keep you here all day chatting in the lobby."

"No, that's fine. It's refreshing, actually. I just got back from school myself and haven't seen a lot of people. Let's walk and talk."

"You got it. What would you like to start with? The smallest units in the new section are two bedrooms, and the largest take up half the floor near the very top. Everything on the last twenty is private express elevator."

"Let's start at the very top. We'll work our way down."

"All right, follow me."

Although he didn't mean to, it was hard for Jack to not notice her figure as she took a few steps in front of him to lead the way.

Buy a condo, Jack. Don't check out the sales associate.

They made their way to a set of unadorned elevator doors and got in. Each chose a chair and strapped themselves firmly into it.

"Maybe I shouldn't ask, but how high up are we going?" Jack asked.

Betty smiled, perfect white teeth set against her red lipstick. "About a mile, give or take."

"Pretty far up there, don't you think?"

"Oh, I don't know. Some of the skyrises in New Beijing reach half again as high. And then there's the ladder itself. That make these buildings look like ant hills."

"Fair point."

"So you think I'm fair, do you?" Betty raised her eyebrows. "You'll like this feature. Jeeves! Top floor, please."

"Good morning, Ms. Martin. Top floor it is," a disembodied voice rang through the service car.

"Just myself and Jack here, a potential buyer. We're ready when you are."

"Nice to meet you, Jack. The trip will take about two minutes. Mind your ears," Jeeves intoned.

The elevator began its ascent and Jack noticed the digital walls change to project the outside. At first the view was crowded with dozens of nearby buildings, but one by one they dropped off until only a handful could be seen, far off in the pixelated distance. Jack closed his eyes.

"Boy this is really high," he said, working his jaw to pop his eardrums every few seconds.

"Isn't it great? They say at night that the light pollution really drops off for the top floors and you can see, like, hundreds of stars," Betty said.

"Hundreds, huh? I bet people really like that." He kept his eyes shut as visions of the sky he lived under in Boulder danced through his mind.

The two continued to work their jawlines and eardrums as the car rose ever higher. As Jeeves promised, the ride came to an end two minutes after it started, and they got off.

"So this top floor has two units. Both have east and west views. One wraps around the north half of the floor, and the other wraps around the south half," Betty said.

"The south side one. Let's see that."

"Sure thing. I also wanted to let you know that if you sign for anything today, we can offer you discounts on upgrades, customizations, and preferred interest rates if you go with our in-house lender and finance through us," Betty said. She rattled off the available upgrades as they walked the hallway to a solid, wooden door.

"Real wood?" Jack gave it a knock. "Wow, real wood. Oh and I'll be paying cash if I like what I see. But we can still talk about upgrades."

Betty stopped short. "Cash? But you're just about my age. Are you pulling my leg? Because I don't have time for joyrides."

"I can promise you this is for real. Shall we take a look around?"

"Yes. Yes, I'm sorry. That probably came off as incredibly rude. Let's go in."

The big wooden door opened into a fully furnished floor, almost exactly as Jack expected to see it. In each room, the floor-to-ceiling windows showed the lake in every east and south pane, and the western ones showed the city and its many thousands of buildings clear to the horizon. The star ladder, far to the north, was somewhat blocked from view. Jack walked around for several minutes while Betty waited. Eventually, he wandered over to the main room's south face and looked outside.

"An open balcony so high up? I figured they'd all be enclosed," he said.

"You'd be surprised how many people comment

on that, no matter the floor. But yes, an open balcony. Sort of. Go ahead, open the door."

Jack grabbed the handle and started to pull, but as soon as he made the barest of movements, the door began a slow roll of its own. It slid back silently on its runners, with no help from anyone.

"That's cool," he said. All sorts of city sounds filtered up from below. He stepped out through the opening but made no move to get near the balcony's half-wall. "This is crazy, just an open-air balcony a mile up. What if something falls and kills someone below?"

"That's a great question," Betty said. She grabbed one of the apples from the dining table's display and heaved it towards Jack.

Jack ducked, not expecting the flying fruit. He saw the apple pass by him in his peripheral vision and momentarily wondered how fast it'd be going when it finally hit the ground. Then the apple bounced at his feet. He stared at it before picking it up.

"Wait, what? But it was. It flew off the balcony."

"You try."

Jack stood and gave the apple a timid toss towards the ledge. It bounced back to him, just like before.

"Forcefields? Someone finally got those to work?"

"Someone finally got those to work. Actually, it was a couple of years ago. These are now standard on just about every open-air structure, aside from the AIER bridges. I'm surprised you didn't know."

"They didn't have these out where I went to school. No real need," Jack replied, still staring at the invisible barrier.

"Oh? And where was that?"

"Way out west. Boulder."

"The outpost science school? I've never met anyone that went there."

"It's quite the place," Jack said, examining the balcony further.

"So, uh. Back to here. What do you think of the unit?"

Jack gave it one last look. "I'll take it. But I'd like to speak to a manager about some upgrades and further construction. And I'd like the furnishings to come with it."

Betty looked as though someone had just handed her a wrapped box at Christmas. "Absolutely. We can probably work with whatever requests you have."

"Let's go get started," Jack said. He walked back to the front door.

The two headed to the elevator.

"When did you want to move in?" Betty asked. They were strapping in for the trip down.

"Tomorrow."

Betty's mouth hung open.

Jack grinned. "I assume that with all cash, things move much faster. And it's not like anyone needs to do a title search."

"Yes. Yes, I mean we can, we will accommodate you. You're going to excite my boss, that's for sure. Jeeves! Lobby floor," Betty said.

"Yes, Ms. Martin. I see everything is secured. Your trip will take about fifteen seconds."

Jack barely registered what the AI was saying until it was too late.

"Wait, fifteen seconds? But howwwwww!" Jack stopped as the bottom dropped out and the elevator car went into its express mode. Betty laughed and Jack held on as though he'd fly right through the pixelated walls. "Ahhhhhhhh!"

This made Betty laugh even more as their short trip ended. Jack exited, white as a cloud and feeling nearly as delicate. Betty took his hand as she walked them back to the sales office.

"That was terrifying. Is that the only way to go down?"

Betty shot him a glance but decided to play it straight.

"No, that's the express service. Fast up, fast down. You can go slower, too, if you want. I personally like to move fast. Hey, don't faint on me now. I don't think I've ever had anyone so surprised by that. You're very pale."

He gripped her hand in return. "Yes, thank you. That was fast, indeed." He tried a weak smile.

"You're an interesting guy, Jack. You come here wanting to see the top floor. You want to pay cash.

You want to move in tomorrow. And I don't think you've ever been in an express elevator until now. Is this legit? You're not from some ground-sunk crime syndicate, are you?"

"I think once I start filling out all the paperwork, you'll understand. But before I do that, I was wondering. If it's not too forward, I have a foundation event to attend tomorrow night, right across the street at that little school you'd like to see razed. Would you like to go with me?"

Betty held his gaze for the same length of time the elevator ride had just taken.

"Sure. You did just get me a commission that'll pay for a whole year of school, after all. I guess I can go to...a function, you said?" Betty handed him a stack of papers to fill out.

He began going through the first one, talking as he went.

"Yeah, my family has a foundation that helps out with the school and I've got to show up. It's full of people I don't know, and aside from my dad, you're the only other person in the city that I've met since coming home. And I've smiled through *almost* all of this today, so I thought I'd take a shot and ask you. I think you'd make it a much more enjoyable night." Jack finished the first sheet and handed it back to her. He moved on to the next one, but watched Betty in his peripheral vision as she scanned the document.

"Is that right? In that case, I think it'd be an

enjoyable night for me too, Jack..." Betty looked at the form, searching for something. "Wilson. Jack Wilson. Holy shit."

28

Jack continued to look at the dim star that shone over the nearly dismantled town. As the final memories washed over him, a rustle focused his attention back to the present moment. He turned from the ruins and looked back.

A slow mound of a silhouette shuffled in from the night.

Clod. Man, that guy doesn't miss a beat.

Jack slunk back down the low hill towards Clod and put the drones and their quarry out of view.

"Hey, buddy. I didn't mean for you to track me down like this. Sorry if I woke you," he whispered.

Clod snorted.

"Okay, let's go."

Jack flashed a blue line from his cube for half a moment and oriented himself to the next cache. In the darkness, the two walked onwards. Behind them, the drones and ancient remains of civilization remained, motionless.

After several hours, another morning greeted Jack. For once, the novelty of his circumstance began to wear off.

I must have gone over six hundred miles at this point. Counting the detour down the Mississippi. And then the dam. How much farther? Two hundred miles? Three?

He glanced at Clod. "What am I going to do with you?"

The idea that his journey might be nearing some sort of conclusion pushed Jack on that day and the next. He reached the sixth cache late in the afternoon the day after he left the abandoned little town.

This time, Harold had deposited the cache only a hundred yards or so from the south bank of a broad, shallow river that seemed to originate out of nowhere and flowed, unhurried, to the east. Clod lumbered over to get a drink as Jack opened up the hollowed out rock. He went through the familiar process of swapping out empty containers and spent supplies for new ones. As he reached the bottom, he found a note:

"Jack, your next cache will be similarly near this river. When you reach it, wait. This is your last entangled pair.

                    -H"

"Wait? Whaddya mean, wait? Wait for what?"

Jack flipped the note over and held it up to the sun, then re-read the brief message a second and third time.

Wait for what?

If the earlier thought of the journey's end had propelled Jack the last couple of days, Harold's note really gave him reason to hustle. Before he started towards whatever waited at the next cache, he cleaned himself in the shallows of the nearby river, relieved that he'd have as much water as he could possibly need for this final leg.

If I really press on and push myself, I could be there the day after tomorrow. Or the day after that.

"Okay, Clod. I hope you're ready for this, because at least one of us should be."

Jack changed out the cartridges from his cube's quantum interface and the rock cache, and wondered if this really was the last blue line he would have to sight and walk. The line that stretched out from Jack's cube ran parallel to the much bigger one a hundred yards to his right. He took off without any hesitation, forgetting completely about the little town, the dam, the old rusty signs, the odd hill, and anything else that he'd passed by over the past months.

* * *

Aramae was amazed at the changes on the landscape. The pine forests were behind her and a flat, grassy plain widened out before her. A river, broad and slow, lay a quarter mile to her left. The only trees anywhere on her journey were now found sporadically near that waterway. Everything else was short grass.

This is both boring and fascinating at the same time.

As she hiked through the shin-high patches of grass and flowers, auburn with the receding colors of fall and changing seasons, she wondered how much of Jack's journey had similarly been a monotonous, boring slog, with nothing of interest happening along the way to break up the tedium. The stark reliefs, quick streams, and high trees of the first leg of her trip made for some interesting miles, but this...this was just an endless horizon. One with tufts of short grasses that clung to dry ground.

Once she saw, in the distance, a small herd of elk moving towards the river. And at night, she heard wolves howling in the far, far-off yonder. But aside from those, and an occasional rattling bugle call from high overhead as sandhill cranes migrated by, the landscape was deserted.

Well, no hurry. I should be at the next waypoint in a few days.

Back in Chicago, Jane sat with her analyst. They had moved off the main floor, away from the busy daily grind, and headed far below ground. Under the building and under the shuttle garage. Underneath the maintenance tunnels and the rescue caverns and even under the city cisterns. The analyst hadn't known of this place before Jane had come to her desk that morning, instructing her to stand and follow.

The two hadn't spoken in months, ever since the tornado. Nobody else had ever asked about it and she hadn't told a soul, either.

"Taylor, grab a seat," Jane said. The two walked through a door at the end of a very long hallway chiseled directly from bedrock.

The room held a card table, a handful of folding chairs, some corner lamps on old, dusty end tables, and a single adjoining washroom, no bigger than two of the chairs placed side by side. It didn't even have a door, just a frame with a yellowed curtain.

"This room got some people through the Great Drop," Jane said. "It's where leaders meet, unseen, to hammer out agreements. When colonists went to Proxima Centauri, the North American contingent was chosen right here. The Wilson Solution was presented here, for the first time. Knowledge of this room is passed down orally. No written record of it exists. You are the first new visitor here in over two decades. There are no cameras, devices, listening equipment, nothing down here. Nobody can eavesdrop. Nobody even knows we're here."

Taylor looked around at the tiny space and wondered if she'd ever see another room again. "Ma'am," she began.

"Jane."

"Ma'am, I haven't told anyone about the man from the tornado. Not a soul. I wrote nothing down. Why am I here?"

"What do you remember from that day, from the tornado?" Jane asked.

"Not much. I've tried hard to actively forget it all, to be honest. The storm blew through and the tornado spun right over the top of where the man was, and then the drone was destroyed."

"The turbines that were damaged near that storm. When they were repaired, did anyone find a body? Parts? Was anyone ever aware of finding his remains, at any point?"

Cold terror gripped Taylor as images of the little raft floated through her mind. The raft passed under the bridge again, just as it had before.

"Taylor! The storm!"

Taylor's hands shook as she looked at Jane. "No, ma'am. Nothing was reported, nothing was found." Her mind replayed the bridge scene again.

Jane keyed into Taylor's fear and sat down next to her. "Taylor, what is it?"

Taylor looked at Jane. "Ma'am, I don't want to be here right now. I want to leave."

"Taylor, if you don't tell me what's going on right now, you'll never leave this room."

Now Taylor's arms shook so much that she curled up in the chair and tucked her knees under her chin to steady herself. "Ma'am. There was a raft.

Some time after the tornado. Along the Mississippi. It passed under the East-West Bridge. Like a week, or two weeks, I don't remember. But it was after the tornado."

"Why wasn't this reported to me? Never mind, I think I can answer that one. What happened to this raft? Where is it now?"

"I, uh, I destroyed it. I landed a drone on it, took control of the drone, and cut the raft up so it would break apart. Whatever was left has long since washed ashore or gone out to sea down by Memphis."

Jane sat back and stared at her underling. Gears within gears spun through her mind as the beginnings of an idea began to coalesce within her. She thought back to her conversation with Betty and she remembered the inside of the condo. The unused kitchen. The office study placed in the middle of a forest hologram.

"Taylor, what do you know about Jack Wilson?"

"Ma'am?"

"Jane."

"Ma'am. I don't know what your real name is, but I know it's not Jane. So, ma'am. Jack Wilson. I don't know much. I know he's a Wilson. The last Wilson. With any luck, he's dead. His family got rich from killing half the planet. Nobody who profited from that deserves to keep all that money and command so much influence after a century. That wealth could be seized and put to such better uses."

"You don't think they deserve what they got?" Jane asked.

Taylor looked at Jane without flinching. "Look at what they did! Even people completely unrelated to them decided to change their last name to get away from being associated with them. There are two people on the planet with that last name now. Jack Wilson and his dad."

"Three people. His wife took his name. Why, I can't imagine. Such a quaint tradition. But she did."

"Ma'am, what's this got to do with any of this other stuff? Who cares about this guy? Most people assume he's dead. Sure, the first month it got a lot of attention, but people moved on after that."

"Taylor, I would like you to create a paper map. Nothing digital. Just North America, black and white. Major sinking boundaries, bodies of water, that's it. I don't care how you get it done. Just get it to me, in my office, by the end of the day. And don't involve anyone else."

Taylor paused for a moment before she answered. "Right away, ma'am."

Jane returned to her office and filled the rest of the day by diving into Jack's past. Such a notorious name meant there was plenty in the public record to keep her busy. And Jack, she determined, had led a most interesting life up to this point. He had lived near Chicago's last old forest to get cut down. His parents had fought bitterly to keep it up. His dad had been part of the rewilding efforts. There wasn't much about his mom, other than her suicide. Of course, everyone knew about his great-grandmother.

And Jack had gone to school out west in Boulder, instead of his family's namesake science center. Jane found that odd, and spent time going through his class list and contemporaries, to see what they ended up doing and where they were living.

Harold Predmoor now taught alongside Jack at the Wilson Science Center. That couldn't be a coincidence. And researchers from that school conducted sporadic field work out in the sinking lands her company owned. She'd have to look into this Harold fellow a bit closer. Hadn't Betty mentioned something about him, that he likely knew where Jack would be, when they had talked some time back? Plus, Harold had seen Jack before he had disappeared. She had been remiss to ignore Betty's ideas.

Yes, Harold looked to be someone she wanted to talk with. There didn't seem to be anyone else left in Jack's orbit from Boulder after so many years.

"I need an AI," she said to her empty office.

"Yes, director. What can I do for you?" a voice answered.

"I need to see a Harold Predmoor here, today if possible. Tomorrow at the latest," she said.

"One moment, director."

The room went silent: first for a moment, and then for several more moments after that.

This shouldn't take too long. I should have spoken to this guy weeks ago.

"Director, Harold Predmoor is unavailable."

"Excuse me? I don't care what he says. Tell him if his school wants to continue to research on our land, he better get here in an hour."

"I wasn't clear. I apologize. Doctor Predmoor is not in Chicago. It appears he left some time ago. According to records, he is currently in Boulder, although I am unable to confirm that."

"What?! He's where?"

"Boulder, director. Boulder is an outpost college approximately nine hundred miles from here, in what used to be Colorado."

"I know what it is!" Jane roared. "Why is he there?"

"I don't have that information. I know he left Chicago, but I don't have a reason why. It doesn't appear that anyone inspected him along the way."

"No, of course not. Why would they? Shit!"

A knock at the door redirected another outburst.

"Come in!"

Taylor walked into the office with a big piece of rolled-up paper tucked under her arm.

"Ma'am? I have what you asked for. I couldn't figure out a way to print it, so I projected the whole thing onto a wall and stuck the paper to the wall, then traced it with a pencil. I figured nobody could find out what I'd done this way, either," Taylor said. She unrolled the map over the room's big, central conference table.

"That was very wise, Taylor. Don't leave. I need your knowledge of things. What you see and hear doesn't get repeated to anyone."

Taylor nodded.

"Is the AI still here?" Jane asked the room.

"Yes, director."

"Good. Encrypt everything from this session and require an entangled pair to access the information stored in your memory."

"Yes, director."

Jane took a red pen and put a dot down on Chicago, right next to the lake.

"Show me where Boulder is on this map," Jane said.

A little red light, no more than a handful of pixels, glowed from beneath the paper. Jane made another dot with her pen.

"Okay, Taylor. Where was the tornado and our mystery man, roughly?"

Taylor looked for a moment and pointed to a spot west of their city. Jane made another dot.

"Now, you said this raft was at the East-West Bridge."

"Yes. But that raft could have floated for days or weeks, really. Who knows where it started."

Jane nodded and drew a red line that traced the

whole length of the river, all the way to its delta in Memphis. Then, she stood back and stared at the map. After a minute, she put an X through a spot along the river.

"That's not enough though, is it?" Jane said to herself.

"Ma'am?"

Jane thought for a while longer.

"Show me research locations operated by the Wilson Science Center."

Two dozen pixels from the conference table lit up around the continent.

"Ha. Good to know they're doing so well. No, this is too much. Eliminate sites east of Chicago or west of Boulder."

Half the pixels dimmed beneath the paper.

"That's not much better. Did any of the reports from any of these sites over the past three months seem unusual?"

"Please specify unusual, director," the AI replied.

"Oh, for crying out loud. I don't know. Injuries, extensions, equipment problems. Requests for more supplies."

Four clusters of pixels remained, scattered around the continent's interior.

"Now we're getting somewhere," Jane said. She touched one cluster with a finger. "Tell me about this one."

"Plant survey team, five members. They

reported the largest populations of several rare flowers ever recorded, and one of their supply cases was attacked by a bear."

"A bear?"

"Yes, director. A bear is a large, omnivorous mammal with several species still alive in some places of the planet. A drone retrieved the case and brought it back here."

"*I know what a bear is!* Who oversees this survey?"

"Doctor Harold Predmoor, Wilson Science Center."

Jane raised an eyebrow. "Did Doctor Predmoor have anything to do with this case being retrieved?"

"Yes, director. He retrieved the footage of the drone pickup and watched it several times. He also traced some lines and had the room's computer run an extrapolation."

"There's footage? Play it."

Jane and Taylor both watched the same scene that Harold had viewed many weeks ago. When it finished, Jane slowly put another red X on the map.

"That was not a bear."

Taylor spoke up. "Ma'am, I think I see what you're driving at. We can't be certain about our mystery man's identity, although the pieces do fit together nicely. Assuming it's Jack Wilson, that does leave one obvious question. *Why?* Why would he be doing this? There's just no reason to be out there on his own, unless he's got a death wish. But if that were the case, he wouldn't have pressed so far out. What's keeping him going?"

"All good questions, Taylor. And I don't know the answers to any of them. But it seems clear that Doctor Jack Wilson is likely very much alive. And he's headed to Boulder. On foot."

29

My god, do my feet hurt.

Up until now, Jack had barely given any thought to his well-worn footwear or the daily aches he had suffered through. But with the end possibly in sight, Jack's mind fixated on every little thing he'd ignored for months.

The last three days had passed in a blur. To his right, the river cut an unerringly straight line over the land, and aside from quick detours to top off his water supply, Jack had not strayed from his parallel track.

The thick, impenetrable grasses he'd started off with in his dad's back yard so long ago were now totally replaced by short, tussocky bunchgrasses, low flowers and forbs, and sagegrass. Even the trees had thinned and shrunk considerably as the land edged higher.

I wonder if Harold found a tree to put the cache under.

He glanced back to see Clod continue his meanderings, sometimes wandering near the river, sometimes over by some thicker clump of grass or flowers blooming late in the season. Since their run-in with the partly dismantled town, nothing else had piqued Clod's interest other than the constant search for something to eat. Clod's breath was visible as he exhaled, even from this distance, and Jack looked ahead at the beet-red sun, hung low in the sky.

This is going to be a cold night.

A single bump on the horizon held Jack's interest as he crested the thousandth low hill of his trip. The bump disappeared again as Jack walked down the hill's other side, only to reappear a few minutes later as he followed the same blue line that he'd followed now for the past two days. Another low ridge. This time, the top of the bump stayed visible. And Jack's blue line aimed straight towards it.

Thirty more minutes of walking took Jack to where his line ended. He walked a full circle around the rock just to make sure. His blue line pointed towards it the entire time.

"Okay, Clod. Apparently, this is the end of the

road. Well, not the road. There is no road. But you know."

Jack looked around. No trees. Nothing in sight but the same stuff he'd walked through for weeks.

Some ending.

He sat down against the supply cache to rest. Three hard days of hiking had strained him for sure, but they hadn't broken him. Still, he was tired, and he had plenty of supplies and water nearby.

Time for a nap. This thing isn't going anywhere.

Jack got out his blankets. He had three of them by now, but he needed only two. Toggling them to heat, rather than cool, he wrapped himself up and wedged himself against the rock, out of the way of what little wind decided to blow across the great plain. He was asleep before he could count to five.

The setting sun had brought the same beet-red sky to Chicago a short hour earlier. Jane had dismissed Taylor and stayed in her office long past dinner. She stared at the map's red markings and their clear progression towards Boulder.

But why?

It was the question that overshadowed every other question in Jane's mind. And she couldn't puzzle it out. The longer she stared at the map, the more she imagined the sheer gall it'd take to strike out alone and walk such a distance.

"How's he even feeding himself?" Jane muttered. "If he'd taken a shuttle, he could have just packed the food for a day or so, but he's been out there for months, if I'm right. He'd need to resupply."

Harold Predmoor. Of course. This whole enterprise always winds back to Harold Predmoor.

"I guess we're just going to have to wait for Jack to show up in Boulder. Or maybe I should go there myself and pay the good Doctor Predmoor a visit."

Jane had nothing else to attend to and nobody waiting for her at home, so she grabbed a go bag that she kept in her office and booked a shuttle before heading to the street. Once there, it didn't take long for her ride to pull up. Like the hundreds of millions of other Chicagoans, Jane slipped inside unnoticed, and the shuttle whisked her away under the cover of night. By the time she woke up the next morning, she was more than halfway to her destination. She'd get her answers soon enough.

30

Jack woke, shivering. Clear skies had bled heat out into space after the sun set. At some point before dawn, the blankets ran out of juice and lost their heat too. Jack grabbed the one remaining blanket that sat unused with the rest of his supplies and turned it on, wrapping it around himself. For nearly the hundredth time, Jack sat to watch the sun rise.

I didn't think I'd be asleep this long. I must've been more tired than I realized.

"Good morning, Clod. Nice walk to the river?" Jack asked as the glyptodont came back from the waterway they had followed for days.

Clod looked at him and snorted, sending two

jets of water vapor into the cold air. He walked past Jack and momentarily eclipsed the rising sun with his rounded carapace. Jack laughed.

Fifteen minutes later, the brilliant morning colors began to fade, and Jack knew it was time to start his day. He tidied the primitive camp, laid out the blankets to charge, and cracked open the supply cache he had spent the night sleeping against. He dug around and pulled out the usual stuff Harold had included. At the very bottom, a small silver cylinder rested against the rough-hewn rock. The size of a fat pen, Jack stared at it for a moment and then brought it out into the light.

He sat down against the rock, turned the cylinder between his hands, and twirled it with his fingers. Then, he felt the familiar seam in the middle, unscrewed the two halves, and screwed them back together again.

Quantum mechanics lab. I gave this to Aramae. I told her they were a matched pair and said they should always be together.

Jack made a fist around the cylinder and stood so quickly that he nearly sat again from lightheadedness. As the spots in his vision cleared, he looked west: sagegrass, more scrubby vegetation, and a flat horizon, as flat as he'd seen at any point in his travels.

"I suppose that was expecting too much, Clod," he said as he glanced south towards the foraging mammal. "Now what?"

Jack paced around, tidied things that had already been tidied, changed his clothes, and then found the sudden urge to bathe and shave and generally clean himself.

"Make sure nobody takes the gear, Clod. I'll be back in a bit," Jack said. He grabbed his toiletries and walked towards the river.

You're ridiculous, Jack. It's freezing cold. You've been out here for months, and no amount of river water is going to replace a hot shower. And your hair is a shaggy mess, no matter what.

Aramae's morning started much like Jack's: cold and clear. A proper sleeping bag and one-man tent made things much more bearable for her, though, as had pitching the tent in a shallow ravine, out of the way of the wind. She packed out her gear and extracted herself up the ten or so feet of the ravine's gradually sloping end. It opened onto the otherwise utterly flat landscape all around her. She had made good progress the day before, pushing on past dark, and stopping only when she had nearly fallen into what became her camping spot. She took it as a sign to not try her luck.

"I wonder if Harold or Jack ever thought about cold weather," Aramae said.

She took out her little pen-cylinder, flashed its green laser line, and turned herself nearly due east before setting off. After almost two weeks of walking, she thought today should be the day.

I'm not sure how this is going to go. We haven't really talked in years.

The little pyramid she carried out with her all this way pulled on her attention. *At least I can hand this thing off to someone that won't vanish if it turns out to be authentic. Maybe then I can walk back home again and get on with life.*

Thoughts of a quiet house, engineering plans for deep space probes, and paperwork gave way after a few more minutes of walking. Her mind filled instead with memories of a lecture hall, a shy young man, and a lot of nights filled with a small group of friends.

"He chose to leave and you stayed. Neither of you were wrong. And you're doing good work and making breakthroughs you only imagined of, way back in those days. Hell, this pyramid might turn any other discovery into a footnote."

Two small lumps on the horizon appeared and interrupted her thoughts. No more than a couple of blips at first, they grew but remained hard to make out against the slowly rising sun.

"Is that rock moving around?"

Twenty minutes later, she approached. It was clear to Aramae that she was looking at the last cache, along with a creature that by all accounts had no right to be there, but also seemed completely unafraid of her. She walked up to the cache and looked around.

"Where did he go?" she said, noticing the tidy

but empty site. "This isn't quite how I imagined things, but I guess I'll wait. What's your name?"

She walked towards the shambling boulder, crouched, and in short order found herself scratching the top of its head.

Jack walked back from the river. He shivered and shook from the cold, clear water. The breeze didn't help. At least he felt a bit cleaner. He wrapped a towel around himself and used a second one to dry his shaggy hair. He silently thanked Harold for the flip-flops in this final supply cache.

I wonder what made him think to add these.

Jack looked ahead to his campsite and wondered how long he should wait. Clod stood nearby, facing south. *Looks like Clod found something to occupy his attention while I was gone.*

Jack walked back to a clean pair of clothes and started to dress.

Aramae stood as Clod's ears turned to the side and he moved his face away from hers. A naked man's butt caught her full attention. Her eyes went wide and she stifled a laugh.

Jack spun around as soon as he heard the laugh, one boxer leg in and the other halfway there. Instinct fought with gravity, and gravity won. Jack spilled over onto his side as he searched for the voice and struggled to dress himself. A blur of a face registered before Clod's frame blocked his view again.

He scrambled to get his pants on and forgot completely about his blue fingers and toes. He heard the same light laughter that he'd only heard in dreams for so many years.

Aramae stepped out from Clod's giant profile and walked towards Jack. She picked up a shirt lying nearby and handed it to him, then took his hands in hers and pulled him up. She was surprised at how rough and cold they felt.

"You're freezing, Jack. But you're also blushing, just as much as you did on that other cold morning so many years ago," she said, still holding his hands.

"I don't feel cold at all," Jack said through chattering teeth. He looked at her, here in the middle of nowhere. "I had no idea you were coming here until I saw the p-p-pen. The one we made in lab together. The one I said should always be with its p-p-partner."

"Not cold? Jack, you're about to convulse. Come here." She grabbed a blanket and wrapped it around him. "What were you thinking, jumping in the river like that? And remember about those two pens. If they hold an entangled pair, it doesn't matter how far apart they are, because part of them will always be linked with the other one."

"I didn't want you to see me all gross and dirty. You should have seen the grime that flowed downstream."

Aramae pursed her lips. "I wouldn't have cared, Jack. You're still shaking. Come here."

She took Jack in her arms and wrapped herself around him, and wrapped the blanket around them both. They stood like that until Jack's shaking stopped.

Gradually, his hands and arms warmed and turned pink again, and he broke his arms out from between their two chests to return Aramae's embrace. He closed his eyes and felt a tear run down his face.

"Aramae, I missed you. I...oh, you have no idea. I missed you so, so much. I don't want to ever miss you like this again. I'm so sorry!" More tears ran. "I should have stayed. I should have never, ever left. I'm sorry. I'm so, so sorry."

He hugged her tighter now, finally able to feel warmth radiate from her.

She rubbed his back and ran a hand through his shaggy hair. "It's okay. It's all right. I'm here now. I'm here now and so are you."

She pecked his cheek. Jack reciprocated, and the two of them searched each other's faces. They recognized their old selves, each in the other, and realized that even as years had passed, part of them had remained with the other and never moved out of that small space they occupied in one another's heart. Maybe buried, or ignored, or denied, but never gone. Distance and time changed nothing. The fears of both would not be realized.

Broad smiles found their way towards each other and the two, after knowing each other for nearly half their lives, finally shared a kiss.

For some time after that, Aramae listened as Jack told her about everything that had happened since he'd read her cryptic message. The disastrous trip with Betty and his decision to leave the city. Seeing his dad, the tornado, building the raft, the bison, the mammoths, every storm, the researchers, almost constant searches for water, the strange hill, the dam, the town, all of it. Jack showed Aramae the faded bruises where the mammoth had rolled him around like a log. He told her how he'd lost his dad's canteen flying down an embankment. How he'd thought about his mom as he lay under the stars and remembered the quiet song she had sung. The memories from college. And when he felt comfortable, he told her about his dreams, wondering what she would think of him once he finished. She never let go of his hand.

Eventually, the sun moved well past overhead and the stories wound down. Aramae reached into her pack and took out the small pyramid. She set it down on the ground between them.

"So this is it, huh?" Jack asked.

"This is what started the whole mess."

Jack reached out and picked it up. It was lighter than he expected, far lighter. The scans he'd seen in his Chicago office months ago didn't do justice to the intricacies of what Jack now saw. For starters, the pyramid had a full range of colors that he hadn't seen before. The colors helped him see that each side was, indeed, some sort of orbital body. He looked at Aramae.

She smiled. "I know. It defies thought. Back in Boulder, I did every non-invasive thing I could think of to it. It took forever. I had to wait until the whole lab cleared out every night, and then I had to run everything manually. When I finished, I made sure there was no residual trace of anything on a memory chip or a maintenance log. But tell me what you see. I've got my own ideas, but I want to hear yours."

He put the pyramid back down between them and pointed.

"This side is Earth, and that side is Mars. But my guess is, you already knew that. Earth is from a quarter-billion years ago. So maybe Mars is too? That's if we're saying this thing is authentic. These other two, now that I see it in color. This side. Could this be Europa? But it's not frozen solid, just at the poles. And then this last one. It looks a lot like the Europa side, just without the poles. The line making up the outline of this one is also a lot thicker. And hold on," Jack said, picking up the pyramid. He looked closely at all four triangular sides again. "Is this moving? It looks animated. Like, I can see movement if I look close enough."

Jack rummaged around for his cube and turned a small part of it on, and glanced back at Aramae.

"You already knew all of this, didn't you? I can see it in your face, you've already figured it out."

"Maybe."

Jack used the cube's powerful cameras to zoom in on each of the four sides' pairs of hemispheres. For five minutes, he looked back and forth, shaking his head the whole time.

"They *are* moving."

"Yes."

"But that's not possible. This is solid metal."

"No. I don't know what it's made of. I put down metal just to cover it in the report. If I'd written down 'Unknown Exotic Material,' that'd have drawn a lot of attention."

Jack continued to study the pyramid's markings through the high magnification of his cube.

"These are oceans. And weather patterns, atmospheres."

Aramae put a hand on Jack's thigh. "Jack, I think this shows these places as they looked whenever… whenever this thing got left here," she said. She squeezed his leg.

"But Mars has been dry for a billion years. At least."

Aramae shrugged. "I know what things look like today. And I know what the data says, but look. Earth, Mars, Europa, and I think this last one is Ganymede. We know today there's water frozen in the last three, and some liquid water too. Just not as much as we're seeing here. Ganymede has more water than Earth, and it's also got a magnetic field. It's just cold."

Jack picked up the train of thought.

"What if this is some sort of map? One that was made two hundred and fifty million years ago?"

"I think it's more than that, Jack. Look at the bottom."

Jack flipped the little mystery over and looked at the square bottom.

"Just a few dings and scratches," he said.

"Jack, this thing doesn't have dings and scratches. That isn't what those are, I'd bet my life on it. I haven't figured out what they are yet, but those were made purposely."

"So now what?"

Aramae laughed. "I don't know. This is where I got stumped and figured you might have some ideas. Plus, you know, this thing's radioactive, metaphorically speaking. If it's actually authentic, then there's going to be a lot of interested parties. And Boulder is really isolated out here. I'm not equipped to deal with this safely. I don't think anybody ever thought about what to do if someone running asteroid contracts, you know, actually *found* something like this."

"Maybe I should contact Harold," Jack said.

"I left him in Boulder, at my house. He wanted to be the one to trek out here to meet you. Can you imagine?"

"I'm glad it was you."

"I know. Me too."

"We probably need to get this back to Chicago, though. What do you think? Do you agree? I don't think it can stay in Boulder, you're right."

"Neither should Harold. He could probably meet you back in Chicago," Aramae said.

Jack grabbed his cube and started to fiddle with various toggles and switches, then stopped.

"I've been off-grid since I left Chicago. Once I turn this thing all the way back on, it's going to attract a lot of attention. I'm going to flag a drone from the university first, and then once *we* get underway, I'll call Harold. That sound okay? And you're coming back with me, this is your discovery. I'm just your human shield."

Conflicting emotions played over Aramae's face for a moment.

"What is it?" Jack asked.

"I'd ask if I can crash at your place, but…"

Jack put both hands in front of his mouth as though in prayer. He exhaled very slowly. "I haven't even thought of Betty. How horrible of a person am I?"

Aramae hesitated before answering. "Jack…you told me what happened. On the vid with her. While you were supposed to be celebrating an anniversary, if I understand things correctly? It's not my marriage, but between that, and you forgetting about her, and then this," she reached out to take his hand, "what's left to worry about?"

Jack put his other hand on top of hers. "Something tells me I'll be sleeping at the office. Won't be the first time. And I know a very quiet house you could stay at for a few days."

"We'll deal with the rest as it comes. No sense in wringing your hands over it now. You haven't been seen in months, and who knows what's going to happen. You ready?"

"Yeah. Yes, I am. Let's get out of here."

Aramae looked over at Clod. "What about him? I think he's grown fond of you."

Jack walked over to the big beast and dropped down to look at him. "Hey, buddy. I don't want to leave, but I can't stay here any longer. I know you'll be okay. And who knows, maybe someday I'll be able to get out and track you down again. I hope you find someone your own size to follow around, though. I think you'd be happier."

He scratched the top of Clod's head and rested against his huge carapace as he put his fingers on the familiar corners of his cube and squeezed. Its lights turned on for the first time in a great many weeks. Soon enough, he interfaced with the Wilson Science Center and dispatched one of the long-range survey drones to their location. For the second time in his life, he used his family's special commands to override any need to justify sending the drone to the middle of nowhere. It was on its way, and it would land in a couple of hours.

31

After they packed up the site, put trash and unneeded items in the cache for later pickup, and set the rest of the stuff off to one side, Jack and Aramae spent some time wandering around. They watched the river, scratched Clod's head, and ignored Jack's cube, which lit up nonstop with people trying to contact him. Eventually, both heard the only man-made noise either had heard for quite some time. A short-nosed little craft set down vertically near the camp, like it was just any other day for the drone. It waited patiently while the two loaded their gear and said a final goodbye to Clod, who was completely nonplussed by the whole commotion.

After they both entered the cabin, Jack closed the door and spoke up.

"Good afternoon! Who am I speaking with today?"

"Good afternoon, Doctor Wilson. My name is Frederick," said a voice.

"Frederick, hello. First, a question. Did you file a flight plan to this location?"

"No, sir. As asked, I filed a flight plan to Boulder, but then ignored it and landed here instead."

"Thank you, Frederick. Now, an odd request. Can you take us to the AIER bridge connected to the Wilson Science Center?"

"That is an unusual request, Doctor Wilson. Let me check," Frederick paused. "Doctor Wilson, I am too wide to safely land on the bridge. The best I can do is hover over it at a height of fifteen feet, if you would like to jump out," Frederick answered.

Jack glanced at a skeptical Aramae. "No thank you, Frederick. Please just land where you normally would land when returning a survey crew."

"That would be the roof, sir."

"Then the roof it is. One more thing, Frederick. Please don't list either of us on your declared manifest. Wilson command override," Jack said.

Aramae leaned over to Jack. "Look at you, Mister Bigshot. Impressive."

"Thank great-grandma Becky, not me. I've now used that birthright twice today, which is twice as much as I've ever used it before today."

"Anything else, Doctor Wilson?" Frederick asked.

"No, Frederick. Let's go home," Jack said. He took Aramae's warm hand in his and closed his eyes as the little craft rose and got underway.

"I'll vid Harold right after this. I hate takeoffs."

Harold looked around Aramae's big empty house and saw early snowflakes fall on the other side of many windows. Beyond them were several old school buildings he had revisited over the past couple of weeks, and a vast coniferous forest that he studiously avoided going anywhere near.

He heard a buzzing from downstairs and went to investigate, figuring correctly that someone was trying to vid him.

That's the second time today.

The name that popped up above his tablet on the tabletop brought a huge smile to Harold's face. This was someone he knew, not like that Jane woman he had spoken to an hour ago.

"The prodigal son! Am I right, am I looking at the man, the myth, the legend?" Harold asked, seeing Jack's face for the first time in months.

"Hi, Harold," Jack said.

"Jack, you look both happier and more worn out than the last time I saw you. Where are you?"

"We," Jack's eyes darted away from the screen for a moment, "are in one of the university's survey drones, headed back to Chicago. We should be there in a couple hours. Aramae tells me you're out in Boulder? I thought you said it'd be too dangerous to get involved like this. You just wanted a vacation, didn't you?"

"You know I can't let you have all the glory and attention. That's how it is, I'll never be second fiddle."

"Can you two ever take *anything* seriously?" Aramae's voice cut through the two of them, resulting in a pair of chuckles.

"Aramae! I'm glad you're there. I wanted to ask you, how I should handle your housekeeper in a little bit? She vidded me about an hour ago. You didn't tell me about her before you left."

"Who? Harold, I have no idea what you're talking about," Aramae said. She moved around the drone's cabin and brought herself into focus.

"Your housekeeper, Jane. She said she'd be by. She should be here any minute. I just figured you told her I'd be staying here."

"Harold, I didn't tell anyone that you're in my house. And I don't have a housekeeper."

"Then who is Jane?"

Jack, listening in, got a sinking feeling in his stomach.

"Harold, get your shoes on. Fast."

In the background, Jack heard a doorbell chime.

"Don't answer that! Run!"

"Harold, take the tablet with you!" Aramae yelled.

The connection died and Aramae looked at Jack. "Can we track him if he doesn't have that tablet with him?"

"He doesn't wear lenses. I'm not sure. Frederick!"

"I'm here, Doctor Wilson."

"Frederick, I need you to find and follow the device I was just connected to. Put it up on a map so we can see exactly where it is."

"One moment."

Jack's leg jittered as he waited for something to appear. It felt like minutes, but after a few seconds, a little map popped up in the middle of the drone's cabin.

"Bigger, please. Double the length and the width," Jack said.

Aramae pointed at a blue dot that rested over the top of a roof. "That's my house. Come on, Harold. Grab the damn tablet!"

At that exact moment, Harold grabbed his jacket, hat, and gloves and ran for the back door. The person at the front door continued to ring and then started to pound on the door itself.

Harold flung the back door open and took a step outside, looking at the woods in front of him. Then he remembered the tablet.

"Shit!"

He turned and pushed partly back into the house, but his outside foot slipped on the fresh snow and he fell in the doorway, taking a nearby shelf and a container of laundry detergent with him as he went down. He got up and ran back for the little tablet, and then hightailed it once more out the rear door.

Jane heard the muffled fall and took a step back. She surveyed the house's second story, roof, and sides. She glanced over her shoulder and tiptoed around, heading through dense foliage and landscaping as quietly as she could.

Back on the big survey drone, Jack pointed to the little blue dot, which was now rapidly moving away from Aramae's house and into the trees behind it. Jack exhaled and held Aramae's hand as the blue dot continued to move.

"After this, Harold's never going to step foot in those woods again. Any idea who that woman is?" Jack asked.

"No, I don't. I don't think I've ever even *worked* with a Jane. And how did she know Harold was there?"

"I don't know, I don't know. We've got to send him some help, fast. And anything from Chicago would take too long."

"I could get something out to him. Get him out of those woods, at least. But then what?"

"Frederick! Are there any ground shuttles near the device we're tracking?"

"One moment, sir." Silence. "There is one, sir. It

arrived an hour ago."

"Gee, I wonder who was in that," Aramae said.

"Frederick, I want you to commandeer that shuttle right now and send it on the road back to Chicago. I don't care who's booked it, I'm using my override again. And Frederick, I want it to stop and pull off to the first available spot on the road and wait for a passenger there."

"Doctor Wilson, there's nobody in that shuttle, and it'll be pulling off to the shoulder about ten miles into its trip."

Jack glanced at Aramae and raised his eyebrows.

"It'll be close. Our stuff doesn't have great range. And I don't think I can use what Harold brought out with him. Does this thing still work like I remember?" Aramae asked. She grabbed Jack's cube. Up popped her own interface after a few seconds. "I guess that's a yes."

Jack watched her work, fear mixed with confidence and anticipation.

"Okay, I got a drone to fly to the tablet's location. Let's hope this works."

Harold continued to run through the woods. Snow cut down his visibility somewhat, but he kept moving. After a couple minutes, he thought he heard a twig snap far behind him, but when he looked, he couldn't see that far back in the falling snow and diminishing light. After another minute, he stepped onto something hard and flat and loud, and he stopped short to look around.

That road.

Harold looked back again and noticed the footprints he was leaving in the snow.

Well, that's not good.

He kept going and soon recognized the shapes of what used to be homes popping up beside the road. A footstep, pounding asphalt far behind him, sent a wave of shivers down his spine.

He ran on.

A minute later, he heard a dull hum far off to his right as he kept moving. Both it and the footsteps gradually got louder, but the hum was getting louder much quicker. After several more minutes, Harold started looking for the source of the noise as he ran, glancing to his right, then over his shoulder, and then to the front again as he stayed on the road for as long as he could.

Now the hum turned into a low roar and drowned out any other noise. Harold couldn't see whatever it was, but it was close. Then he heard Jack.

"Harold! Grab it! Grab the sides! Now!"

Out of the murky sky emerged what looked like an open, flying briefcase. Two massive rotors spun within either side of the rectangular housing. Two handles, one on each end, beckoned Harold to reach out and grab hold.

He did.

As he grabbed on, a scream from behind him made it through the noise of the little craft. He ignored it and closed his eyes as the flying briefcase strained to gain altitude. Slowly at first, but then quicker as the fans spun even faster and whined in their housing. Harold hung on for dear life, expecting the footsteps behind him to jump up and grab his leg at any second. After moments that felt like minutes, he opened his eyes to white on all sides. The old houses were gone and he couldn't even see the trees.

"Harold, just hold on. I know you can't talk back to us, but just hold on. This time, it's someone else's turn to save you."

The flight lasted about ten minutes, and Harold was starting to wonder how much longer his hands could grip their handles when the pitch of the fans and the direction of the air around him started to change. He felt himself slow, and then the ground appeared under him. There was a shuttle fifty yards from where the briefcase set him down.

"That's your ride, Harold. You might get a little hungry on your way back, but it'll drop you off at the science center's entrance," Jack said through the craft's speakers.

Harold looked up, threw a salute Jack's way, and ran to the waiting shuttle.

32

Jack sat back in his seat and turned off the cube. The map hanging in front of him and Aramae disappeared. He looked over and saw the same crazed expression on Aramae's face as he imagined was on his.

"What's gonna happen next?" Jack asked.

"I'm not sure, but we've only got about an hour until it happens. Look, you can see the ladder already," Aramae said. She pointed out the window. Off in the distance, a thin black line led straight up into the sky.

At that moment, back in Chicago, the clinic Betty

worked at was buzzing with idle chatter amongst the staff. Quiet conversations let out occasional excited outbursts, and anyone not seeing a patient was glued to their lenses, or talking to a co-worker, or both.

Betty left an exam room and looked around. She had been slammed with back-to-back appointments all morning and was barely staying on time.

"Hey Susan, what's going on? This place is on edge," she asked a passing nurse.

"Betty! What are you still doing here? I thought you'd be long gone."

"What are you talking about?"

Susan looked at Betty as though she were mad.

"Your husband! They're saying he popped back onto the grid this morning. And he might be heading back here right now, although nobody can really confirm that part. You should go home!"

Betty stood there, stunned. It had been more than two months since she'd had any contact with her husband. And now he was coming home? It was almost too much to process. She sat down and stared at the wall. After ten minutes, she took Susan's advice, booked a shuttle for home, and left in a daze.

The ladder grew larger in the survey drone's windows. Low outlying buildings on the edge of the city's hard border transitioned to a tight mass of skyrises and vertical farms stretching towards the lake for a hundred miles. The drone whizzed past them all, settling high into open airspace between the superstructures.

Aramae spoke up.

"I haven't been in this much humanity in a very long time, Jack. I've forgotten just how dense and colossal the ladder cities really are. I'm out of here the first chance I get. Back to school for me, back to the middle of nowhere."

Jack looked at her pert nose and long brown hair, which he now saw was shot through with a few streaks of grey as well, with tighter lines near her eyes.

Neither of us are getting younger.

"Aramae, I," Jack's voice faltered, "Aramae, I want to go back with you. I don't know what's going to happen with this pyramid we're traveling with, but after a few days, it's going to be someone else's problem. And I don't want to continue here, not with the life I've got."

He took a deep breath and continued on.

"The last few months, being out there, I wasn't pressing on to get to you because of what you found. Sure, circumstances at home gave me a good kick at the start, but I never turned around, never turned on my cube to call for a ride, even with everything I dealt with. I never wanted to come back. I wanted to see you. No matter what. I knew if I shuttled out, I wouldn't get the world's attention, and it might put you in danger, so I walked. Which turned out to be really, really dumb, because I had no idea what I was doing. But I'd do it again in an instant to see you.

"I don't exactly know how you feel about me. Us. But I know I feel more strongly about you than I do about anyone else on Earth. That probably makes me a shitty husband, but right now I don't care, and I can't change how I feel. Sometimes I wish I could. I wish I could change my feelings because it is so, so hard to live with them every single day. But I can't. They're there, they're strong, they never diminish, and I don't want to deny that any longer. I've denied it for years and it's only made me miserable. And so I want, I need to change things. You're right, my marriage is over. I am better off single than staying married. I just didn't want to face that until very recently. I don't know if this between us would work out, or if it's all just a mirage or in my head, but I want to try. If you do too, I want to try and see what happens.

"And I'll leave everything here. Just give me a few days to settle things. Then, I can come back to Boulder with you. If you want. I love you. I have loved you for half my life."

Aramae sat there, looking at Jack. Their survey drone began to slow and descend. As it bumped and landed on the roof of the Wilson Science Center, she placed her hand in Jack's. It was slightly smaller but much warmer than his.

"Yes. I'd like that very much. I know things will be a little crazy for a bit, but I want you to come to

Boulder. And I know I'm not supposed to say this to a married man, but I love you too. And I've loved you just as long as you've loved me. That night we talked about the colony during freshman year. It was then, wasn't it?"

Jack nodded.

"It was exactly then."

33

The roof of the Wilson Science Center had an unfettered view of Lake Michigan, but on all other sides it was surrounded by buildings two orders of magnitude taller than it. Jack and Aramae exited the survey drone and hauled out their gear, descending from the roof's maintenance access stairs to the top floor of the building. Jack hadn't been back since his meetings with Harold. It was Aramae's only visit. He led them down a wide hallway, past dozens of students studying in their usual spots. None bothered to look up at first, but gradually more and more eyes and lenses recognized the man in front of them and began transmitting what they saw.

Hundreds of eyes turned into a million, and after only a minute or two, tens of millions of eyes were watching through the vision of those few students lucky enough to be studying on the top floor, just as the missing professor and his mystery guest strolled on through.

Jack cracked opened the door to his office and Aramae walked straight in, aware of the small crowd growing behind them. The door clicked shut and they both dropped their packs and sat down. Aramae rummaged through her stuff until she found what she sought. The pyramid that'd started everything rested in her hand. She looked at Jack.

"Ready to do something decidedly unscientific?" she asked.

"You mean, make a wildly unsubstantiated claim that'll be sure to slingshot from ladder to ladder?"

"That's exactly what I mean. Once the cat's out of the bag, and with the whole world watching you, there won't be any way to bury it. It'll see the light of day. The truth about this little thing will come out, whatever that truth is."

"Let's do it."

Aramae took the pyramid in one hand and Jack's hand in the other. Together they walked out of the office, past the hall with Jack's sketches, and out to the top floor's terraced balcony, which overlooked the projection of Earth hovering in the huge open space of the Wilson Science Center. They stood there, side by side, and watched as every face turned up to look at them. Every voice in the building quieted. Jack had never heard the place as silent as it was at that moment.

"You start," Aramae whispered.

Just pretend it's a really big lecture hall, Jack.

"Folks, ladies, and gentlemen! Judging from the stunned silence in this great hall, I see that you all recognize me. And to those watching through the lenses of those gathered here, I can assure you that I am very much…present. I can only assume that there must have been many reports and much speculation about me during my absence. Those reports, as the saying goes, are greatly exaggerated.

"I have spent the last few months out beyond the city's borders. I have seen things and ventured through places that I did not know existed. I have crossed hundreds of miles of rewilded carbon sink on foot, to meet this woman here beside me. I believe she has discovered something so important, so impactful, and so life-altering for every person alive today, that no word and no trail of my actions could be known without putting her in acute danger. Because what she is about to tell you will challenge the entire way our planet has functioned since my great-grandmother's discovery led to the Great Drop and the star ladders we take for granted today.

"I am sure I will be asked to recount my journey in a great many interviews. Maybe I'll even write a book about it. But for now, I would like each and every one of you to listen to what she has to say. Record it, broadcast it, tell your friends, make as many copies as you can, because there are people out there that would see this discovery sunk, buried and forgotten. Because their way of life and their beliefs about what makes us human would be shattered.

"I have known this woman for half my life, and she is unimpeachable. In the coming days and weeks, what she is about to say will be borne out to be truth. Ladies and gentlemen, here she is: Doctor Aramae Cate Moreau."

Jack stepped back and left Aramae at the front, all eyes on her. He smiled.

"Thank you, Doctor Wilson. Folks, for parts of two different millennia, we have searched for an answer to the ultimate question: are we alone? Of all the stars in the sky, only one has ever spoken to us, and it speaks to us in languages we already know. Today, that all changes. What I have here today is the first proof of intelligent extraterrestrial life, and I believe it goes further, much further, than even that extraordinary statement. Let me tell you about our discovery..."

34

Aramae finished addressing the crowd, plus a good portion of the planet watching from afar, after a long and detailed explanation on everything she knew about the pyramid. Some of what she said undoubtedly went over most everyone's head, but enough had gotten through and resonated to mark the day as a pivot point for humanity. Everyone alive would remember where they were when it happened.

As the two of them retreated from the overlook and headed back to the office, Jack took her hand and guided Aramae to a nearby door, one whose handle required a thumbprint. He took her hand

and pressed her thumb against the sensor. The door opened. After they went through, he closed it behind them.

Aramae stopped, looking first at the AIER bridge and all the skyrises around them. Then, she walked around and noticed every plant, insect, bird, and other critter that made the bridge home.

"Harold mentioned this place to me out in Boulder. Before I left to come find you. He said only five people in the world can get out here."

"He's right. I thought we needed a moment. *I* needed a moment. What you did just pushed civilization onto a new path."

"Oh, stop. I bet you bring all the girls out here when you want 'a moment.'"

"Right. That's me, the big-time player here in the big city."

Aramae's face fell as she looked past Jack's shoulder. Jack turned to follow her gaze. The door at the far side of the bridge opened.

Jack turned back to Aramae.

"Can you wait here? I don't want to drag you into this, but I don't want you to vanish on me, either. This won't take long, I don't think."

"Yes."

Jack walked down the length of the bridge connecting the two buildings, heading towards the person standing near the door. She didn't come out to meet him. As he made his way towards his wife, he noticed subtle changes about her, and then he realized what those changes meant.

"Hello, Betty."

"Hello, Jack. I'd ask where you've been, but I just saw it live, back in our condo," she said, tilting her head in the direction of the skyrise she had come from. "Who is she?"

"You said you saw the news, so you already know. I think that's the question I get to ask anyhow. Not you," he said, looking down. "Who is he? I know it definitely can't be mine."

"I...I don't know. I never got his name. But don't change the subject. You abandoned me there, Jack. And then you vanished for months. I thought you were dead! How could you?"

Familiar feelings dredged themselves up from the pit of Jack's body, feelings he hadn't needed to contemplate for quite some time. He knew where this was headed. For once, he spoke how he really felt.

"Betty, stop. Just stop. Stop. I'm not doing this. Even before I saw you here, like this, I knew this was coming. This is over. I want out. I want a divorce. I wanted it a year ago. I wanted it two years ago. I should have said it then, and I'm sorry. But this is over. You can have the condo. It's yours. I'm leaving Chicago and I don't think I'll be back here again any time soon. I might never return."

"You're going with her?"

"Yes. I should have never left her in the first place, and that mistake is mine. I am sorry that you, us, this, is fallout from my screwup a very long time ago. Good luck. I hope you find some happiness in your future. You deserve it just as much as anyone."

Betty stood there, speechless. Jack turned and walked away, taking Aramae's hand. He did not look back.

35

Harold enveloped Jack with a big bear hug in their office as Aramae watched the two old friends.

"Congratulations, Harold. You'll do a better job running the foundation than I ever did, and now I have an excuse to come back and visit. Just promise me you'll keep our office the same."

"I promise. I'll have an excuse to come out and visit you too," Harold replied. "But I think I'll take a *shuttle* to Boulder when that time comes."

"Ha ha. It feels like it's been a year since we helped get you back here in one piece, but it's barely been a week. What an insane week it's been too."

"It's a whole new solar system again," Aramae

said. "I'm surprised they got the pyramid's square side figured out as fast as they did, but wow, it was even bigger than I thought. Early reports are saying the information they're seeing will let them warm all three worlds. Just think! The asteroids we're mining are just the start. Three new worlds we can live on and walk around on, once we undo the pause 'they' did for us two hundred and fifty million years ago. It's like someone knew life on Earth would be able to use the other worlds, once it evolved. But they also knew if they didn't pause the other places, those worlds might never be usable. Someone out there wanted the life on this planet to succeed. I wonder if they're still out there and if we'll ever find them. They left us three seeds and instructions for how to grow them. In a place that we'd never find unless we were ready."

Jack took her hand.

"Beautifully put, Aramae. Maybe someday we'll meet them. Until then, three seeds. And they also left one tree."

-END-

About the author

Carl Armstrong lives and works in the suburbs of Chicago, Illinois. When not moonlighting as an author, he teaches high school science. Frequent trips to prairies and forests with a dog, a thermos, and a camera are par for the course. Occasional twenty- or thirty- mile bike rides aren't out of the question when it's warm out.

They Left One Tree is his debut novel.

How to contact

If you would like to contact the author, there are several options for getting in touch:

https://www.instagram.com/authorcarmstrong

https://authorcarlarmstrong.com

https://twitter.com/AuthorCarlArm

Any of these platforms have options to send me a message. I hope you enjoyed this novel. I look forward to hearing from you!

-Carl Armstrong

Dalea Publishing can be reached at daleapublishing@gmail.com. We are a small house and the mailbox is opened only once a month.